Praise for the novels of

MAGGIE SHAYNE

"Shayne crafts a convincing world, tweaking vampire legends
just enough to draw fresh blood."
—*Publishers Weekly* on *Demon's Kiss*

"Maggie Shayne demonstrates an absolutely superb touch,
blending fantasy and romance into an
outstanding reading experience."
—*RT Book Reviews* on *Embrace the Twilight*

"Maggie Shayne is better than chocolate.
She satisfies every wicked craving."
—*New York Times* bestselling author Suzanne Forster

"Maggie Shayne delivers sheer delight, and fans new and old
of her vampire series can rejoice."
—*RT Book Reviews* on *Twilight Hunger*

"Maggie Shayne delivers romance
with sweeping intensity and bewitching passion."
—*New York Times* Bestselling author Jayne Ann Krentz

MAGGIE SHAYNE

Twilight Prophecy

MIRA

Recycling programs for this product may not exist in your area.

ISBN-13: 978-0-7783-2980-0

TWILIGHT PROPHECY

Copyright © 2011 by Margaret Benson

All rights reserved. Except for use in any review, the reproduction or utilization of this work in whole or in part in any form by any electronic, mechanical or other means, now known or hereafter invented, including xerography, photocopying and recording, or in any information storage or retrieval system, is forbidden without the written permission of the publisher, MIRA Books, 225 Duncan Mill Road, Don Mills, Ontario, Canada M3B 3K9.

This is a work of fiction. Names, characters, places and incidents are either the product of the author's imagination or are used fictitiously, and any resemblance to actual persons, living or dead, business establishments, events or locales is entirely coincidental.

MIRA and the Star Colophon are trademarks used under license and registered in Australia, New Zealand, Philippines, United States Patent and Trademark Office and in other countries.

For questions and comments about the quality of this book please contact us at Customer_eCare@Harlequin.ca.

www.MIRABooks.com

Printed in U.S.A.

To Sharyn Cerniglia, a woman who is so special, so beautiful and so pure of spirit that her aura sparkles and shines with it. Sharyn has shared many things with me, among them her wise advice, her keen insights, her motivational pep talks, and the source of her knowing, which has changed my life. But above and beyond all of that she has given me her friendship, the worth of which cannot be measured. Thank you, dear Sharyn, for being my sister-friend.

1

James dressed in white. White lab coat, white scrubs, white cross-trainers. Sometimes he broke it up with a colored shirt, but for these visits, he mostly stuck with white. Made him fit in.

That was important to him. Fitting in. Though deep down, he knew he didn't. Not anywhere. He was one of a kind. One of a pair, really, but even his twin was his opposite.

Fitting in here, though—or at least, projecting the appearance of doing so—was necessary. A matter of life and death, and maybe part of the elusive thing he'd been seeking his entire life: a reason for his existence.

He nodded in a friendly, confident way to the people he passed in the antiseptic, cluttered corridors of New York Hospital for Children. It was a busy place, even after visiting hours. As soon as he saw his chance, James ducked into one of the patient rooms.

And then he paused and went silent as he turned to look.

There, asleep in the bed, lay a little girl who slept with a knit hat pulled down over her head to cover the fact that she had no hair. No eyebrows, though that was harder to hide, despite the dimness of the room. There was a sickly sweet scent clinging to her, the scent of cancer. And while most human beings wouldn't have been able to detect it, he could. He wasn't entirely human, after all, much as he hated to admit that. Vampiric blood ran in his veins, heightening his senses well beyond the norm. So he smelled the cancer mingling with the stronger scents of antibiotics and the iodine concoction that stained her skin near every puncture wound. The little girl's arms looked as if they'd been used for pincushions. It was barely 9:00 p.m. but she was asleep, her body exhausted. Her spirit worn down. Her name was Melinda. She was ten years old.

And she was terminal.

His eyes on the sleeping child, he moved closer to the bed. Watching her, keeping his steps silent, he reached out his open hands and laid them gently on the center of her chest, palms down, thumbs touching. He closed his eyes, and opened his heart.

"Doctor?" a woman asked.

James opened his eyes but didn't move his hands. He hadn't noticed the woman sitting beside the bed. Hadn't even checked to be sure the room was empty. This little girl had been his entire focus. And he thought that for as long as he'd been sneaking in and out of hospital rooms by night, he really ought to know better.

He just got so caught up in his work....

"What are you doing?" the woman asked.

He smiled and met her eyes, willing the unnatural glow in his own to bank itself, to hide from her. "Just feeling her heartbeat."

The woman—the little girl's mother, if physical resemblance was anything to go by—lifted her brows. He saw her clearly, despite the darkness of the room. "Isn't that what your stethoscope is for?"

"Do you mind if I finish?" He inserted authority into his tone this time. That was what a real doctor would do, after all. "You're welcome to stay, but I do need silence."

Frowning, Melinda's mother rose from her chair to watch him. He kept his hands on the girl and felt them growing warmer, knew that soon he would give himself away. He had to distract her. "Would you mind getting me her chart? It's over on her nightstand, I believe."

Nodding, though still obviously suspicious of him, she moved to the nightstand. And James let the power he'd felt rising up in him continue to move through him, into his hands and into the child. A soft golden-yellow glow emanated from his palms for a long moment, and he let it, not stopping even when he knew the mother was turning back toward him. Even when he knew from her sharp gasp, that she'd seen.

The power would flow as long as it needed to. Sometimes it took a second, sometimes a minute. But only it knew when it was finished.

"What is that?" the woman asked. "What the hell are you doing?"

"Shh," he whispered. "Just a moment, please."

"A moment my ass. Who are you? Why haven't I seen you before? What's your name?"

The light beamed brighter.

"God, what is that?" And then she was striding to the door, flinging it open. "Help! Someone help me, there's a stranger in here and he's—"

He lost her words in the softness of the hum that filled his head. It was a vibration, a harmonic tone that made his entire body vibrate in resonance with it, and it felt like…well, he couldn't describe what it felt like. Never had been able to. But he thought it must be what it felt like for one's soul to leave one's body at death and to emerge into oneness with the universe. It felt like bliss and perfection and wonder and ecstasy.

The glow died. His hands cooled. A nurse came running, and the room's lights came on. Blinding and harsh. As he lifted his head and finally refocused on the here and now, he became aware of several people standing in the doorway, frozen in that suspended moment before action set in.

But his main focus was on the little girl. Her eyes were open and staring into his, and she knew. He knew she knew. The exchange between them was real and utterly silent, overloaded with meaning. She might

not be able to describe it or explain it or even understand it, but on a soul-deep level she knew what had
just happened between them. He smiled warmly and
gave a nod of affirmation, and he saw the relief, and
then the joy, in her eyes.

She smiled back at him, and then someone was
grabbing him, pulling his arms behind his back and
holding them there, while another someone snatched
the name badge from the lapel of his white coat and
said, "Call the police."

"The police are already here," said a familiar—and
welcome—female voice. "He's been lurking around
here for a while," the uniformed "officer" explained.
"Someone already called it in." She took hold of his
arm. "Come on, buddy. Let's you and me have a little
talk in private."

"I want to know what this was all about," the
mother demanded.

"Can I see some ID?" one of the nurses said at the
same time, addressing his captor.

"Yeah, yeah," Brigit said, her impatience palpable.
"How about I get him out of the poor kid's room first,
huh? I'll need to question each of you just as soon as
I have him securely tucked away in the backseat of
my car. Do not go anywhere."

She moved behind James as she spoke, and he felt
metal on his wrists, then heard the telltale click of
handcuffs snapping tight. She certainly was pouring it on. She took him by an elbow and turned to
lead him out of Melinda's room. As the door swung

closed behind him, a tiny, beautiful voice said, "It's okay, Mamma. I think he was a angel. Not the kind that comes to take you away. The kind that comes to make you better."

He smiled as he heard those words. Yes. This was his purpose. It was the only thing that gave him any pleasure at all in this isolated, lonely life of his: using his healing gift to save the innocent.

Then his captor shoved him into the elevator, and they rode in silence to the ground floor. He looked her up and down. Her Goldilocks curls were bundled up tight, and her pale blue eyes, with their ebony rings, refused to meet his. When the elevator doors opened, she escorted him unceremoniously outside to her waiting car—a baby-blue, fiftieth anniversary edition Thunderbird—where she opened the passenger door.

He got in. She went around, got behind the wheel and started the engine. Then she reached into her pocket and pulled out a key. "Turn toward the door," she ordered.

James turned toward the side window, so his back and cuffed wrists faced her. She inserted the key, twisted it and the cuffs sprang free. But even as he brought his hands around in front of him, he saw one of the nurses from Melinda's room coming through the hospital doors, frowning as she moved toward the car.

"Incoming," he muttered.

And then the nurse had rounded the car and was tapping on Brigit's window.

Brigit rolled it down in the middle of the nurse's "I knew it! You're not a cop at all, you're—"

Brigit released a growl like that of a panther about to strike. Not human, that sound. It sent chills up even James's spine. He knew she'd exposed her fangs, and probably showed her glowing eyes, as well.

The nurse backed away so fast she fell on her ass, and then Brigit hit the gas and they pulled away, tires squealing before catching pavement and launching the T-Bird into motion.

"That was unnecessary."

She glanced his way, fangs still visible, eyes still aglow. "Says who?"

"Says me. And will you put those damned things away?"

She shrugged, but relaxed enough to let the razor-sharp incisors retract. Her eyes returned to their normal striking ice-blue shade. "So are you done bitching now? Ready to throw in a 'Hi, sis. Thanks for saving my ass back there. Great to see you again.'?"

He sighed, shaking his head. "It is good to see you again, little sister. How are you?"

"I'm good. So far. And you?"

"Fine."

"Typical. One-word answers always were your thing. And I see you're still trying out ways to use your gift. You decide to eradicate death altogether now, or just for those you deem too young to die?"

He lowered his head. "I didn't need your help, you know. I do this sort of thing all the time."

"I know you do. Unlike you, big brother, I care enough to keep track of my kin."

He closed his eyes. "I'd see you more often if you didn't give me this lecture every single freaking time."

"What lecture? The one about abandoning your family? About turning your back on what you truly are, J.W.?"

"It's James."

"It's J.W. It's always been J.W., and it'll always be J.W."

"And I didn't abandon my family or turn my back on what I am."

"No? When's the last time you exposed your fangs, J.W.? When's the last time you tasted human blood?"

The last time…? It had been when he and his sister—his twin—had been adolescents, and their honorary "aunt" Rhiannon had insisted they imbibe. From a glass, not a warm pulsing throat, and still it had repulsed him.

"You're lying to yourself," Brigit said. "It was delicious. It set your soul on fire and left you craving more, and you know it as well as I do."

He was startled, but only briefly. "I'm not used to being around someone who can read my every thought."

"Yeah, well, whose fault is that?"

"Look, I admit, the blood was…appealing. That's what repulsed me. I don't want to be…that way. And I'm not denying who I am, I'm choosing who I want to be, even while trying to discover why I'm here, why I was given this power." He turned his palms up and stared at them, as he had so often throughout his life. "Power over life and death."

"You've always been so sure there's a reason," she said softly.

"I *know* there is, Brigit."

She nodded. "Well, I hate to admit this, bro, but you're right. There is a reason. And I have recently discovered what it is."

He stared at his beautiful twin, his opposite in almost every way. And yet they were the only two of their kind. He was certain she was kidding at first, because she had always teased and taunted him about his yearning for meaning, his quest for understanding. His innate sense of goodness and morality. But she didn't laugh or even smile at him this time. And her face was stone serious.

"You think you know why we were born?"

"Yeah. And it's not to run along the seashore revivifying dead starfish and tossing them back into the waves like you did when we were kids, or to cure little girls with cancer." She licked her lips and shot him a quick look. "That's what you did, just now, isn't it? Cured her?"

He felt warm all over, and his smile was genuine. "Yeah. She's gonna be just fine."

Brigit's lips curved upward, too, before she bit back the smile and put her trademark stern expression back in place. She was a hard-ass. Or at least she liked people to think she was. They'd played these roles all their lives, and he often wondered why she'd taken to hers as easily as he had taken to his.

His was easy. He was the good twin. The healer. The golden child.

Hers was a harder role to embrace. She was the bad twin. The destroyer, in a manner of speaking. And yet she'd never once complained about the label, even mostly seemed to try to live up to the tag—or rather, live down to it.

"Well?" he asked at length. "Are you going to tell me?"

"I think I have to show you." She nodded at a magazine that was rolled up and tucked into the cup holder between them.

He sighed, about to argue with her, but when he met her eyes, he found her mind open, as well. Nothing hidden, no barriers, which was a very rare thing for his sister. He narrowed his eyes and felt only sincerity coming from her. No pretense, no hidden motives.

"The end of the world is coming, bro. It's coming—and we're the only ones who can prevent it. That's why we were born. To save our entire race. Read the article while I drive. The page is folded over. I just hope we're not already too late."

"Too late?"

"I think it's going to start tonight," she told him.

He shook his head, still not following. "You think *what's* going to start tonight?"

Brigit licked her scarlet-stained lips and sighed. "Armageddon. At least for our kind, and maybe for theirs, too."

"We're one-quarter human, Brigit. Their kind is also our kind."

"Fuck their kind." Her eyes flashed.

"Either way," she went on. This might be it for everyone. Unless we do something about it." She looked at her watch. "In the next forty-five minutes, as a matter of fact."

"And where, exactly, is Armageddon going to break out in forty-five minutes?"

"Manhattan," she said. "At a taping of the *Will Waters Show*." She looked his way again and caught him staring at her as if she'd been speaking in tongues. "Will you just read the damned article? And buckle up. We've got to move."

Frowning, he buckled, then opened the copy of *J.A.N.E.S. Magazine* to an article about a recently translated Sumerian clay tablet, written by someone by the name of Professor Lucy Lanfair. He found himself stuck on the tiny head shot of the professor herself, almost unable to tear his eyes away to read the piece that had his sister so wound up. It seemed as if the professor's brown eyes were staring straight off the page and directly into his soul.

Brigit pressed harder on the accelerator, and the car's powerful engine roared like a vampire about to feed.

2

Lester Folsom wasn't enjoying life anymore, and he was more than ready to leave it behind. But he wasn't willing to take his secrets to the grave with him. Those secrets were worth money. A fortune. And hell, he'd risked his life often enough while learning them that he figured he'd earned the right to spill his guts and reap the benefits before he checked out for good. So he'd spent the past year doing exactly that.

He was old and tired, and he was damned achy. And it had happened all at once, too. None of this gradual decline one tended to expect from old age. Not with him. One week he was feeling normal, and the next, he noticed that it hurt to lift his arms up over his head. The balls and sockets in his shoulders felt as if they'd run out of lubrication, stiff and tight. And he felt something similar in his knees and wrists and even his ankles now and then. It had happened right about the same time his eyesight had gone to hell. And it had all been downhill from there. His hair had thinned, and what remained had gone silver. His back had grown progressively more stooped, his skin more papery, with every passing year.

The beginning of his end, as nearly as he could pinpoint it, had been fifteen years ago, right after he'd retired from government work. His pension was a good one. But not as good as the advance River House Publishing had given him for his tell-all book. That money had allowed him spend the past twelve months on a private island in the Caribbean, basking and writing. Reliving it all, and yes, occasionally jumping out of his skin at bumps in the night. But they'd all been false alarms.

They wouldn't be, after tonight. If his former employer didn't get him, the subjects of his life's work would. Either way, he was history. And that was fine.

He'd had that year in the tropical sun. Sandy beaches and warm saltwater made bifocals and arthritis a whole lot more bearable. And now the year was over. The book would hit the stands one month from today. He figured he'd be dead shortly thereafter. But he was ready. His affairs were all in order.

"Five minutes, Mr. Folsom," a woman's voice said.

He glanced up at the redheaded producer who'd poked her head through the door into the greenroom. It wasn't green at all. Go figure. "I'll be ready," he replied.

And then she opened the door a bit farther and

allowed another woman to enter. "You'll go on right after Mr. Folsom," the redhead told her.

"Thanks, Kelly."

Kelly. That was the young redhead's name. You'd think he could have remembered that from twenty minutes ago, when she'd first introduced herself. Didn't much matter, he supposed. She was gone now.

The newcomer—he immediately labeled her an introverted intellectual—nodded hello, then looked around the room, just the way he had, taking in the table with its offerings of coffee, tea, cream and sugar, and its spartan selection of fruit and pastries. There was a television mounted high in one corner, tuned to the show on which they were both soon going to appear, but he had turned down the volume, bored by the host's opening segment.

The woman finished her scan of the room and looked his way instead, then lowered her eyes when he met them. Pretty eyes. Brown and flighty, like a doe's eyes, but hidden behind a pair of tortoiseshell-framed glasses.

"Well," he said, to break the ice, "it seems Kelly isn't much for introductions, so we'll have to do it ourselves. I'm Lester Folsom, here to plug a book."

She smiled at him, finally meeting his gaze. "Professor Lucy Lanfair," she said, moving closer, extending a slender hand. It was not a delicate, pampered looking hand, but a working one. He liked that. She had mink-brown hair that matched her eyes, but she kept it all twisted up into a knot at the back of her head.

He took her hand, more relieved than he wanted to admit that it was warm to the touch. "Pleased to make your acquaintance."

"Likewise." She withdrew her hand, wiping it on her brown tweed skirt. "Sorry about the sweaty palms. I'm a nervous wreck. I've never been on TV before."

"Nothing to be nervous about," he assured her. "You look very nice, if that's any comfort to you."

"I've never been too concerned with how I look, but thank you very much. I appreciate it."

A woman who didn't care about looks. Well, now, that was interesting. "What is it you've come to talk about?" he asked.

She sank into a chair kitty-corner from his and un- rolled the magazine she'd been clutching in one hand. "A rather startling new translation of a four-thousand, five-hundred-year-old clay tablet."

He lifted his brows, his attention truly caught now. "Sumerian?"

"Yes!" She sounded surprised. "How did you know?"

"Not many other cultures had a written language in twenty-five hundred BCE. May I?" He nodded at the magazine, and she handed it to him. The *Journal of Ancient Near Eastern Studies, J.A.N.E.S.* for short, had a classic image of a ziggurat tower on the front, beneath which the headline screamed, New

Translation Suggests Another Doomsday Prophecy for Mankind. He glanced from it to her. "This is your piece?" When she nodded, he said, "You made the cover. Impressive."

"Yes, of a scholarly journal with a readership of about three thousand. Still, it's nice to get the recognition. Though I could do without the sensationalism. What the prophecy predicts is meaningless."

"Oh, don't be so sure about that." He shifted his gaze to the book he carried with him everywhere he went. "And you should be grateful for the sensationalism. You might not have gotten any coverage at all without it."

"No, I guess not."

"So, you're a translator?" he asked, as he flipped pages to find her story.

"And an archaeologist, and a professor at Binghamton University," she said softly.

Not bragging, just particular about getting her facts straight, he thought. She was a pretty thing. A bit skinnier than he liked, but women had been curvier in his day. She dressed down, though. Probably to be taken more seriously in her career. Pencil skirt, simple white blouse with a thin, cream-colored button-down sweater over it. Very plain.

"And now an author to boot," he added.

"It's mandatory in my field. 'Publish or perish' is more than just a figure of speech."

Or in his own case, *publish* and *perish*, he thought. He found her article and, without time to read it all,

skimmed ahead to the actual translation. Within the
first few lines, he was riveted.

> The offspring of the Old One,
> All the children of the Ancient One,
> Of Utanapishtim,
> In a stroke, are no more.
> In the light of his eyes, they are no more
> To the last, to the very last,
> Unless Utanapishtim himself… (Segment
Missing)

"As I say, it's not what it says that's so interesting," the skinny professor said, her voice breaking
into his reading. "It's that the Sumerians simply were
not known to prophecy. But—"

He held up a hand to stop her distracting chatter
as his eyes sped over the lines.

> When light meets shadow,
> When darkness is well-lit,
> When the hidden are revealed,
> War erupts.
> Like a lion, it devours.
> Like a tigress, without mercy, it destroys.

> For the end is upon them,
> The end of their kind,
> The end of their race,
> The race that sprang from his veins.

The door opened, and the redhead—Kelly—poked her head in again. "Time to go on, Mr. Folsom."

"One moment!" he barked, startling both women. He had to finish reading. He could not stop there. He had to know.

> Only the Old One… (Segment Missing)
> The Flood-Survivor
> The Ancient One
> Utanapishtim
>
> The Two must bring about… (Segment Missing)
> The Two who are opposite
> And yet the same,
> One light, one dark,
> One the destroyer.
> One the salvation

"The twins," he whispered. "This is about the legendary mongrel twins."

"Excuse me?" Professor Lanfair asked.

"Mr. Folsom," Kelly said. "We have to go."

Ignoring them both, he flipped the page, but there was no more. Lifting his head, he speared the professor with his eyes. "That's it? That's all? They printed all of it?"

"Yes. At least, that's all so far. There are still hundreds of broken pieces of clay tablets from that particular dig site in storage. There may be more to this tablet, but at the moment—"

"Mr. Folsom!" Kelly was not taking no for an answer.

He nodded, closing the magazine and handing it back to the doe-eyed bookworm. "It's not a doomsday prophecy at all, Professor Lanfair. Not for humankind, anyway. This is about them."

"About whom?"

He sighed, glanced at the redhead and then leaned close to the professor and whispered in her ear, "About the race no one believes exists—the very one my book is about to expose on national television tonight." A sudden chill raced up his spine, and he glanced at the TV screen in the corner again, then narrowed his eyes and looked more closely. As the camera panned over the studio audience, he spotted a dark-suited man standing near the back, and then another near the exit. Both wore tinted glasses in the dim studio. His mouth went dry.

But he couldn't back down now. He had to see this through. Returning his attention to the pretty professor who had stumbled upon what might be the key to everything, he pressed his personal copy of his soon-to-be-released book into her hands. "You'd better hold on to this. Don't let anyone know you have it, and don't let it out of your grip. No matter what."

"I don't under—"

"I'm about to tell the world that vampires really do exist, and that our government has known about it for the better part of a century. The darkness, my dear girl, is about to be well-lit. The hidden is about to be revealed. And there are those who don't want that to happen. But the proof—" he tapped the book's cover with a forefinger "—the proof is in there."

Then he straightened away from her, nodded at the television set and said, "Turn up the volume and pay attention, Professor. Somehow, this involves you, too." Then he walked out the door, letting it swing closed behind him.

He followed the youthful and impatient producer, who all but trotted down one long corridor after another. It was all he could do to keep up, and he was literally out of breath by the time she pushed open a pair of double doors and held one with her back while ushering him through. "Take your time crossing the stage," she told him in a whisper. "Wave hello to the audience. And watch those cables on the floor."

Will Waters, twenty-five-year news veteran, retired network anchor and current host of the nation's top-rated prime-time news magazine, rose to his feet and extended a hand in Les's direction. "Please welcome Lester Folsom to the show."

Struggling to catch his breath, Les lifted his chin and began walking forward, his pounding heartbeat barely audible to his own ears due to the live studio audience's obedience to the glowing "applause" sign. Silently, he wished he hadn't missed Will Waters's entire introduction. But he could guess at what it had entailed. The true contents of his book had not been revealed to anyone besides the publisher, only the barest of hints had been released to the press.

That he had worked for a top-secret sub-division of the CIA for more than twenty years, a sub-division known as the Division of Paranormal Investigations, or DPI. And that his book would reveal the existence of things formerly believed to live only in the realms of fiction. Just what sorts of things—that was what he would talk about tonight. If those fellows in the back of the audience let him get that far, anyway. He'd have to get straight to the point with Will Waters. No time for small talk.

He stepped over a pair of heavy cables that snaked across the floor and made his way to the host, one of the most beloved newsmen in the world. Will Waters extended a hand.

And just as Lester Folsom closed his own hand around it, he felt something like a sledgehammer pound into his chest. And then again. And again.

It was only as he sank to the floor that the accompanying sounds—*Pop! Pop! Pop!*—registered in his brain. Not hammer blows. Gunshots. Bullets. They felt nothing like he'd expected. And vaguely, he became aware that the famous veteran newsman was on the floor beside him, jerking spasmodically as he bled out. Collateral damage. That was what those suits would call it.

As the light of this world began to fade and the light of another appeared on a distant horizon, Lester thought that they had got to him even faster than he had anticipated.

He'd done the right thing, though. And despite

this sloppy effort at containment, there was no way they could keep his secrets quiet now. He'd opened Pandora's Box, then made a graceless but timely exit before the havoc he'd unleashed could play out. From the sounds of the skinny professor's prophecy, it wasn't going to be pretty. He hoped she would survive, now that she was the only one with the proof.

The light on the distant horizon grew brighter. He could see it clearly even without his glasses. And then his shoulders stopped aching at last.

When the crazy old man left the greenroom, Lucy finally allowed the amused smile she'd been holding back with all her might to take possession of her face. She even laughed a little, quickly clapping her hand over her mouth in case he might hear beyond the heavy door. That would just be cruel. But really, *vampires?* Lester Folsom was obviously suffering from some sort of delusional break with reality.

Poor Kelly. He'd given the girl an awfully hard time. Lucy made a mental note to go a lot easier on the young producer when it was her turn to go onstage.

Sighing, she glanced down at the book the old man had pressed into her hands.

THE TRUTH.

Unimaginative title, but memorable in its simplicity. There was a string emerging from the top of the book, and a tiny jade Kwan Yin, goddess of mercy and compassion, pendant dangling from the bottom. A necklace. Pretty. What an odd thing for a man to be using as a bookmark. She wondered if Mr. Folsom was a practicing Buddhist or just fond of Asian art. She removed the necklace from the book and hung it around her own neck, tucking the pendant underneath her blouse, so she would remember to return it to the man when they passed again. She was sure she would see him on her way to the stage.

She stuffed the book into her satchel so she wouldn't forget it and offend the old guy when he came back to the greenroom for his coat and saw his gift, abandoned there. Then she dropped her bag into an empty chair and went to the television to turn it up the old-fashioned way, since she didn't see a remote, curious to see how the fearless vampire hunter would come off to the viewers.

She'd always had a lot of respect for Will Waters. She hoped that wasn't about to be shaken, but she suspected it was. There were only two ways this interview could go down, the way she saw it. Either Waters was going to expose the old man as confused and possibly senile, or he was going to play along with this sensationalistic vampire nonsense for the sake of his ratings. Either way seemed a breach of what used to be known as journalistic integrity. She hoped she was wrong.

Lucy sat down, waiting for the commercial break to end. She had been pleased at the invitation to appear on a serious news program. Not because she had any desire to grab her fifteen minutes of fame. God knew she preferred solitude. Her favorite place in the world, aside from a dig site in the middle of nowhere, was the dusty basement of the archaeology department at BU. And she certainly wasn't going to jump onto the 2012 doomsday bandwagon, as the show's producers seemed to be expecting her to do. No, she was going to stick to the facts. This translation was an extraordinary new bit of information about the ancient Sumerians, how they lived and how they thought. Period.

Sensationalism was something she didn't need. And she wouldn't take fame if they gave it to her. Recognition for her work, that would be okay, because it might just result in good PR for the university, which might persuade the powers that be to further fund her work.

She was picking over the fruit tray on the table, looking for grapes that hadn't yet made it more than halfway to raisinhood, when the show's theme music announced that the break was over. As it faded away, Will Waters introduced his dotty next guest.

Lucy looked up at the screen, absently popping a grape into her mouth, and watched as Mr. Folsom made his way toward the set. His gait was slow and shuffling, his posture stooped. He took his time crossing the stage, then finally extended a hand to shake the host's.

And then there was a series of popping sounds that Lucy recognized all too well. She froze in place, not believing what she was seeing on the TV screen, as both men fell to the floor, red blooms spreading on their white shirts.

Shock gripped her as her brain tried to translate what her eyes had just seen. The cameras began jostling amid a cacophony of shouting, rushing people. Some seemed to be racing toward the stage, but most were running away from it, stampeding for the exits.

The screen switched abruptly to a "technical difficulty" message, and it took Lucy a few seconds to realize that the sounds of panic she could still hear were coming, not from the television set, but from the hallway beyond the greenroom door.

And for just an instant she was back there again, sleeping in her parents' tent on the site of an archaeological dig in a Middle Eastern desert.

There were motors roaring nearer, and then a series of keening battle cries and gunshots in the night. She felt her mother's hands shaking her awake in the dead of night and heard her panicked, fear-choked voice. "Run, Lucy! Run into the dunes and hide. Hurry!"

At eleven years old, Lucy came awake fast and heard the sounds, but what scared her more was the fear in her mother's voice, and in her eyes. It was as if she knew, somehow, what was about to happen.

"I won't go without you!" Lucy glimpsed her father as he shoved his worn-out old fedora onto his head. He was never without that hat on a dig. Said it brought him luck. But it wasn't bringing any luck tonight. And then he was taking a gun from a box underneath his cot. A gun! She'd never seen him with a gun before.

Her parents were a pair of middle-aged, bookish ar-
chaeologists. They didn't carry guns.

"You have to, Lucy. Go! Now, before it's too late!"

"Obey your mother!" her father told her.

Her mother pushed her through a flap in the rear of
the tent, even as men in mismatched fatigues surged
from a half-dozen jeeps, shouting in their foreign
tongues, shooting their weapons. Lucy's feet sank
into the sand, slowing her, but she ran.

There were screams and more gunfire. Every crack
of every rifle made her body jerk in reaction as she
strained to run faster through the sucking sand, until
finally she dove behind a dune, burying her face.

But worse than the noise, worse than the shouting
and the gunshots, was the silence that came after-
ward. The vehicles all roared away. And then there
was nothing. Nothing. Just an eleven-year-old girl,
lying in a sand dune, shaking and too terrified to even
lift her head.

Something banged against the greenroom door,
snapping Lucy out of the memory. Blinking away the
paralysis it had brought with it, she realized that she
had to get the hell out of this place, and she had to do
it now. The door through which she had entered was
not an option. There was what sounded like a riot
going on beyond it. Turning, she spotted the room's
only other door, one marked EMERGENCY EXIT
ONLY.

This qualified, she decided, and she grabbed her
satchel and jacket, shoved the emergency door open

and ran through it into a vast concrete area with an open, overhead door, like a garage door, at the far end, and the city night beyond. She raced toward that opening, onto the raised platform outside it—a loading dock, she guessed—and jumped from that to the pavement four feet below.

Running full bore now, she followed the blacktop that ran between two buildings until she emerged onto a New York City sidewalk. Blending with the masses of humanity, she walked as fast as she could away from the violence she'd just witnessed.

Sirens screamed as police arrived. She smelled fast-food grease from somewhere nearby. Across the street, four men emerged from a black van. They wore suits and long dark coats, and they strode very quickly toward the building she'd just exited. One glanced her way, but she quickly averted her eyes and kept on walking. The wind swept a playbill over her feet and on down the sidewalk, and air brakes whooshed in the distance. She kept going.

Guilt rose up to nip at her heels. She was a coward for running away. Surely she ought to seek out a police officer, and tell him what she had seen and heard.

But everything in her told her to do just the opposite. So that was what she did. Running away, saving herself while others died—that was she did best, after all.

And yet it didn't work out quite that way for her this time. From behind her, Lucy heard a voice say,

"Hold it right there, lady." And somehow she knew he was addressing her.

Her feet obeyed. But her heart raced even faster. The fight-or-flight impulse was coming down with all its weight on the "flight" side of the coin. And every cell in her body was already in motion, pushing her, making it almost impossible to stand still.

"Are you Professor Lanfair?" the man asked. He was one of those men in black she'd spotted earlier. She could see his warped reflection in the back of a chrome mirror, affixed to the side of a hot little sports car she wished she could jump into and drive away.

"I'm afraid you're going to have to come with me, ma'am."

No, I don't think I am.

Her brain argued, told her to just calm down, take a breath and cooperate. The guy was official in some way, right?

And then he started toward her. His footsteps on the wet sidewalk were like a starter's pistol. And they had the same effect on her. She burst into motion like a racehorse when the gate flies open, but in three strides she felt an impact in the center of her back. The force sent her falling, as if she'd been slammed by a speeding truck. She was already colliding with the sidewalk by the time she actually heard the gunshot.

The pain of it came last, like a red-hot poker had been driven right through her spine and out through her sternum. Her bag went skidding along the sidewalk, into the alley, everything flying out of it in a hundred directions.

Shot. My God, I've been shot. I've been shot, I've been shot.

She lay there, facedown and shocked beyond thought, in a warm and spreading pool of her own blood. *See?* A voice in her head whispered. *I told you not to run.*

3

James took off the lab coat in the car and was wishing he had something besides the white scrubs and cross-trainers he was still wearing when his sister pulled the Thunderbird to a stop in a convenient spot she'd no doubt had some part in orchestrating. Her mind was far more powerful than his. He could read thoughts and impose his will on mortals, too, but she made him look like a rank amateur in both areas.

Feeding on human blood enhanced the vampiric powers they'd been born with. Or so she kept telling him. He hadn't imbibed enough himself to know. Nor would he—ever.

Brigit stopped the car abruptly. "Here we are. And we're late, just as I feared." She looked at her watch again while she got out on the traffic side and hurried around to the busy Manhattan sidewalk. There was a lighted marquee above the entrance to Studio Three, but Brigit was moving too fast for James to spend any time reading it if he hoped to keep up with her.

She got to the door, where a man in a dark suit said, "I'm sorry, ma'am, the taping is already underway. You'll have to wait for a break to go inside. May I see your tickets?"

Brigit smiled her sweetest smile and beamed her ice-blue eyes at the man. At first he reacted just as any male would, with pure sexual interest, but then it went further. His eyes began to glaze over. His smile died, and his entire face went lax. Expressionless. He opened the door and stepped aside to let them pass.

"Nice guy," she said. "Strong, silent type."

"Yeah." James didn't hide the disapproval in his tone. It was wrong to manipulate human minds that way just because you could. "Really, sis, would it have killed you to just get the damned tickets?"

"Who are you, the ticket police?"

James ignored the question and moved with his sister into the darkened studio, where Will Waters was delivering his opening monologue—his customary commentary on the week's news—on a soundstage in front of a live audience. Something prickled along the back of James's neck. He stopped and gripped his sister's forearm until she stopped, too.

Standing along the rear wall, behind the spectator seats, was a man in a long dark coat. In the dark, James's vision was excellent. He'd inherited that ability, among others, from the vampire side of the family. It was one of the traits he didn't mind making use of.

And he wondered again, as he often had, whether

it was hypocritical of him to embrace the traits he approved of, while rejecting the ones he didn't. Seeing in the darkness, however, did no harm. And it was almost as handy as the ability to walk around in the sunlight without becoming a living torch, a trait he'd inherited from the human branch of the family tree.

Who do you think he is? his sister asked without speaking aloud.

James had to focus to reply. It had been a long time since he'd tried mental communication on this level. Picking up thoughts, sensations, vibes was one thing. Conversation—language—that was far more complex. It came back to him easily, however. Like riding a bike, he supposed.

Don't know, but there's another on the right, and two more up in the balcony—one on each side. Look like government types.

Hmm. Men in Black. Brigit pretended to study her nails as she furtively looked in the directions he'd indicated. *Do you think they know about the prophecy's connection to the undead?*

How could anyone know about that but us?

A lot of people know about vampires, J.W. DPI, the government. They might be after the professor.

Could they be bodyguards or something, maybe for another guest? James watched the men, feeling more alarmed by the moment and knowing better than to ignore his instincts.

I don't even know who else is on tonight. Oh...

Brigit's mental communiqué came to a halt as Will

Waters's words came clear. "Next up, our surprise guest. A man who worked for what he claims was a top-secret subdivision of the CIA for more than twenty years. Now he's written a tell-all book, which he says will prove the existence of things he calls... paranormal. His book was due to hit the shelves next month, but we've just this minute had word that it has been abruptly pulled, its production stopped by the Department of Homeland Security. A DHS spokesman says the book divulges classified information that could put undercover agents and operations in jeopardy. As to the author's claims of government knowledge of supernatural matters, the spokesman laughs and asserts that the author is clearly suffering from some form of dementia, but that despite his delusions, he's still in possession of sensitive information that must be contained.

"Here to answer those claims and talk about what his book would have revealed, retired CIA Field Agent, Lester Folsom."

James and Brigit stared at each other, stunned. "They're talking about the DPI," Brigit whispered. "And Folsom...haven't I heard that name?"

"You didn't know about this?" he asked.

"No, and from what Waters just said, I don't think anyone did." The old man who had to be Lester Folsom was already walking unsteadily across the stage, moving slowly. He stretched out a hand toward the host's outstretched arm, and then suddenly gunshots rang out. The two men jerked with the impacts and blood spatter sprayed behind them.

James was riveted as the old man fell to the floor, and the famous newsman with him. His gaze shot upward instinctively, to the balcony, where the shots had originated, but he could no longer see the man in black up there. The crowd was on its feet, and people were rushing for the exits.

He started to move forward, toward the dead men, but his sister grabbed his shoulder. "Not them. Her. We have to get to her."

"She can wait," he said, turning and gripping her hand tight, as people hit and jostled them on the way out. "They're dying."

"They're dead! And if you try to help them, those bastards will just kill them again and you with them," Brigit shouted over the increasing din. "You think it's coincidence Folsom and Professor Lanfair were on the same talk show, on the same night? The suits will get her if we don't. Come on, she'd be backstage somewhere."

"But, Brigit—"

"We need her, J.W. We need her to save our entire race, and maybe hers, too, if you need some added enticement. Come on."

They ducked out the door, and he found it much easier to move with the flow of panicked audience members than against them. Sirens were wailing already as they emerged into the night and hurried up the sidewalk. James looked and looked for the woman whose photo had appeared in the magazine his sister had shown him. The translator. Professor Lanfair. But the crowds and now the cops—who were rushing up and pulling people aside, trying to contain their witnesses—were making it harder.

"That's her, J.W. Just came out of the alley, and she's flying! In heels, too!"

James looked in the direction his sister was pointing, but there were dozens of panicked individuals on the sidewalk. And then he heard a voice shout, "Hold it right there, lady."

He saw one of the men in black leveling a gun at the back of a slender woman in a tweed skirt. He could only see the back of her head, but he *felt* her.

Turning wide eyes on his sister, he said, "Why didn't you tell me she's one of the Chosen?"

"I didn't know. What the—"

Just then the professor jerked forward, even as James held up a hand, an unthinking reaction. He shouted "No!" but it was too late. The man in black's gun went off, and the bullet tore through the professor's body. James saw, as if in slow motion, the blood explode from the exit wound like a mist in front of her, even as her back arched and she slammed facedown onto the sidewalk.

And then there was no stopping him. He launched into motion, passing by the killer, falling to his knees beside her. Her brown hair was coming loose from its tightly wound bun, and it was glittering, too, with the rainy mist now falling on the city street. He rolled her onto her back, very gently, and his gut-level, genetically encoded need to aid anyone of her kind compelled him to help her. To save her.

She was one of the Chosen. One of the rare mortals who possessed the Belladonna Antigen and, with it, the potential to become a vampire. Vampires sensed her kind, smelled them, and could not fight the instinct to protect them. He'd inherited *that,* too. But in the professor's case, it felt like something more.

He had rolled the professor onto her back, so the misty rain fell on her cheeks now. Vaguely, he heard his sister trying to hold off the man in black, who was trying to get past her. She was exerting her will, but he was fighting it as if he knew how. Further support of her theory that he was DPI, which would have given him training in dealing with preternatural mind control. Luckily a huge crowd was closing in, too, giving James a heartbeat more time.

"I said stay back!" Brigit shouted. Her voice in that moment was something beyond human. The power it carried could not be resisted. Even James looked up at her, then from her fierce expression to the dazed faces of the people around them. They'd inexplicably stopped in their tracks and were unable to convince themselves to move forward again. The government man included.

"Stay back," Brigit kept saying, holding her hands up, palms out. She was really straining. Her eyes were beginning to emit a soft glow.

"Easy, Brigit," he warned. "Don't go too far."

"You handle your gift and I'll handle mine. Get on with it, J.W."

He nodded, looking down at the woman again. Her eyeglasses were crooked and her eyes were closed, thick sable lashes lying on her smooth skin. Upturned nose, full lips, Audrey Hepburn cheekbones. Her life was fading. James turned his palms up and stared down at them, and then he felt them begin to warm. Turning them downward again, he laid them over the exit wound in her chest, ignoring the blood and gore.

Her blood was flowing as his hands grew warmer, and he sensed very strongly the extremely rare Belladonna Antigen every vampire had possessed as a human. She was almost family.

The part of his family he had rejected. And yet, he could not turn away from her. Wouldn't have, even if he could.

As his hands grew hot, he pressed them between the woman's breasts. His palms immediately began to emit that familiar, yellow-gold luminescence. He shifted his body and tried to block the light from the spectators around him, and prayed that his sister would be able to hold their attention long enough.

James felt the professor's chest grow hot, matching the energy of his palms. He saw the glow of his hands reflected there and knew the healing was beginning to take. He felt that sensation again, the one of his soul sort of reaching out from his body to connect to something more, something bigger, far beyond any individual sense of self. There was a greater whole and it was one, and he was part of it, in those moments.

His gaze shifted suddenly and without warning to Lucy Lanfair's face, and at that same instant her eyes flew open. Brown eyes. Staring straight into his.

"I know you," she whispered.

"Easy. Take it easy."

"But I know you. I know you."

And then her eyes shifted lower, to his hands on her chest, and she saw all the blood—and there was a lot of it. She started sucking in openmouthed, shallow breaths, and he knew she was on the edge of panic. "Oh God, Oh God, Oh God—"

"It's okay," he told her. "It's okay. It's not as bad as it looks."

"What…what's that light? What are you doing?"

The glow intensified, just as it always did at the end of a healing. It grew brighter and then died, just that fast. Like the flash of a firefly on a summer country night.

"Get the fuck off her, pal!"

A pair of hands gripped his shoulders, jerking him bodily up and away from her. He'd been unaware, for a few ticks of the clock, of what was happening around him. Other black coats had emerged—some from the studio, others from the dark-colored vans that were lining the street. An ambulance had backed up to the curb, and the medics sprang into action the second James was no longer blocking their way.

He was weak. He was always a little weak after

a healing, and this made two in one night, only a bit more than an hour apart. He felt disoriented, too. Illogically, he didn't want anyone else near this woman, and he started to push his way back to her, but his sister touched his arm.

There's nothing we can do now, she said, mentally. *Too many witnesses, and we don't want these suits to know who the hell we are, J.W. Not if they're who I think they are.*

But they're taking her—

We'll get her. We will. But later. This is too risky.

Even as they carried on the mental conversation, one of the medics looked up. "There's not a mark on her. I don't understand. Where the hell did all this blood come from?"

"Just get her into the ambulance," one of the men in black ordered, and then he turned, scanning the crowd—in search, James knew, of him.

The man had a scar running from the outer corner of his left eye, across his cheek, reaching almost to the center of his chin, and eyes the color of wet cement.

"You," he said loudly, pointing at James, who was some twenty feet away. "I want to talk to you."

Brigit tugged his arm. "We have to go. Now."

He knew she was right. But it was killing him to leave Lucy Lanfair. Even as his sister tugged him toward her waiting car, James was looking back, watching them lift the gurney on which the beautiful professor lay, strapped down now, into the back of the ambulance.

She was looking straight back at him. She didn't reach out, and she didn't speak, but she couldn't seem to take her eyes off him, either.

And then they closed the doors, and Brigit gave him a shove.

"I said wait!" Scarface commanded. He was reaching into his coat now, and James had little doubt he was about to pull a gun.

They'd made it back to the car, and James reached for the passenger door just as Brigit started the motor with a roar. Her window was down, and she was looking back at the man. As James predicted, he was leveling a gun.

"Freeze! Don't make me—"

Brigit lifted a hand, palm up, fingers loosely touching her thumb.

"Don't kill him!" James shouted.

She flicked her fingers open as her gaze intensified, and a beam of light pulsed from her eyes toward the man. Something exploded, shaking the sidewalk, and even the street, so powerfully that several onlookers fell down. Dust and rubble rained down as people ran screaming for cover. At the same instant, Brigit was gunning the motor again, spinning the tires, shifting rapidly through the gears as she sped away.

James turned in his seat, wondering if the debris falling on the crowd included bits of Scarface. But no, it seemed to be a magazine stand that had stood a few yards from him.

"Don't worry," Brigit told him. "The vendor had

left his post to gawk at the lady who was gunned down on the sidewalk. No casualties, though I think letting that scar-cheeked bastard live was a mistake."

"You sound just like Rhiannon, who, I think, originated the phrase 'Kill them all and let the gods sort them out.'"

"Funny you should mention her."

He closed his eyes. "Tell me that's not where we're going."

"Who the hell else is going to be able to tell us what's going on, J.W.?"

"I keep telling you, I go by James now."

"Yeah. You *do* keep telling me that. It's irritating. I wish you'd stop."

She took a corner so fast that he was mashed up against the door, and he knew there was no going back now.

He'd been sucked back in. Just as he'd always pretty much known he would be. His family were not the kind who let go easily.

The ambulance attendant was sticking a needle into her arm the second the doors swung shut, and Lucy gasped at the unexpected pinch of it. Then she looked up at the young man and said, "I really think I'm all right."

"Just relax, Professor Lanfair. You're in good hands."

"How do you know my na...uh..." Ocean waves came washing into her brain, crashing and then slowly sucking her logical mind back out to sea again. "What did you…give me?"

"Just relax now. It's all fine. Just relax."

He was smiling and his eyes were kind and sort of hazel. But they weren't those other eyes. Those piercing, electric-blue eyes she'd been lost in moments before. And this medic's hands, while soothing and strong, were not the same hands she'd felt on her before, either. That other touch had been so powerful she'd felt it in every cell of her body. A touch that she knew had somehow…healed her.

And that man. That face. That familiar, beautiful face. Something in her, something deep inside her, had recognized him—though she knew she had never seen him before in her life.

Perhaps, she thought, he was an angel.

"Time to wake up now, Professor. Come on. You've had a good rest. Wake up. We need to talk."

Lucy opened her eyes. But the white room was tipping slowly one way, then the other, growing on one side, shrinking on the other, then reversing itself before just spinning slowly. There was a woman. Black hair with a white streak. A man with a big scar on his face. It must have been his voice she heard.

That was all she noticed before she slammed her eyes closed again.

"I'm going to be sick."

"No, you aren't," the woman said softly. "Do you remember who you are, dear? Hmm?"

"Am in the hospital? Did I die?" God, she was so disoriented.

"You're safe, and you're fine, and you're going home soon."

Her voice was deep. A little gravelly. A Stevie Nicks voice. Lucy loved Stevie Nicks, mainly because her mom had.

"Now, tell me your name," Stevie Nicks said.

Lucy smiled, remembering the soundtrack of her childhood, before it had all gone so dark. "Lucy. Dad used to call me Lucille. But I hated it. I wouldn't hate it now, though. I'd love to hear him call me Lucille again."

She tried opening her eyes again, but the room was still all out of sorts. She saw the man with the scar leaning close to Stevie—no, that wasn't Stevie. She wasn't wearing a scrap of lace or fringe, or a single trailing shawl. No, she was wearing mannish blue trousers with a white shirt tucked in, a thin belt, and a white lab coat, like a doctor.

"Can you get her to focus?" the scarred man said.

"If you get what you need, does it matter if it's couched in her life story?"

"Time is of the essence here, Lillian. All hell's breaking loose out there, in case you hadn't noticed."

"Maybe your containment team should have considered not having their work televised, then. Back off and let me do my job."

The scar-faced man huffed, but he moved away from the bed.

Oh, Lucy thought. She was in a bed. And that white lab coat—yeah. Okay, this must be a hospital, then.

"Lucy, what's your full name, dear?"

Lucy tried to focus, because for some reason she was afraid of making that man angry, and he already seemed awfully impatient. "Lucille Annabelle Lanfair."

"Very good. And what do you do, Lucy?"

"I work in the Ancient Near Eastern Studies Department at Binghamton University," she said, wondering why her tongue felt too big and her esses were lispy.

"And what does that work entail?"

"I teach classes about ancient Sumerian culture and the Sumerians' written language. It was the earliest form of writing, you know."

"No, I didn't know that. That's fascinating. Why don't you tell me about this most recent translation of yours? The one that got you noticed by Will Waters."

At the mention of the talk show host's name, she cringed, squeezing her eyes tightly shut once more, and hearing again the gunshots, seeing the chaos, feeling the horror. "He's dead, isn't he? And that crazy old man, Folsom, too? I saw it."

"Yes. Yes, they're both dead. Some crazed fan. Did you meet Mr. Folsom?"

Keeping her eyes closed, she said, "In the green-room."

"And did you talk to him?"

She nodded. "He was…a little crazy, I think. Said vampires were real."

"That is crazy. Did he say anything else to you?"

"Said this involves me, too. Said my translation wasn't about humans, that it was about vampires, and about…them."

"Who?"

She shook her head. "Twins, he said. Mongrel twins. Crazy."

"I see. And did he say who or where these twins are?"

"No. He had to go." Lucy felt her heartbeat quicken, and her breath came a little faster. "And then someone shot him—" Her voice broke as her throat went too tight for words to fit through, and hot tears surfaced in her eyes.

"It's all right, Lucy. It's all right. You're safe here," the woman who sounded like Stevie said softly. Lucy wished she would sing. "Now I want you to think about what happened right after that terrible shooting. What did you do?"

Lucy kept her eyes closed, but the scalding tears slipped through anyway. "I ran."

"And why did you run?"

"It's what I always do."

The woman was silent for a moment. "When have you had to run before, Lucy?"

But before Lucy could answer, the man spoke, his voice deep and low and rough, like sandpaper. "When she was a kid. Eleven, I think. On a dig with her archaeologist parents in the Northern Iraqi desert, by special arrangement with the government. Bandits raided the campsite by night, shot the entire team and took everything that wasn't nailed down. She was found cowering in a sand dune, sole survivor. It's all in her dossier."

Lucy felt the woman's hand covering hers. "That must have been awful for you."

"It was the worst day of my life. Until today."

"I'm very sorry, Lucy. And I'm sorry to have to make you relive this, too. But we're nearly done. Now, I want to get back to what happened at the studio. You were in the greenroom, but you saw the shooting. How did you see it, when the greenroom is so far away from the soundstage?"

"I...I saw it on the TV."

"I see. So you saw it happen on the TV in the greenroom, and then you ran."

"Mmm-hmm."

"And then what happened?"

Lucy sniffled hard and wondered why she was spilling her guts this way. But she couldn't seem to stop herself. "S-Someone told me to stop. He was dressed all in black, I think. And he had sunglasses. So I froze, and I tried to stay still, like he said, but I just...I just couldn't. My legs just wouldn't obey. And I ran. And he...he shot me. He shot me."

"But you're all right now," the woman said.

"There was all this blood. It was everywhere. And I fell down, right in it. And it started to hurt. And then…and then he was there."

"Who was?"

"I don't know." She frowned, her eyes still closed, as if to keep the memory inside. "He touched me, and I felt like I knew him. And he had these eyes…"

"And what did he do to you, Lucy?"

"Nothing. He just touched me."

"How, Lucy? Where did he touch you?"

"My chest." She lifted a hand to press it to her own sternum, where she was sure there had been a gaping, jagged hole before. But there was only soft fabric, not her own clothing, and though she explored with her fingers, she felt no sign of any injury beneath it. "And then the man who shot me and…other men who looked like him were pushing him away and putting me in the ambulance. And now I'm here."

"But you don't know his name?"

"No."

"But you said you felt like you knew him?"

"And yet…not. You know?"

"No. No, I don't."

"Ask her what she felt when he was touching her," the scarred man barked.

She didn't like his voice, and she didn't like him speaking as if she wasn't even in the room. And she wanted to go home. To her cozy one-story house with the flower boxes in the windows and the neat sidewalk that was all bordered in flawless flower beds, just like the house itself. Her house was sunny and yellow and orderly and neat, and above everything else, it was safe.

Safe. Like the big maple tree at her grandpa's house, when she used to go there as a child and play tag with her neighbors. The giant tree was always safe. She'd convinced herself that her home was the same way. Off-limits. No one could get to her there. No pain, no violence. Home was her haven.

"When the stranger put his hands on you, what did you feel?" asked the woman with the Stevie Nicks voice and Cruella de Vil hair—Lillian, Lucy remembered.

"I was terrified. I'd just been shot. At least…I thought I had. I was covered in blood, and it hurt, it really did. But I guess I must have…hallucinated it, or maybe I hurt myself when I fell down."

"What did you feel *physically?*" the woman went on. "When the stranger put his hands on you?"

"Oh, that. Well…his hands felt…warm. And then hot. And it seemed like there was a light sort of… coming from them. And it filled every part of me. And for just a second, I thought I might be dying, and that he was an angel."

"An angel," the man said, nearly spitting the words.

"That's an interesting thing to say."

Lucy sighed. "I really want to go home now. I'm

all right, aren't I? I mean, I wasn't shot after all, right?"

"Well, there are certainly no bullet holes in you now," the woman said, sounding cheerful. And then she got up and joined the man, then spoke in a very, very soft whisper, "The pentothal is wearing off. Is there anything else you want, before...?"

"Ask her about her blood type. We tested her, came back positive for the antigen. I want to know if she knew."

Why, Lucy wondered, did they think she couldn't hear them?

But Lillian was returning to her bedside now. Lucy heard the woman's footsteps on the floor tiles. Smelled the soap she used, too.

"Lucy, do you know if there's anything...unusual about your blood type?"

"Yes, there is. It's...very rare. Only a few people have it. It makes me bleed easily. And it's hard to find a donor to match me, which is why I donate regularly and have my own supply in storage. But that's at Binghamton General—and I keep some at Lourdes, too. That's another reason why I was so afraid when I saw all that blood all over me." She paused, opening her eyes now. "If it wasn't my blood, whose was it?"

"We don't know. Can you tell me any more about your blood ty—"

"But how can you not know? If someone else was shot on that sidewalk, how could you not—"

"Lucy, I'd like you to take a breath and calm yourself." The woman put a soothing hand on Lucy's forehead. "A lot of people were shot at that studio last night. Inside and outside. It was chaos. And I wasn't there. I'm sure someone knows the answers to your questions, but it's not me."

Lucy sighed. "I want to go home." She sat up in the bed and looked around the white room while waves of dizziness washed over her brain. "Where are my things?"

"Lucy, about your blood type," Lillian said. "Is there anything else you can tell me about the Belladonna Antigen?"

Lucy blinked and met the woman's eyes. Her head was beginning to feel clearer. "How do you know? I never told you what it's called."

"We want to know what you know about it."

"What kind of a medical question is that?" Lucy narrowed her eyes, suddenly suspicious of this woman, who she'd assumed was a doctor or a shrink—or maybe a grief counselor, sent in to help her process what had happened.

"You want to know if I'm aware that I'm going to die young? I am. There's no treatment, and there's no cure. People with this antigen usually die in their thirties. And I'm in mine now, but so far I feel fine. No symptoms."

"And what would those symptoms be?"

"You tell me, you're the doctor." Lucy watched the woman's face and knew, just knew. "Or if you're not, then I'd like to know who you are."

"I am a doctor. And I work for the government," Lillian said. "And I think we're all through with your questioning now. You can relax. I'll be back in a moment."

"I don't want to relax," Lucy said. "I haven't done anything wrong. I've told you everything I know." She was suddenly terrified, and while she thought she might benefit by demanding her rights or a lawyer, she decided to wait until those things were truly necessary. She didn't like conflict or confrontation, but she liked the unknown even less. And she had no idea who these people were or where she was being held. And it was feeling more and more as if she was… being held. She'd assumed she was in a hospital, but she wasn't so sure anymore.

The woman crossed the room to where the scarfaced man waited near the door, and then they stepped through it, leaving her all alone.

Lucy got up and went to the door—the windowless door—as well. And as she did, a feeling of fear rippled up her spine, because she had a pretty good idea of what she was going to find when she got there.

She closed her hand around the doorknob and twisted, her heart in her throat—and then it sank to her feet when the knob didn't budge an inch.

Locked.

She was being held by people who had drugged her and questioned her. And might even have shot her.

But then her hands rose to her chest, and she pulled the fabric away from her skin and looked down her neckline. The necklace she'd found inside the crazy author's book was still hanging there, Kwan Yin looking serene and gentle. But there was no sign of any wound in her chest. Not a mark.

And yet she remembered it all so vividly. She'd felt that bullet tear through her.

God, she wondered, how could that be?

But she knew how. It was that man. That angel. He'd healed her.

She closed her eyes and whispered a prayer to him right then and there. "If you really are my guardian angel, please, come find me again. Save me again. I need to get out of this place. I want to go home."

4

"Well? Where is she?" Rhiannon demanded.

James tipped his head to one side and met the eyes of the most powerful vampire he had ever known. Also the most beautiful. And the most dangerous. Rhiannon stood beneath a crystal chandelier in the foyer of the Long Island mansion that was her summer home, or one of them. She wore her usual choice of attire, a floor-length gown, with a slit up to her hip on one side and a neckline that plunged to her navel. Black satin that was almost as shiny as her endless raven hair, or the black panther, her beloved pet, that rubbed against her legs as she spoke.

"Good to see you, too, Rhiannon," he said. "It's been a while." He glanced at the cat. "Hello, Pandora."

Rhiannon made a dismissive sound like a set of air brakes releasing a brief spurt of excess pressure. "You walked away from us, J.W. Not the other way around. Don't expect a warm welcome when you finally deign to honor us with your presence."

"Rhiannon, he's—" Brigit began.

"Where is the professor?" the arrogant one asked again, and this time her tone brooked no argument. No discussion.

"She got away," Brigit said softly.

"She got away?"

"She was taken, actually." Brigit lowered neither her head nor her eyes. She held the regal Rhiannon's gaze firmly and strongly, and for just a moment James was amazed and impressed by his sister's moxie. She'd grown up just as tough as everyone had known she would. And even though she'd been Rhiannon's favorite, he hadn't expected her to be able to stand up to, much less hold her own against, the most feared vampiress of them all. He could do so, always had. But that was because he didn't particularly care whether or not he gained her elusive approval.

"Taken by whom?" Rhiannon asked, taking a step nearer, so the two women stood nearly nose-to-nose on the imported Italian marble floor. Black with swirls of silver. Pandora tensed, her sharp cat's eyes watching every move, as her tail twitched.

"DPI," Brigit said, not backing down a single inch. "Or that's my best guess. There's more going on here, Aunt Rhiannon. A lot more."

"Such as?"

Leaning still closer, looking as if she was either going to kiss Rhiannon on the mouth or bite her nose off, Brigit said, her tone dangerously soft, "Why don't you back up out of my face and I'll tell you?"

Rhiannon's eyes narrowed. "You're treading on dangerous ground, Brigit."

"Just like you taught me to do."

Rhiannon's scowl lasted a few more seemingly endless ticks of the clock. Pandora flattened her ears and a deep, soft growl emanated from her chest. And then, finally, Rhiannon rolled her eyes and paced away, almost gliding, despite the four-inch stiletto heels she wore. "Fine. Talk. Take your time about it, too. It's not as if our entire race is at stake, after all."

"Drama queen," Brigit muttered.

Rhiannon whirled. "Excuse me?"

They stared at each other across the room for a long moment, and James tensed, wondering if the great Rhiannon, formerly known as Rianikki, the daughter of an Egyptian Pharaoh who never let anyone forget her rank, was going to try to annihilate his twin sister. He was about to step between the two women when Rhiannon smiled. It was a slow, gradual smile, but a smile nonetheless.

"You are extremely fortunate that I love you as I do, firecracker."

"And I know it," Brigit replied. But her own face and voice softened, as well. "All right, come sit. Here's the deal." Moving to the nearby sofa, the two sat down, and Brigit began recapping everything that had happened. Relaxing, the large cat curled up at Rhiannon's feet and closed her eyes lazily.

James ignored them, for the most part. He hadn't been home in a very long time, and while this was not his parents' place, he had spent a large portion of his childhood here. "Aunt" Rhiannon had insisted on having a hand in raising him and Brigit. And he'd always been secretly glad of that, too, because while he, already adored by all, hadn't needed the extra attention, his sister had thrived on it.

After all, to everyone else, she was the bad twin. Oh, no one ever said it that way. Not out loud. But she'd been born with the power of destruction, and she'd spent her entire life having to listen to her parents and every other role model in her life telling her that her power was bad. That it was dangerous and must be controlled, contained, kept on a tight leash. While he had been born with the power to heal, with everyone always oohing and ahhing over it, telling him how special he was, how someday he would do great things with his powers. How he was meant for something very special.

No one had ever blatantly compared the twins, called him the good one and her the bad one. But it was still the impression they'd both received from the adults in their lives. And it was an impression that ran deep. It had filled him with a perhaps unwarranted sense of pride and of goodness that had eventually led him to leave his people in search of meaning. While it had, he sensed, left his sister with a feeling of unworthiness. Or would have, if it hadn't been for Rhiannon.

She alone praised Brigit's ability as something special, something worthy, something good. She was constantly telling Brigit how there could be no creation without destruction. How goddesses of death were also goddesses of rebirth. How sacred her power was, how holy. And how James's talent meant nothing without Brigit's to balance it.

He'd never really believed any of that. He'd figured Aunt Rhi was probably just trying to make Brigit feel better, feel worthy. And he loved her for it. He'd never liked thinking that his sister's feelings were hurt just because he was born with the gift of healing, even restoring life, and all she got was the ability to blow things up.

"Did the healing take?"

It was a beat before James realized the two-thousand-year-old vampiress was addressing him. "Yeah. I think so."

"You *think* so?" she asked.

"I can't be sure. They took her away before I had the chance to—"

Rhiannon was glaring at him, her full lips as thin as they could get, arms slowly crossing over her chest, forcing her breasts together.

He looked away, sighed. "Yes. It took."

"Are you sure?"

He thought back, relived it all in his mind, and then got stuck in remembering those eyes. Those doe-brown eyes, and the fear and confusion in them when they'd opened up and stared so deeply into his.

I know you.

What the hell was up with that?

"J.W...." Rhiannon prompted.

"Yes." He knew the light and the heat flowing from his hands had peaked, then just begun to ebb when he'd been forced away from her. "I'm sure. The professor was fine."

"*Was* being the operative word," Brigit said. "We can't be sure of anything now that those bastards have her."

"You're sure it wasn't an ordinary team of paramedics?" Rhiannon asked.

"Men in black were giving the orders. We both saw it." Brigit glanced at James, who nodded in confirmation. "We're going to have to plan and execute a rescue," she said.

"What could the DPI want with her?" James asked, trying to force his focus to stay on the matter at hand.

Rhiannon leaned forward to stroke her panther. "They must know about the prophecy, and that it applies to us. Our race. The descendants of Utanapishtim. The tablet says our race will be no more. And believe me, nothing would make the DPI happier than that. They see us as a threat. They've been hoping to get the green light to wipe us out for as long as they've known of our existence."

"Why haven't they gotten it?" James asked.

Rhiannon leaned back on the sofa, which was as ostentatious as everything else in her homes. Red velvet, with gold braid and fringe. "There are a few leaders wise enough to know that war with our kind might not be easily won. By keeping our existence secret, they've managed to maintain a tense but fragile, and entirely unspoken, truce. Now, though…" She lowered her head with a sigh.

James had never seen Rhiannon this worried before, and it got his attention. He moved to the sofa and sat down beside her. "Now?" he prompted.

She lifted her head, looked him right in the eyes. "Now, thanks to Lester Folsom and his book, the entire world knows we exist."

"The book was pulled." Frowning, James shot a look at Brigit. "Isn't that what Will Waters was saying in the intro? That the government had banned it, called a halt to the release, confiscated every copy before it ever hit the bookstores?"

"Yeah, J.W., but you've gotta know when the author of a banned book is taken out on national TV, the public will start turning over every rock to find out what the book had to say," Brigit said.

"And I have no doubt there are copies somewhere. And there are certainly people who know what was in those pages. His publisher, for one," Rhiannon added.

"No doubt the DPI has already absconded with every computer that ever came within reach of the manuscript," she went on. "But that won't stop word from spreading. No, this cat is thoroughly out of the proverbial bag."

"We need to know what's in that book," James said softly.

Rhiannon nodded. "I agree. But we also need to keep our focus here. Our main goal has to be to prevent the foretold annihilation of our race. And to do that, we need to understand the parts of that clay tablet that were incomplete, the missing pieces. And the other clay tablet in our possession, the one we've kept for centuries, never quite sure why."

"I'd forgotten about that. Legend has it that clay tablet will one day save our race," James said, recalling the tales told to him over and over throughout his childhood. The legends of his race, how they began, and the story of the tablet that must be protected. "Where is it?"

"Damien has it," Rhiannon said. "I'll get it from him. The prophecy suggests that all of this so-called Armageddon is heavily dependent upon the involvement of two things."

"Yeah," Brigit muttered. "Us."

"And him," Rhiannon said.

James frowned. "Him? Him, who? You mean Utanapishtim?"

"Precisely." Rhiannon rose from the sofa, paced across the room, then turned and paced back again. "So what Folsom wrote in that book, and what the government intends to do about it, and whether it becomes public knowledge—all of that is on the back burner. Our first goals are these—we have to find and rescue the professor, so that she can help us locate and translate the rest of that prophecy. And we have to enlist the help of the very first immortal. The

Ancient One. The Flood Survivor. The father of our race. Utanapishtim."

"How the hell are we going to do that?" James asked. "A séance?"

"Of course!" Brigit said. "Aunt Rhi was a priestess of Isis—"

"Not was, is. And that's high priestess," Rhiannon corrected.

"Yeah, yeah," Brigit said, no doubt pissing Rhiannon off again, James thought. "But that's not the point. The point is that you know how to contact the dead and all that shit, right? Right? So is that it? Are we going to have a séance?"

"Not exactly," Rhiannon said. "We don't need to speak to the dead if Utanapishtim is alive."

"But he's not," Brigit said. "He's been dead for more than five thousand years, Aunt Rhi."

"Yes, well, that's where your brother comes in."

Rhiannon speared James with her eyes, even as he felt his own widen. "You can't mean…you want me to—"

"Raise him, J.W."

He shot off the sofa as if it had electrocuted him. "I can't!" The panther's head came up, and she looked irritated at being disturbed from her nap by his sudden movement.

"How do you know?" Rhiannon asked him.

"For the love of—how could I not know?"

Rhiannon shrugged, graceful, sexy. "I've seen you raise the dead, J.W. You've been doing it since you were born. You started with your own sister, stillborn, blue, no heartbeat, not a breath of air in her lungs." Rhiannon moved closer, reaching out and grabbing James's forefinger, enclosing it in her fist. "You took hold of her just like this," she said. "And she breathed, J.W. She breathed. You healed her. You brought her back to life."

"I know. I know. And yeah, I've been successful a few other times since then, but only when the subject has just died. Never with anyone who's been dead for long."

"But have you tried?" Rhiannon asked.

"What, restoring life to a rotting corpse? Yeah, yeah, that's how I spend my Halloweens. Are you fucking crazy?"

"So you've never tried, then," Brigit said. She was rising now, too, growing excited, he thought, at this impossible, insane notion.

"No, I've never tried."

Rhiannon nodded. "We'll start small, say with someone a week dead. And we'll build from there. We'll need to find corpses in various stages of decomposition, of course, and—"

"Shit." James's stomach convulsed. He took an involuntary step backward. "No. No, this is sick."

"Call it what you will. It's necessary," Rhiannon said.

"It's to save our race," Brigit added.

"No way. No way in hell." James was shaking his head slowly in dawning horror. "And it won't work. And even if it did, Utanapishtim isn't going to be in some stage of decomposition. He'd be dust by now."

Rhiannon shrugged. "Dust, bones, rotted flesh, all just different phases of the same basic components. If you can do it with one, you can do it with the others."

"You're out of your mind, Rhiannon."

She lifted her perfectly arched brows and sent him a look that told him he was getting close to the danger zone.

And then Brigit's hand landed on his shoulder. "J.W.… James. You've spent your entire life asking yourself, and the universe, why you were born with this power. Maybe this is it. Your answer. Maybe this is why. To save your family. Your *people*. There's not much that could be bigger, more important, than that. Is there?"

He stared at her. And he could barely believe that he was letting her talk him into it. Because she had a point. He had always wondered why. He'd always known he had this power for a reason, a big reason, and he'd been searching for it all his life.

Maybe this was it. And if there was any chance it was, then he couldn't very well turn his back on it, now could he?

He lowered his eyes, released all his breath at once, swallowed hard and whispered, "All right. All right, I'll…I'm in."

"Good." He heard the smile in Rhiannon's voice, felt his sister's arms close around him in a relieved hug.

"We're going to have to get out of the city," Rhiannon announced, moving quickly toward the nearest window, her cat at her heels. "We need someplace with privacy for these experiments. We'll leave as soon as possible."

"But, Rhiannon," James said, lifting his head. "What about Lucy Lanfair?"

"Lucy...oh, the professor? Obviously we're going to have to take her with us. We'll pick her up on the way." She glanced out the window. "But not tonight. It's nearly dawn. I must rest. I suggest you do the same."

Lucy opened her eyes and felt an odd, moist breeze on her face. Almost as if she were outside. She'd been sleeping very soundly and wondered what on earth had awakened her. Something had. And she was nowhere near ready to get up, not after...

No, she wouldn't think about that. She needed to pull up the covers, roll onto her other side and...

Where were the covers?

Wait, where was the mattress? The bed? All she felt was sand and very finely ground pebbles.

Her eyes popped open, and the first thing they focused on was the giant orange curve of the sun, just beginning to rise over a distant horizon. She was... outdoors. On the shore of the ocean. She was grasping handfuls of sand and shells in search of blankets.

Waves whispered soothing sounds as they whooshed up over the sand, then burbled back out again. The wind smelled like seaweed and brine. She brushed off her hand, rubbing it against her shirt, then paused, because she was wearing clothes. A pair of jeans that were a size too big, and a white button-down shirt. A man's shirt, she thought. Sitting up, she pushed a hand through her hair, which felt vaguely like a rat's nest, and tried to remember how she'd ended up here. The last thing she remembered…

They'd fed her. She had supposed that was a plus, even if the food was tepid and sticky, and almost certainly prepared by peeling back the plastic and nuking for five minutes on high. Meat loaf with gravy, soupy mashed potatoes, green beans that tasted the way she thought paint would taste and some kind of cherry dessert that was so tart it made her pucker. About two tablespoons of each, whether she needed it or not.

Famished, she'd wolfed the food down so fast there hadn't been time to ponder the taste overly much. A blessing in itself.

Or not. Because she didn't remember anything else. Nothing at all. Apparently they had tranquilized her with something. It hadn't hit her with the potency of the first injection, in the ambulance, and it didn't have her spilling her guts on any subject they broached, like the one they must have given her just before starting their interrogation. And she didn't have any doubt that was exactly what it had been. An interrogation by some secret government agency that wanted to know how much she knew about the murders of Lester Folsom and Will Waters.

Only that wasn't what they'd questioned her about, was it? They'd seemed far more interested in what she knew about her angel. Her savior. That beautiful man who'd saved her.

Or had it all been some kind of a dream?

Maybe. Or maybe not. She couldn't be sure, because she didn't know anything for sure anymore. Except that there was someone walking toward her now, along the sand. Walking at a brisk but unhurried pace. She blinked, but her eyes were so unfocused that it was as if she were peering through a dirty window. She squinted, thought she saw a baby-blue car on the side of the road, some distance beyond him, then shifted her focus right back to him again. Yes, him. Definitely male, tall. And as he drew nearer there was something…

It was him!

She scrambled to her feet, forgetting all about the lingering effects of whatever dope they'd used to season her food. Unconsciously, she pushed one hand through her hair, even as she backed up a step, wobbled, then caught her balance again. Her brain was still foggy, her equilibrium off-kilter. Should she stand there, waiting, or run away? She didn't know whether she was afraid of this guy or not. She didn't know anything about him, except that he'd been leaning over her after she'd been shot down on the street outside Studio Three. And that she'd felt as if she knew him from somewhere. And that it had seemed as if he had…helped her. Healed her. Saved her.

On the one hand, if he'd helped her then, maybe he wanted to help her now, too.

On the other, if he were involved in any of that violence that had unfolded back there last night—God, had it only been last night?—then she wanted no part of him.

He stopped walking, maybe sensing her distress as she stood there with one hand trying to hold her wild tangles of hair to the back of her head and the other arm wrapped around her own waist, as if she could somehow protect her vital organs simply by covering them with a forearm.

He wore a tan, short-sleeved shirt with the top several buttons undone, khaki trousers, rolled up a little, and his feet were bare and sinking into the sand. Bare feet. That made him seem less scary, somehow.

"It's all right, Lucy. It's me. I'm the one who helped you, after—"

"I remember."

He tipped his head to one side. "You look as if you've had a rough night."

She blinked. "Rough? I witnessed a double execution, ran for my life, was shot in the back and somehow yanked from the brink of death by whatever magic it is you wield," she said, and the words came pouring out, faster and faster. "Then I was kidnapped, drugged, held prisoner, questioned, drugged again. And now I wake up in the middle of nowhere in clothes that aren't my own, and I don't even have my purse or a hairbrush or—" Her throat closed off and her face pulled itself into an embarrassing grimace as tears strained to break through whatever invisible barrier had held them back so far.

And then they escaped, just as her knees weakened and her entire body went lax, as if there was simply no more fight left in her. She sank to her knees in the warming sand, her head falling forward.

But before she could collapse entirely, he was there. He caught her beneath the shoulders, his arms powerful and strong, holding her upright, and then... And then he pulled her gently to her feet and closer to him. So close that her body rested against his warm, solid chest. So close that she could inhale him, feel him all around her.

"You're freezing," he muttered into her hair, and those iron arms tightened just a little to hold her against his warmth. Just enough. She absorbed his heat and his strength as if he were feeding her very soul. And maybe he was. "It's okay. It's okay, Lucy. I have you now. I'm not going to let anyone hurt you again, I promise."

She shook her head against his chest. "Who are you, that you should even care?"

"What the hell did they do to you?" His voice wavered a little as he dodged her question. "How did you escape?"

"I di-di-didn't," she managed in between chest-wrenching sobs.

"I'll ask you to explain that…but later. I think right now you need a warm, soft bed and a decent meal."

"I need to go home." She lifted her head and stared up into his eyes, ashamed that her own were probably pleading and needy. And yet, she couldn't help it. "I just want to go home."

"I know. I know you do." He scooped her up, right off her feet, and he carried her across the sand, away from the sea, as gulls cried and swooped overhead. The sounds of the waves washing over the shore grew fainter, and soon they were approaching his car. A shiny car, pale blue with a white convertible top that was currently up, not down. Probably one of those new versions of an old classic. He set her on the white leather seat as carefully as if she were an injured dove, even leaned over to fasten her seat belt for her. And then he got behind the wheel and pulled away.

Yes, she thought, as she drifted to sleep in the comfort of his car, he was definitely a good guy. He was going to take her home. She rested her head against the big soft seat, closed her eyes and basked in the warm air that was blowing from the car's heater. Thank God.

"Thank you," she whispered.

Soon she would be safe and sound in her own bed again. And then she would try to figure out what on earth all this was about. Not that she even cared. None of it had anything to do with her. And it was all fairly ludicrous, as far as she could see. Vampires and secret agents and tell-all books and public executions.

Drugging and questioning and cloak-and-dagger nonsense. None of it concerned her, other than to make her think a letter to the president was in order, and maybe a change of party affiliation soon, if this was the way her side wanted to run the world. Assassinating senile old men with vivid imaginations in the name of "national security" seemed beyond the pale, frankly.

And yet, something very remarkable had happened to her. There was no doubt in her mind that she had been shot and lying in a pool of her own blood on that Manhattan sidewalk. And then that man…this man…

She opened her eyes slightly and looked at him, behind the wheel of the blue car. He was a beautiful man. He had skin that was so flawless he almost seemed like a figure in a wax museum—the kind that looked just like the real person except for being perfect. That was how he looked. Perfect. And not just his skin, but his hair, which was shiny and appeared to be made out of strands of silk, in shades of honey and caramel and gold, one color blending into the next. And his eyes were that way, too. Vivid, electric blue, with a very fine black outline around the irises, and some kind of mysterious backlighting thing going on behind them. Or there had been when he'd been leaning over her on the sidewalk with his hands on her chest. Not pressing, to stanch the flow of blood. No. Not pumping, as if he'd been attempting CPR. He hadn't been pushing against her. It was more like he'd been pushing something into her. Out of him and into her.

And there had been that glow from his hands and from his eyes.

God, he was unearthly. And so very beautiful.

She remembered that there'd been a woman with him, a blonde who'd hustled him away. And she'd been gorgeous, too, in the fleeting glimpse Lucy had of her.

He looked her way, then looked again as he caught her perusal of him. She was too tired, her brain still too numb from all the chemicals swimming through it, to be embarrassed at being caught. Still, she thought she ought to say something.

"I don't even know your name." It was better than nothing.

"It's James. James Poe. Although my sister refuses to call me anything but J.W."

"Your sister?" Ridiculous that she felt such a silly spark of hope that maybe he wasn't romantically involved with the gorgeous blonde after all. It wasn't as if she herself would ever see him again once he dropped her off at the bus station or airport or wherever it was he had in mind to dump her.

"Brigit. She was there, too, when…everything happened."

"Oh."

"We're twins, you know."

That made her smile a little. "Twins. That must

be amazing. To have someone that close to you, who knows you that well."

"It's wonderful. And it's horrible. Depends on the day."

She breathed and relaxed. "I think you saved my life on that sidewalk, James."

His face seemed to tense a little, and she thought he was trying to decide how to answer her. Finally he just said, "You should really get some sleep. We've got a bit of a drive."

"But…you realize I need to know, right? I don't give a damn about any of the rest of this. But what happened there on that sidewalk—when you put your hands on me—that I need to know."

When he still didn't say anything, she went on. "I felt the shot hit me—it was like being pounded by a sledgehammer. And then it burned straight through my body. Like how I would imagine a white-hot blade would feel." As she spoke, she straightened up in the seat and pressed her palm to her chest. "And then I was on the ground in a pool of blood. So much blood. And all of it mine. I'm sure it was mine." She lowered her eyes. "Or else I'm hallucinating, maybe losing my mind. Because it was that vivid. That real."

He glanced her way briefly, and when she met his eyes, he gave her the validation she sought with a single nod. "You didn't imagine it. It was real."

She wondered if she could accept that.

"And then you came," she said softly. "And you put your hands on me. I thought I felt heat, and I thought

I saw…a light. It came from you, from your hands on me. Was that real, too?"

He didn't answer.

"Are you an angel? Are you some kind of…guardian angel, James?"

He licked his lips as if he were nervous, and then nodded once, as if having made a decision. "You're going to have to know sooner or later anyway, I suppose."

She wanted to ask why he would say that, since she would probably never see him again after he took her wherever he was taking her and dropped her off. Right? She wanted to ask but couldn't bring herself to interrupt just when she thought she was about to get some answers.

"I was born with a…a gift," he told her.

"A gift?"

"An…ability that most people don't have."

She tipped her head to one side, watching him. "The ability to…heal gunshot wounds?"

"Yes. Or just about anything else."

Her brain told her that the man was clearly delusional, and she thought what a shame it was that such a gorgeous specimen was mentally warped. But she couldn't really brush off his claim that easily when she'd been on the receiving end of his healing touch. Could she?

"You don't really believe me."

"I…I don't how I can doubt you. And yet, it just doesn't seem…plausible."

He shrugged, drove for a while in silence.

She rested, waiting, wondering if she'd offended him somehow, regretted it if she had. He'd saved her life. And then found her on the beach.

How had he done that?

"Here we are," he said, and he pulled the car carefully over onto the shoulder of the road and brought it to a stop.

"Here we are where?" There was nothing around them.

"Proof." He opened the car door and got out, and to her surprise, he moved toward a black bit of road-kill just ahead. A crow, its feathers all askew, its body limp.

She frowned, intent on James as he crouched down beside the bird. A car sped past, its back draft blasting his hair and clothes briefly, but he didn't even seem to notice. He was holding his hands over the bird. "Good," he said. "It's still warm."

Compelled beyond resisting, she opened the car door and got out, moving closer to him without even planning to do so. She squinted, leaning forward. Was there light coming from his hands? There was. A soft yellow glow that seemed to emanate from his palms.

Shifting her focus to his eyes, she thought she glimpsed a similar light there, but then he closed them. She kept moving nearer, then knelt right beside him.

There was a sudden flapping, and then he was

holding the crow between his hands, wings contained. The bird's black-currant eyes were open, and it parted its large dark bill to release a series of loud squawks that did not sound like gratitude.

Then James rose, lifted his arms, parted his hands, and the crow flapped its big wings and took flight.

Lucy stood there for a long moment, watching until the gleaming black corvid was out of sight. "That bird wasn't injured," she said quietly. "That bird was dead."

He shrugged, saying nothing.

"Are you telling me you can raise the dead?"

"Sometimes."

He had avoided her eyes until then. But he looked into them now. "But besides that—I'm really just an ordinary man, Lucy."

"There's nothing ordinary about you."

He shrugged, lowered his gaze. "I just…I don't want you to be afraid of me."

"Afraid of you?" She continued to stare at him, her mind lost in wonder. "You're some kind of an angel, or…or a superhero. I'm not afraid of you."

"Good." He met her eyes again, and for the first time she saw his smile. "Good." Then he took her arm, and they started back toward the car.

"How did you find me?"

"All too easily, I'm afraid," he said, opening her door for her.

She got in, and he rounded the front of the car and got in, as well.

"What do you mean?" she asked when he was seated.

"I need to know how you escaped," he told her.

She shook her head. "As I said before, I didn't. I was there—"

"Where?"

She frowned, thinking back. "I don't know. I was unconscious for most of the ambulance ride—they drugged me. I woke in a hospital-like room, but it wasn't a hospital. Or at least, not an ordinary one. I was interrogated as if I were a terrorist or something."

"About what?" he asked. "The shooting?"

"A little. But mostly about you, and then they started asking me about my blood type, which is rare. And I have no idea how they knew that." She shook her head, more confused than ever. "Much less why they would even care. Eventually they fed me, and then I was out again. I suspect they drugged the food."

"Probably."

"I woke up on the beach." She met his eyes. "And you were there."

He had been about to put the car into gear and pull away, but he stopped in midmotion and looked at her. "They just let you go? Just dumped you on that beach for me to find?"

"I don't know that they could have expected you to be the one to find me there, but yes."

"Oh, they expected it." He drew a deep breath. "Do you trust me, Lucy?"

She tilted her head to one side, searching his eyes. "I think so, yes."

"Good, because I have to ask you to do something for me."

She nodded. "I guess I owe you a favor, given that you've saved my life—maybe twice now. What is it?"

"Take off your clothes."

5

James tried not to notice the things he couldn't help but notice as the frightened, introverted professor stood behind a conveniently located grove of trees in her bra and white cotton panties, with her arms up over her head.

He tried not to notice, but he noticed anyway. Her skin, smooth and tight. Her lean body. She wasn't curvy. She didn't have mounds of cleavage busting out of a lacy push-up bra. She was lean and toned. Her skin didn't sport a dark coppery tan but was almost as pale as his undead relatives'.

And warm, as he ran his hands over it. From her shoulders to her wrists. Underneath her arms and down to her lithe waist and then to the barely flaring hips. From her soft belly over her rib cage and all around her breasts, all the while trying not to touch the breasts themselves. Then he turned her and examined her nape, her shoulder blades, her lower back. He stopped where the underpants began, crouching down to begin checking those long, lean legs of hers.

He found the telltale bump, no bigger than a mosquito bite, in the delicate crease where buttocks met thigh, and she jumped when he ran his finger over it.

"Hey!"

Her voice was raspy, a little bit breathless. She was either humiliated or as turned on as he was, and then he wondered if it might be a little bit of both.

"Sorry. It's right here."

"What's right here?"

"I'll show you in a sec. Grab hold of the tree, this might pinch a little."

She did as he told her, and he squeezed the tiny bump like a blackhead. It popped like one, too, except that the object that came out of it was tiny and metal.

To her credit, she didn't squeal. She flinched hard and sucked in a sharp breath, but that was all.

He said, "All done," and held the thing on the tip of his forefinger as she turned.

She frowned at it, wishing for her glasses. "What is it?"

"A tracking device. It sends out an electronic signal so that someone on the other end knows where you are at all times."

Lifting her eyes to his, she said, "They put that in me?"

He nodded at her clothes where they were hanging

over a nearby limb. "Better get dressed. Now that we're rid of this, we can be on our way."

"But why?" she asked, grabbing the jeans and stepping into them. "I mean, if they wanted me, why let me go? And if they didn't want me, why implant that…that thing in me?"

"So you could lead them to me," he told her.

She stopped with the shirt in her hand and studied him for a long moment, then resumed dressing. "Why are they looking for you?"

"Because I'm different. And with the DPI, that's pretty much all the reason they need."

"What's the DPI?"

"A government agency," he said, and didn't elaborate. Instead, he refocused on the device, already thinking up ways to get rid of the little unit. "You ready?"

"Yes. Ready." She looked at his hand. "Are you going to crush it under your shoe, or bury it, maybe throw it into a stream or something?"

"Or something," he told her. And then he started walking back toward the car. As they reached the winding road, he waited. Two other cars went by, followed by a pickup, all headed in the direction she and James had come from. When the truck passed, he tossed the tiny unit and it landed right where he intended it to: in the bed.

"Now they'll be looking for us in the opposite direction."

"You're brilliant."

He smiled at her and opened her door. "You can barely keep your eyes open, can you?"

"No." She got in, leaned her head back and closed her eyes.

"Maybe you can relax enough to sleep for the rest of the ride. They can't follow us now, and I think you're finally convinced that I'm one of the good guys." It was a real shame he was going to have to prove otherwise to her when they reached their destination, he thought grimly. But in this case, the ends justified the means. And he couldn't be sure she would refuse to help his cause, once they got there, so maybe she could go on thinking he wore a white hat.

But if she did balk, then he would have to force her cooperation.

For a moment he went still, stunned by his own train of thought. That was not the kind of thing James Poe ever did. Force someone to do something they didn't want to do. Much less someone like her. Innocent, frightened, delicate.

Beautiful.

He wondered what was happening to the moral code he'd lived by for his entire life. But he didn't really have a choice in the matter. The existence of his entire race was at stake.

Brigit paced and worried. She had taken Aunt Rhi's advice and headed into her bedroom for a nap, but she had awakened the moment she sensed that J.W. was gone. She felt him more acutely than she felt anyone else. Upon rising, she'd made the unfortunate choice to turn on one of the twenty-four-hour news channels to hear what was being said about the events of the night before.

Veteran newsman Matthew Christopher was in the middle of interviewing a suit-wearing politician who spoke as if from memory. "Lester Folsom's book was pulled for reasons of national security, Matt," he said, as if speaking to a slow student who didn't quite get the point. "As demented as poor Mr. Folsom was, we can't ignore the fact that he did indeed work as a covert agent, and in that capacity, he was privy to massive amounts of sensitive information."

"Apparently enough to get him shot," the newsman replied.

"No one has proven that the murder had anything to do with—"

"Don't give me that," Matthew interrupted. "A guy's about to release a tell-all, an exposé, about his work as a covert op, and he gets blown away, execution-style, on the eve of that. Do I look like I was born yesterday?"

"Matt, you're not giving me a chance to explain—"

"There are sources, Mr. Jenner, who say Folsom's work involved the paranormal. The unknown. Some of the blogs are claiming he was about to reveal the actual existence of a race of vampires. How do you respond to that?"

The guest made a face. "Anyone can post anything

on the internet. You know that. No right-minded person would believe—"

"We might know what to believe if the storm troopers hadn't raided every book distribution center in the country, destroying every copy in existence so none of us could read for ourselves…"

"You'd be reading fiction. With just enough real information thrown in to cause serious problems."

"Are you concerned at all about rumors that there were a handful of advance copies floating around? That WikiLeaks has published what they claim are actual excerpts from the Folsom manuscript on their website?"

The bureaucrat measured his words. "As far as we know, we've managed to find every copy."

"It's for sure you got all of Folsom's. And his notes, and everything else he had in his house in the Caribbean. Relatives claim soldiers gutted the place."

"That's an exaggeration."

"They say you stripped it to the bare walls. Even rolled up the carpets."

"Well, I wasn't a part of that team, and I'm sure the family's feeling very violated, and perhaps, in their grief, might just be blowing things a tiny bit out of pro—"

"Tell me this, Mr. Jenner. Is there, or has there ever been, a secret division of the CIA devoted to investigating cases involving the paranormal?"

Jenner looked Matthew Christopher right in the

eye, leaning slightly forward in his seat. "Absolutely not."

"Who shot Lester Folsom, Mr. Jenner?"

"We don't know. But believe me, the murder of a CIA operative, even a retired one like Folsom, is something we take very seriously. We've put every resource we have on this, and we will not rest until Lester Folsom's murderer is—"

Brigit clicked the remote control, accidentally hitting the channel selector rather than the off button. The riot taking place on the TV screen held her riveted. Flames were licking at the early morning sky, devouring what looked like a brownstone. The tagline on the bottom read Riots Break Out in Brooklyn. The reporter was saying that a gang of self-proclaimed vigilantes apparently believed the residents of the two-family building were vampires, and so they'd set the place on fire and burned them alive.

She hit the remote again, turning the TV off, and closed her eyes. *Where are you, big brother? The world is going insane, and it's not safe out there for you.*

He spoke to her mentally. *I've got the professor.*

You rescued her alone?

They let her go. Planted a chip, but I tossed it. We're on our way.

Not here, Brigit replied, her lips moving as if to give more emphasis to her words. *It's not safe. Word's out. Vigilante vampire hunters just murdered two families in Brooklyn. As soon as the sun sets, I'm taking Aunt Rhi and getting out of here.*

Go to the Byram house, her brother told her. *They think we abandoned it long ago.*

Good idea.

Be careful, Bridge.

I will, bro. You, too. See you in Byram. Wait till after dark.

See you there, he assured her.

Brigit closed the channels of her mind, just in case there might be anyone around trying to pick up on mental transmissions. God, if the mortal world truly knew they existed…then they'd be lucky if any of them managed to survive.

She must have slept all day, Lucy thought as she came slowly awake. The sun was gone, having set beyond the distant horizon sometime before she lifted her head to stare through the car's windshield.

They seemed to be in the middle of nowhere, driving along a narrow, twisting, dark road without a painted line or a streetlight in sight. The pavement was cracked and littered with potholes, and the edges were disintegrating chunks of broken asphalt. Forests stood clothed in a misty purple haze in the distance, and just as she was about to ask where in the name of creation they were, they rounded a hairpin curve and she saw a mansion straight out of an old Saturday afternoon creature feature.

It rose, gothic and dark, with countless sharp spires

stabbing into the deepening twilight sky. A few of its arched windows were lit, but most remained black, like sad, vacant eyes. And the wrought-iron fence that rose tall around the outside leaned lazily this way and that, as if its spearlike points were tired of standing guard.

To Lucy's horror, James turned into the twisting dirt path that passed for a driveway, passing in through the open gate and driving nearer the house she was sure must have been the setting for a plethora of Vincent Price films.

"Where are you taking me?"

"Don't panic, okay? I know it's scary looking, but it's just a house, and it's one of the few where they won't be looking for us."

"They aren't looking for us. They're looking for you. They let me go, remember?"

"This is just a stop along the way."

"Where the hell are we? Why did I sleep so long?"

"We're in Connecticut." He stopped the car, shut off the engine. "And you slept so long because you were drugged last night, and…and because I told you to."

"You told me to." She looked at him as if he were insane.

"The power of suggestion is…it's another of my…"

"Finally!" The driver's door was yanked open, and a pair of female arms wrapped themselves around James before he could get out. The newcomer's blond hair was barely visible from within the car, but her swimsuit-model bosom was level with Lucy's line of sight as the woman released James to kiss his face, then squeezed him again. Lucy relaxed as she realized that it was just his sister, Brigit. Not that she cared. She was angry, she reminded herself. Which, by the way, was unlike her. She didn't get angry. She negotiated; she talked things out with reason and with logic. She avoided conflict.

Until she'd been shot down in a Manhattan street and dragged into some kind of intrigue that had nothing to do with her.

"You said you would take me home," Lucy accused James's back.

"You said I would take you home. I just didn't correct you." His voice was muffled by the hug, until his twin finally released him and straightened away.

"Aunt Rhi and I have been worried sick. You took much longer than we expected. You should have checked in." She peeked around him, smiled and bent down a little to wave her fingers at Lucy. "How are you doing, Professor?"

"I just want to go home."

"Yeah, you look good and pissed off." Brigit grinned. "Glad to see you have it in you, to be honest."

Then Lucy's door was pulled open, and she turned and lifted her head, startled, to find herself staring up into the powerful eyes of a woman who was frightening in her beauty, regal in her bearing and intimidating in her glare.

"One would expect a woman plucked from the very jaws of death itself to show a little gratitude. Wouldn't one?"

She didn't speak so much as purr her words, her voice deep and resonant and menacing.

"Of course I'm grateful. I just…none of this has anything to do with me. I've been through hell, and I want to go home."

"Oh, well, that's different then," the woman said. She looked up, over the hood of the car, to the two on the other side. "She wants to go home, poor little thing. That changes everything, doesn't it? Including the fact that our entire race is facing annihilation?" She snapped her eyes back to Lucy's, and before Lucy could blink, she was pulled from the car, and lifted off her feet and into the air.

The regal one, her endless raven locks waving in the breeze as if with a life of their own, glared up at her, baring her teeth to reveal fangs that gleamed. She was holding Lucy up with one hand, clutching the bunched-up front of her borrowed shirt. And by her side, a black panther—a black freaking panther—crouched and snarled, baring *its* fangs, as well.

Lucy couldn't speak, couldn't scream. She was silent and shaking, and her heart pounded at a rate that had to be dangerous to her health.

"Put her down, Aunt Rhi." James's voice was firm

as he came around the car and put one hand on the woman's shoulder. "She's here to help us, after all."

"Pitiful that the salvation of our race lies in the hands of this puling, weak little mortal." But the woman did lower Lucy to the ground.

Lucy looked back toward the gate at the entrance to this horror film set, her entire being itching to run. But there were others standing there now. And she thought they might be vampires, like this dark-haired one, who surely must be their queen. One of them even wore a cloak that floated and snapped in the wind.

Lucy shot an accusing look toward James, who'd saved her, only to pitch her into a pit of vipers more dangerous than the one he'd pulled her from. He was no hero, no angel. He was one of them.

And why did that realization bring such a crushing sense of disappointment with it?

"Only partly," he said aloud. "I'm part human, too."

She blinked in shock. "Did you…did you just…?"

"Hear your thoughts? Yes, I did. I'm sorry, I didn't mean to intrude, but you were sort of shouting them at me."

"At us all," the one he'd called Aunt Rhi muttered, stroking the panther's head. The cat pressed up against her hand like a devoted pet.

"Brigit and I are the two who are like no other," James went on. "Part vampire, part human. The Light and the Darkness. Opposite, and yet the same."

"One the destroyer, the other the salvation," Lucy

whispered, and in her memory she heard again Lester Folsom's shocked words as he'd read the prophecy.

This is about the mongrel twins.

"Exactly," James said. "We need your help, Lucy. We need your help to figure out how it is that we can avert the disaster predicted in that prophecy. The vampire Armageddon."

"And you're going to give it to us," Rhiannon informed her. "Eagerly, willingly and completely. Anything less, and you'll become…kitty treats."

Her pet growled as if on cue, and Lucy tried to hide the chill that tiptoed up her spine.

6

The mansion was musty, dusty and falling down, but Lucy could tell as soon as she walked through its lopsided front door that it must have been amazing once. A large chandelier hung crookedly, wearing a canopy of cobwebs and grime, from the center of a water-stained cathedral ceiling. It was missing a few of the teardrop-shaped dirt-colored bits that might have been crystal prisms. There were lumps of furniture covered in filthy sheets, bookcases without any books, dust and spiderwebs everywhere. A few paintings still hung on the walls, but they were too filthy to see very well. A woman in a gown from some other century. A man on a horse. A landscape. The place smelled of damp plaster, mothballs and that instantly recognizable old house smell. And it felt sad, abandoned and lonely.

"This way," James told her, leading her through the foyer with one hand on her elbow. The others had remained outside, Rhiannon moving toward the strangers near the gate and into the arms of the one in the cape.

Lucy moved along, letting James guide her toward the curving staircase with the thick banister and twisted newel posts that were probably works of art beneath the years of neglect. She didn't speak. She couldn't. Inspecting the house and musing mentally about what it must have looked like once was her way of trying to distract herself from her almost paralyzing fear and the odd, surreal sense of having just landed in the middle of an old Stoker novel or a Bela Lugosi film. This new reality—this impossible world—was all around her. She could see it, hear it, touch it. And yet it couldn't be real, this world where a pack of vampires lurked outside while their offspring walked her through their haunted mansion.

"I'm sorry about Rhiannon," James said. "She's… not overly fond of mortals."

That comment drew her gaze to his. "She's a… vampire." It was difficult to even say the word. Even more difficult to wrap her mind around the notion that she had just had a conversation—a very one-sided and unpleasant conversation—with a creature she had always known for sure was make-believe.

"Yes." He was leading her up the stairs now.

"And you're one, too."

"I'm one-quarter human, three-quarters vampire."

"I don't think that answers my question," she said softly. "Are you one of them—or one of us?"

He met her eyes. "Both. And neither. I'm...different."

"Because you can heal?"

"That's only one of the ways in which I'm different. There are others."

"Such as?" She was being pushy, demanding answers. That was unlike her. Her voice didn't even sound like her own. And she was as angry with James as if....as if she had a right to be.

He shot her a look, as if he, too, had noticed the change in her attitude. "Unlike our vampiric relatives, Brigit and I can tolerate a normal diet—we can eat steak and baked potatoes if we want to. We don't need blood to survive, the way the undead do. We aren't compelled to sleep by day as they are. They can't resist it, you know. They fall asleep even if they try not to." He looked her way as they moved slowly up the surprisingly sturdy staircase.

"I didn't know that," she said.

"Sunlight doesn't do us any harm, either, though it would incinerate a full-blooded vampire. This way." He took her elbow lightly, turning at the top of the stairs to move along a wide hallway, with doors lining either side. There were light fixtures on the walls that appeared to be gas powered, or at least looked as if they had been once.

"So in what ways *are* you like them, then?" Lucy asked. "Aside from the fact that you believe yourself to be above the law and ordinary human ethics."

He stopped walking and searched her face, but she

refused to meet his eyes, staring instead at the center of his chest, as if willing his heart to explode under the force of her quiet anger.

"Don't judge me, Lucy. You don't know anything about me."

"Don't *judge* you? You've brought me here against my will. You allowed that…that creature to threaten me, and you've made it abundantly clear that you intend to keep me here until I do whatever it is you want me to do." She lifted her eyes to his then, but only very briefly. She didn't like looking into his eyes. They were the eyes of an angel. Out of place and so deceptive in the face of a man whose heart was that of a demon. "For all I know, you'll murder me once you have no more use for me." She faced forward, began walking again, as if she knew where they were going when in fact she had no clue.

He gripped her shoulders, stopping her abruptly and turning her to face him. "Can't you fathom that we're in a desperate situation here? Do you not get that desperate measures had to be taken? We didn't have a choice—I didn't have a choice—in this."

"There's always a choice, James." She lowered her eyes. "God, I thought you were some kind of… guardian angel. My savior. I was such an idiot." Tears burned her eyes.

He gaped for a moment, then tightened his grip on her shoulders, gently, but firmly, as if trying to squeeze his point into her awareness. "I need you to understand that you are in no danger here. No one is going to hurt you. And…and I am not a monster. I'm not even one of them."

"It's true, Professor." Brigit's voice came from the bottom of the stairs, drawing Lucy's gaze her way. She was surprised to see anger—and perhaps hurt—in the female's Arctic-blue eyes. "He hasn't been one of us for a long, long time. He abandoned all of us years ago."

"It wasn't the life I wanted," James said, and he suddenly sounded defensive.

Lucy felt like crawling into a crack in the wood-work. This discussion was personal and passionate, and none of her business.

"You can't deny your own blood, J.W." Brigit skewered him with those potent eyes of hers. "You can't be other than what you are." She jerked her head toward the hallway above her. "And it's the door you just passed."

He looked guilty, then nodded. "It's been a while," he admitted, but quietly. Lucy didn't know if he was talking to her or to his sister, who had already turned away. She, Rhiannon and the other vampires she'd seen coming in through the front gate seemed to have their own business to attend to. And Lucy was re-lieved not to be surrounded by them. Relieved…and terrified.

James opened the door his sister had indicated, and they entered what must have been a beautiful bedroom once. The wallpaper, old-fashioned, gold perhaps, be-neath the grime, bore a pattern of swirls in deep red velvet, and had probably been wildly expensive and elegant at one time. The windows were tall, the glass in them so old it was thicker at the bottoms than at the tops, distorting the view even more than the filth covering them did.

James let go of Lucy's elbow and crossed the bedroom to the far wall, where he grabbed hold of the gaslight that was mounted there and pulled it forward. Lucy jumped in surprise, her mouth going bone dry as the wall began to slide sideways, vanishing into itself at a point that had appeared no more than a piece of wood trim.

Beyond it, she saw a void, total darkness. Until he reached beside him to flip a switch and lights came on. Electric lights. They illuminated a room that was entirely different. Modern. Clean.

Floor-to-ceiling bookcases lined one wall, and they were loaded with volumes. Hundreds of them. To the left stood a large cherrywood desk with lion claw feet. It supported a computer with a thirty-inch flat-screen monitor, a cupful of pens, a stack of file folders. It was so out of place and so…so ordinary…that her brain didn't seem to want to process it at first.

"The DPI knows about this mansion," James told her. "But they believe we abandoned it decades ago. We prefer to keep that illusion intact. Believe me, it's the last place they'll look for us."

"DPI," she repeated. Trying to remember what it stood for. He'd told her, hadn't he? "That's the government agency you were talking about before."

"The Division of Paranormal Investigations. It's sort of a black op division of the CIA. The man who shot you was probably DPI."

"And they shot Mr. Folsom, too?"

"Yes, to keep him from exposing their existence—and ours." The wall slid closed behind them, and James led her across the large room toward a gleaming oval table that matched the desk. It was surrounded by expensive but comfortable-looking swivel chairs, upholstered in burnt-red leather studded with antique brass upholstery tacks. This place looked for all the world like an ordinary office in the ordinary world. But what caught her eye was a familiar-looking slab of hardened clay in the center of the conference table.

James kept on walking, opening a door on the far end of the office. "This hidden section of the mansion is laid out in a straight line, everything end to end, following the lines of the house, so nothing stands out. The outside windows are actually false—opaque. It's ingenious, really. But then, so is its designer."

She barely heard him. Her eyes were riveted to the ancient clay tablet that lay on the table. Its surface was covered with the lines and angles of cuneiform script, marks that had been made by a scribe pushing reeds through the clay when it had still been moist and pliant. Around three, perhaps four, thousand years ago, given the style of the markings.

"At any rate," James went on, "there are bedrooms and a kitchen through here. One working bathroom, too. All of them completely stocked for comfort and emergency use. And while I don't imagine there are a lot of supplies for human beings, there are always at least some basics. At least, there always used to be, back when—"

He stopped talking, and she knew he must have finally noticed that she was no longer behind him nor paying any attention to his guided tour of her prison. Her attention had been caught, and it wasn't coming back any time soon. Lucy laid her palm on the cool tablet, moving it slowly over the markings that another human being had painstakingly pressed into it tens of centuries ago. She closed her eyes, and in her mind she could see the scribe in his pristine white robes, with his bushy dark unibrow. He would have had raven black hair, and deep brown or even ebony eyes. He would have thought of himself as one of the black-headed people, and his job would have been a sacred one.

"Ah, the tablet is here already. Good. Rhiannon said she would try to get it by the time we arrived."

Lucy blinked out of her reverie, though she swore she could still smell the smoke of the scribe's oil lamp. Her eyes still on the clay tablet, she whispered, "Where did she get this?"

"From…a vampire. A very old one."

"And where did *he* get it?"

"Probably from the person who carved it."

Lucy swung her eyes toward his, felt them widen.

"He calls himself Damien now," James explained.

"But that's not his real name. He had to change it. But when he was human, he was known as Gilgamesh."

She searched his face and without a word called him a liar. It couldn't be.

"It's true."

"The Gilgamesh?" she whispered. "King Gilgamesh, of Ancient Sumer, is…a vampire?"

"The first vampire, as a matter of fact." Sighing, James pulled out a chair for her. She only stared at it, her head spinning. "We have a history as old as yours…or nearly so," he told her. "And it begins in Sumer. I want to tell it to you, and believe me, Lucy, that's a big deal, because there are very few living mortals who know any of this, and even fewer who know it all. I would very much like for you to be one of those few. In fact, I *need* you to be one of them."

But Lucy was hardly listening, too busy searching the databases inside her mind for anything remotely like this in all her years of study, and she was finding almost nothing.

"There is no vampire lore in Sumerian legend," she said, though that wasn't entirely true. There was Lilith, but she was just the baby-killing demon invented to explain Sudden Infant Death Syndrome to a primitive people who equated every illness, death and stroke of bad luck to a supernatural being or demon of one sort or another. Lilith had only evolved into a vampire in far later tales, and then, later still, into Adam's first wife. The one who'd refused to submit.

"There is if you know where to look. I'll tell you,

if you'll let me." Again he nodded at the chair he'd pulled out for her.

She stared at the chair. She wanted to argue with him, to refuse to listen or help or do anything at all to involve herself in a mess that was not her own. And yet…this was her area. Her passion. Ancient Sumer, the history, the archaeology, of it, its written language. This was what she did. Hell, it was her life. It had been her parents' lives before her. And their deaths, as well.

For just a moment she imagined her dad, with his sun-worn face, like old, old leather, and that ever-present fedora that was worn almost threadbare. She wondered what he would say if he were here, and she knew immediately that he would jump in with both feet. He would not hesitate out of something as trivial and meaningless as fear. He would dive into this, if only to find out more.

Knowledge was a drug to him. As it was to her, she was forced to admit.

And so she nodded and sank into the chair James offered, grateful to have something to distract her from her bitter disappointment in the man she had, for a few brief moments, thought of as some kind of hero. "All right," she said softly. "You have my attention. I'm listening. Tell me your story."

"You already know a lot of it. The tale of Utanapishtim, for example." He pulled out a chair and sat facing her. "Tell me what you know about him."

She frowned, tilting her head to one side, and fell

into the comfort of the familiar. She began recounting the tale she'd told to countless groups of students. "Utanapishtim, also known as Ziasudra, a great king, was a righteous and wise man, beloved of the gods. And so, when it was decided to send the great flood down to wipe out mankind, he alone was chosen to receive mercy. He was instructed by the gods to build a massive ship, and because he obeyed, he and his family survived the great flood. As a reward for his faithfulness, the ancient one was given the secret to immortality."

When she looked up from her story, it was to see others gathering around her. Rhiannon was there, along with the cloaked stranger, who was dark and handsome and wearing a formal suit beneath the cape, as if he were embracing his own cliché. The black panther sat upright, its body pressed to Rhiannon's leg. Brigit was there, too, holding a bowl of fruit and a tall glass of water, which she placed on the table in front of Lucy.

Looking around at them, Lucy saw in their eyes the same fascination she always felt when she told this story, recorded on clay tablets long before the Hebrew Bible and its account of Noah and his ark had even been thought of. They were absorbed, riveted.

"But the thing is," she said quickly, "it's just a story. A legend. I mean, yes, the latest geological research shows that there probably was a flood at some point in history, one big enough to leave the impression that it destroyed the world and that only a few chosen ones survived to rebuild, but it was more than likely—"

"And Gilgamesh the King," James whispered softly. "Tell us his story, Lucy."

"I thought *you* were going to tell *me*."

"I will. Indulge me."

Blinking slowly, she took a grateful sip of the water. The others were making themselves comfortable, too. Rhiannon leaned against the dark man's shoulder, and his arm went around her. She pressed her free hand to his chest, and the cat lay down, now that she was no longer stroking its head. Brigit perched on the edge of the table, taking an apple from the bowl and biting into it.

"All right, I'll give you the short version," Lucy said, unable to resist her favorite topic. "Gilgamesh was a prideful and arrogant king, and not a very kind one, until he met a wild man of the forest called Enkidu, sent to teach him the error of his ways. Enkidu and the king fought when they first met, and were so equally matched that neither could prevail. They fought until they were too exhausted to stand, and in the end, they began to laugh and fell into each other's arms. From that day on, they were best friends. Enkidu seemed to be the king's opposite, wild, humble, a man of nature, not of palaces, and humility rather than power. And the king learned from him and became a better person. But when Enkidu was killed, the king lost his mind. He set out across the desert in search of the secret to immortality, hoping he could bring his friend back to life again. That search took him to the home of Utanapishtim, the flood survivor and only known immortal human being."

Her audience was riveted. She was almost enjoying herself, immersed in this tale that was, after all, her life's work.

"Utanapishtim gave that secret to him, but as the king set out across the desert again, it was stolen from him by a serpent. And that's how the story ends."

"That's only how you think it ends," Rhiannon said softly. She straightened away from the dark man, becoming the center of attention. Lucy got the feeling that was usually the case with her. "You see, Utanapishtim had sworn an oath to the gods that he would never share the gift of immortality with another living being. He'd obeyed, even to the point of watching his own family grow old and die, while he lived on, ever young, ever alone."

Several heads nodded.

Brigit picked up the tale from there. "But he could not refuse the command of his own king. He gave Gilgamesh the gift of immortality—but it didn't work quite the same way in him, as on the man to whom had been bestowed, because Gilgamesh received it not from the gods but in direct disobedience of their dictates. Gilgamesh became more and more sensitive to sunlight, and he craved human blood, the elixir his new self needed in order to survive. He was, in fact, the first vampire. And yes, he is still alive today."

Lucy could barely believe it. "I must meet him,"

she whispered. And then her gaze shot to the cloaked stranger. "Is it you?"

He smiled, and it was warm, affectionate even. "No, child. Not me. I'm Roland de Courtemanche, and I'm a mere eight centuries old, give or take." He bowed deeply, and she had to blink her vision clear.

"You will meet Damien. I give you my word," James said.

She could hardly believe it was possible. "If he's still alive, then why can't he translate the tablet for you?"

"It's a dialect from a different time than his," James told her.

"And what about Utanapishtim?" she asked, mesmerized by the tale to the point where she had momentarily forgotten that these people were holding her against her will. Or were they?

"He was punished by the gods, who took away his ability to live forever but did not take away his immortality," James said. "I know that seems like a contradiction, but it's how the story came down to us. We don't know what it means. Except that, at that very moment, he began to age, to die. And when King Gilgamesh's mortal enemy, Anthar, arrived later, having followed the great king and spied on events, he demanded that he, too, be given the gift. Utanapishtim tried to refuse, but that evil one forced him, and then he beheaded the old man, leaving him for dead, and took his faithful servant, a young man barely out of his teens, as his own slave."

"So this Anthar was…the second vampire."

"Yes, and he soon made the servant into the third—thinking to make for himself a stronger, more resilient slave. But all that did was allow the boy—a man by then—to escape," James said.

"And the first thing the boy did," said Brigit, "was return to the old man's home to see to his remains. But they were gone."

"We need to know what happened to Utanapish-tim's remains," Rhiannon said. "That is why we've brought you here. We believe there is a clue on that tablet you've been caressing so lovingly throughout this conversation. It's been among us forever. Even Gilgamesh doesn't know its source. But we've always known to keep it safe, because it would save our race one day."

"And you believe that day is here."

Rhiannon nodded slowly. Lucy turned her gaze from the intimidating vampiress to James. "But why do you need to find his remains? Surely there's nothing left but dust by now. What good can that possibly do you?"

He lowered his head. "Can you translate the tablet for us, Lucy?"

She blinked rapidly. "If I had access to my books, to my notes, to my lab…"

"We'll get you whatever you need. But the work will have to be done here," Rhiannon said. "And despite what I said earlier, no harm will come to you. So long as you do as we ask."

"No harm will come to you either way, Lucy," James said.

"J.W." Rhiannon's tone held a warning.

"No, this is bullshit." James put a hand on Lucy's shoulders. "The fact is, Lucy, no one here could hurt you even if they wanted to. They're incapable of it, compelled to protect you instead, as a matter of fact."

She frowned up at him. "But why?"

He shrugged. "You're sort of...related."

Her frown deepened, but he explained no more. Instead, he dropped down to his knees in front of her chair. "Stay with us, translate this tablet for us, and I give you my solemn vow, you'll be safe. And as soon as it's done, I'll personally return you to your home."

She couldn't hold his gaze. If she did, he would hypnotize her into saying yes. They could do that, couldn't they? So she lowered her eyes and found herself struggling, torn between her fascination with the Sumerian connection, her curiosity about what this tablet might reveal, and her lifelong fear of conflict, of danger, of confrontation, of ever getting involved in...much of anything.

"Do I really have a choice?" she asked softly.

He swallowed hard. "No. I'm afraid you don't."

7
___

Why did something very much like relief flutter through Lucy's insides just then? Because the decision had been taken out of her hands? Because she couldn't be brave on her own? Because she knew that not even the most tantalizing opportunity in the world could entice her to overcome her overwhelming cowardice? Yes to all of those, and now, because he'd given her no choice, she didn't need to search for an inner strength that didn't exist. She would do this because she had to, and she would be terrified the entire time because that was who she was.

James was turning away now, his head lowered, his hands in his hair. "I hate this, Lucy. This isn't who I am, and holding you here this way—it's beyond barbaric. It goes against everything I believe in."

Lucy frowned, for the first time looking away from her own torment long enough to see that he was not pretending. This was tearing him apart. Or something was.

"No one will hurt you," he went on. "But we can't let you go until you do as we ask, Lucy. I'm more sorry than you'll probably ever know."

"Shall I just vomit now, or is there a violin solo coming up?" Rhiannon asked, looking from one of them to the other. Roland put his hand on her arm as if to quiet her.

When Lucy did nothing but blink, her mind still on James and the anguish she'd only just now glimpsed in him, along with the hundreds of questions that glimpse had raised, Rhiannon rolled her eyes and went on. "Professor, give Brigit a list of what you need and where we can find it." As she spoke, she crossed the room to the desk, and then slapped a notepad and freshly sharpened number 2 pencil down in front of Lucy. "Feel free to use the internet. The ISP has been scrambled. You won't be traced. Be aware, however, that every keystroke is being monitored, so any attempt to send an SOS will be intercepted. And while J.W. is correct in that we cannot harm you, believe me when I tell you that I can—and will—make your life miserable if you cross me."

Lucy believed her.

"Just translate the tablet, Lucy," Brigit said. "We'll let you go the minute you finish. And that will be faster than anyone could mount a rescue attempt anyway. Besides, just because we can't hurt you—not that we'd want to," she went on, "that doesn't mean we couldn't do some serious damage to anyone who might come charging to the rescue. And you don't want innocent people getting killed over this, do you?"

Lucy nodded slowly, understanding that she was completely at their mercy. And wishing she understood why they couldn't actually hurt her, how she was…related, as James had put it. And more. What were vampires, really? What were their weaknesses? What powers did they possess? Were all the myths true, the crucifixes and holy water and wooden stakes and…?

"Come with me now, J.W.," Rhiannon said, interrupting her thoughts. "We're short on time, and your training is about to begin."

"Take heart, little mortal," Roland said softly, as he passed her on the way out. "None of us are quite as bad as we seem. And you've been told the truth here."

And with that, they all left the room except for Brigit, who sat at the far end of the table, slouched in a chair. She bit into her half-eaten apple and talked with her mouth full. "You must be pretty pissed off right now. I would be."

Lucy looked away, refusing to answer. Brigit leaned forward, reaching for the notepad and pencil, pulling them across the table to her. She took another bite and sat back with the pencil poised. "So? Tell me what you need."

Lucy thought of all the things she needed, and then she thought of the one thing she wanted. She wanted that book by Lester Folsom, the one with the parts of the story these vampires might not be telling her. "My handbag," she said. "I really can't even begin until you get me my handbag."

Brigit frowned, but jotted it down. "I fail to see how your handbag is going to help you translate, but I'll get it. What else?"

Lucy listed several indispensable reference books from her personal collection. She would have loved to have asked Brigit for some of the volumes at the university, but she didn't want to drag any of her colleagues into this mess or put anyone else at risk. So she only named the books that could be found in her own little cracker-box house with its marigold-filled flower boxes in the front windows and its marigold carpets lining the walk all the way to the stoop.

She missed her home. Her haven.

"Got it. And that's upstate, right?"

"Binghamton, yes."

Brigit frowned but didn't argue. "I might need to delegate. Anything else?"

"My laptop. It's there, too, at the house."

Brigit scribbled on her notepad. "Is that it?"

Lucy nodded. "That's it."

"Good. All right, this is going to take some time. Do what you can while I'm gone. Eat some of the fruit I brought you. You must be hungry. And you need to keep your strength up. Also, there's a bathroom all the way at the end," she added with a nod toward the door at the back of the office. "You can wander all you want in this section, but don't go into the main part of the house. We can't afford to have anyone see movement out there. Okay?"

"Yes. Okay."

"Okay. See you in a while. Behave." And with that, Brigit left her alone.

Alone in a crumbling mansion full of vampires and their…kin. In a hidden section, behind a secret wall, translating an ancient dialect under duress.

She couldn't have made this up if she'd tried.

Brigit drove into the city, parked her car in a no parking zone near the curb and walked three of the remaining four blocks to Studio Three. She stopped there, still a block away. She could see the spot on the sidewalk where the spineless little mortal had been shot down.

She frowned and wondered if she was starting to think a little bit too much like Rhiannon. But then, there was no such thing as too much, in her opinion. Rhiannon was Brigit's hero. She wanted to be as much like the ageless, timeless vampiress as possible. And even then, she knew she would never compare.

Rhiannon was surely one of the most powerful of her kind, and there was no doubt she was the most arrogant. She was impatient, demanding, intolerant of weakness or whining and she had a temper that could easily explode into violence. But she was good. Deep down, she was good.

Brigit wasn't. She was the bad twin, always had been. Her brother had been born with the power to heal, to restore life. He'd restored hers—she'd been stillborn. Blue, until he'd wrapped his tiny hand around her fingers, or so the story went.

She, on the other hand, had been born with an opposing power. One she'd been sternly warned not to use, not to play with, not to demonstrate—ever. J.W. was the good one, the hero, the healer, the guy in the white hat. Brigit was little more than a Disney villainess. Every story needed one, after all. She'd accepted her dark nature long ago. She did what she wanted, when she wanted and she made no apologies. There was no point trying to be good. She hadn't been born with a calling, the way her saintly twin had.

Rhiannon had been the only person in Brigit's life to encourage her to develop her power. In secret, without the knowledge of her vampire father, Edgar—who preferred to be called Edge, and really, who could blame him?—and her half-vamp, half-mortal mother, Amber Lily—who would have had a breakdown if she'd known, that was how good and pure she was. As a result, she'd become very good at destroying things. Very good. Rhiannon had told her many times that her power, her gift, was every bit as important as her brother's.

There can be no creation without destruction, child. No life without death. Except for us, of course. No healing power without an illness or injury to heal. Never forget that. He might be the sun, little one, but you, my darling, darkling Brigit...you are the moon.

Brigit smiled as Rhiannon's deep voice resonated

through her mind. Oh, it was bull, of course. Rhiannon only loved her because she was a rebel, a mini-me to the great high priestess. And because her powers of destruction made Rhiannon's pale by comparison.

Still, she appreciated the lies. They'd made her feel a bit more accepted, more worthy.

Pulling herself back to the task at hand, Brigit resumed eyeing the police tape and uniformed cops up ahead. They'd blocked off that section of the street with sawhorses painted in barber pole stripes, from the spot where Lucy had fallen to the far side of the building where the killings had gone down. The alley where Lucy thought her bag had landed was beyond the barricades. Brigit supposed she could create a distraction, then dash in there. But if she had to do any digging through trash to find it, she was likely going to be caught. And she would really hate to have to kill anyone today. What with brother-dearest home doing his best Jesus Christ impersonation, she had to at least try to refrain from playing the role of Lucifer.

There was another alley running beside the building just this side of Studio Three. A Chinese restaurant and camera supply store flanked it. Seeing no other choice, she made sure no one was noticing her and ducked into it, intending to follow it to the end, pop out a block over and approach the alley she needed from behind.

She only got halfway along it, though, when a man sitting on the ground shook a battered paper coffee cup at her. "Spare change?" he asked.

She pressed her lips together in distaste. He smelled to high heaven; even a full-blooded sensory-deprived mortal would have curled her lip in revulsion at his stench. And his milky sightless eyes were all matted together, dried goo in his long lashes. He had salt-and-pepper whiskers that had an ecosystem of their own going on in their depths, and a splotch of white foam in one corner of his lips.

"Sorry, I'm tapped out." She kept walking.

"Cryin' shame. I been waitin' for you all this time, an' now you just walk on by."

Brigit had proceeded a few more steps, but she stopped then, a tingle of awareness dancing up her spine. Turning to look at the old man, she saw that he had a very nice-looking satchel beside him. Brown, leather, with two buckles holding its flap top closed.

"You've been waiting for me, have you?" she asked.

"If you're the one. You got a purpose, have ya? A calling?"

She rolled her eyes. "You must be talking about my brother," she said, a hint of sarcasm welling up in her chest, though she knew the man was just talking nonsense.

"Nope, nope, nope, I think it's you. Came for this, didn't-cha?" He tapped the bag with a flat filthy palm.

She narrowed her eyes. "The one I came for is in the next alley."

"Was. Till I brought it to this one."

"Why did you do that?" She stepped a little closer, growing more and more curious about this blind man.

"It's what I was told to do. Move the bag so those fancy suits snoopin' around wouldn't get their hands on it. Hold it here for you. I got the sight, ya see. Not the eyesight, mind'ja. But the sight."

She frowned, and suddenly she didn't doubt him for a second. Hell, she'd been raised by vampires. She wasn't going to doubt a homeless, blind, self-proclaimed psychic in an alley. Even a skeptical mortal would find this guy a lot easier to swallow than a blood-drinking, night-walking immortal. "You're some kind of psychic, are you?"

"I see things," he said. "Seen you. Pretty thing, you are. Hair like sunlight at high noon, real pale. Pale blue seawater eyes. Power, too. Power they wouldn't even show me. Said I didn't need to know, but that I'd do well not to piss you off. I ain't, am I? Pissin' you off?"

"Depends," she said. "Are you going to give me the bag?"

"Soon as you tell me one thing. I'm s'posed to ask, you see. To make sure you're the one. So here it is, little lady. Here's the question. Makes no sense to me. But here it is, all the same. How were you born?"

"I was born dead," she replied, quickly and without even thinking about her answer.

He pressed his lips tight, shook his head in apparent wonder. "Damned if that ain't what they told me you'd say. Alrighty, then, here it is." He held up the bag.

She took it, surprised by its weight, eager to dig through it to see just what the good professor wanted so badly. But first, she thought she ought to give the old guy something for his trouble. She dug in her pockets, finding a handful of crumpled bills she'd forgotten were there, and, leaning forward, she pressed them into his hand. "Take this for your trouble," she said.

"No need."

"Take it," she said. And then she smiled a little. "Or you'll piss me off."

"Well, now, I guess I don't wanna do that. I thank you, little lady. An' I'll tell you one last thing before you go—which you'd best do soon, since those suits are headin' this way as we speak."

She looked up and down the alley, but saw and sensed no one.

"You do have a callin', a purpose," the old man told her. "You do. An' it's a big one."

Brigit's throat went tight and her eyes burned, even as her mind muttered bullshit.

"Go on now. Git."

"I'm already gone," she told him, and then she was. But as she headed back along the sidewalk toward her car, she spotted the suits hurrying down the sidewalk, intent on the old man's alley. And she had no doubt they had counterparts on the other end. The old fuck had been dead-on balls accurate about those suits heading their way.

Damn. How, then, could he have been so wrong about her?

She hefted the bag's strap up onto her shoulder and picked up the pace.

James followed Rhiannon back through the false wall and into the main part of the dilapidated mansion. Through the bedroom into the second story corridor, and then down the curving staircase into the foyer that had once been fit for royalty.

She led him down another hallway, where the plaster was disintegrating. His steps crushed fallen chunks of it into fine white powder that stuck to his shoes, and the bare lath showed through the walls like the skeleton beneath a corpse's skin.

Funny that he'd chosen that particular mental image, he thought, as she led the way into the pitch-dark basement and yet another hidden room that he knew had once been the laboratory of vampire scientist Eric Marquand. But then something caught hold of his attention. A scent, and a sense, too. Death. There was death here.

He stood motionless, straining his eyes in the darkness. "My night vision isn't as good as yours, Rhiannon, but I don't like what I'm sensing down here."

A light flared, but not from a match. The candles on a nearby stand came to life, the wicks smoldering and then bursting into flame one by one under the power of Rhiannon's intense stare.

Not a vampiric skill, that little trick. That bit was hers alone. The daughter of a Pharaoh and a high priestess of Isis, "Rianikki" knew secrets and possessed powers none of them would ever equal—a fact she wasn't likely to let anyone forget.

"Your first guinea pig awaits you," she said softly, lifting the candelabra and moving toward a table in the center of the room.

The flickering yellow light fell upon a dead woman, her body still and pale and wet. He lowered his head, closing his eyes against the sight. "Shit, Rhiannon, what have you done?"

"Oh, please. I didn't kill her. In fact, knowing your fondness for the weaker race, I asked Roland to find our first candidate."

"Roland brought her here?" James's reluctance lifted a little. Rhiannon's mate wasn't as ruthless or cruel as she was. He was, in fact, calm, logical and kind.

"Yes, and I've sent him out to bring more. As for this one…" She nodded at the corpse. "She's thirty-three, married, a mother of two. Her car skidded off the road into an isolated lake a little over a day ago. Roland pulled her body out only hours ago, after I told him we needed a freshly dead mortal for your experiments."

James stared at the woman. Her hair had dried in tangles, and there was mud caking on her still damp clothes. But her skin was blue. She was clearly dead and far beyond saving.

"Well?" Rhiannon asked. "Go on, do that voodoo that you do so well. We haven't got all night."

He dragged his eyes away from the dead mother. "Rhiannon, I can't."

"Oh, please. You can. You used to run along the beach picking up dead starfish and healing them before tossing them back into the waves. When you were three, you did this."

"Newly dead. And starfish are not human beings. It's not...it's not the same."

"How is it different?"

"What if she's...you know...in heaven, or—"

"If she's in heaven, J.W., then she will return to heaven again in short order. The human lifetime is little more than the flash of a firefly in length. You won't be taking that from her, just rearranging her schedule a bit. Think of her husband, her children, if that helps ease your ridiculously overdeveloped sense of morality."

"No, Rhiannon, that would be playing God." He looked at the dead woman again, shaking his head.

"That's what I said at first," said a deep voice from behind them.

James turned, spotting Roland standing there in his traditional getup. He was the only vampire James had ever known who actually wore a black cape and a dark suit.

"I thought you'd gone for more bodies," Rhiannon chided, but gently, lovingly.

"I prefer to see how this goes first." He nodded. "And to say a proper hello to you, James."

James moved toward the man, who was centuries older, but didn't look a day over thirty and never would. "I'm sorry I didn't greet you properly upstairs," James said. "I was distracted."

"I could see that." The two embraced, Roland hugging hard and clapping James on the back. "It's been too long, J.W."

"It has. And I'm sorry."

Roland released him. "No apologies. We each have our own path to walk. But I'm glad you're here now. We need you, J.W. And as distasteful as this task seems, it is my belief that you have to do it. I'm convinced that your woman's interpretation of that Sumerian prophecy is correct, even more so than I was before."

"She's not my woman." James lowered his head, feeling his face heat and wondering why. "She hates me at the moment, and I don't particularly blame her."

Roland opened his mouth, closed it again. "That's beside the point. The tablet she translated predicts that the world of men will find out about us—and that has happened. It predicts war breaking out—and that, too, is unfolding as we speak. And then it predicts the end of our kind, James, and says that only Utanapishtim can save us."

"I get that, but I don't see how this is going to—"

"Because," Rhiannon interrupted, "we're going to find his remains, and you are going to restore him to life. Therefore, you must begin pushing your powers to their absolute limits and beyond. Making them stronger, until you can do this thing and save your people."

James looked from Rhiannon to Roland. "And you believe this is a good idea, as well?"

Roland lowered his eyes. "Not good, no. But necessary, yes. Since you were ten years old, you've been asking why. Why were you born with this power to heal? What was its purpose? Now you know, J.W. Now you know. You are the only one who can save us. And it begins here. With her." He nodded toward the corpse.

James fought against a full body shudder, but he moved closer to the table, to the dead woman lying there. "And if I manage to wake her, then what?"

"Then we try a corpse that's been dead a bit longer," Rhiannon said. "A week. And then a month. And then—"

"What happens to her?"

Roland's hand closed on James's shoulder from behind. "I'll tend to her. I'll take her to the shore of the lake where her car still lies. I'll erase her memory of us, arrange for a mortal to discover her there."

"Her family will be notified," Rhiannon whispered from his other side. "Her husband and children will meet her at some hospital, and there will be tears of joy. They would thank you on their knees if they knew what you were about to do for them, J.W. That should appeal to your hero complex nicely, if saving your own kind is not enough."

James looked at her sharply. "You just can't let up, can you?"

She narrowed her eyes, telling him without a word that he had better watch his step. He held her gaze without flinching.

"I believe this is necessary. And I've consulted with the elders of our race," Roland went on. "Eric, Dante and Sarafina, Vlad, even Gilgamesh himself—"

"My parents and grandparents?"

He nodded. "Yes. Edge and Amber Lily, Jameson and Angelica—they've been consulted. We all agree. This is the only way."

Drawing a deep breath, James nodded and moved closer to the table. He held his hands over the dead woman and closed his eyes. He focused his energy, and he felt the warmth begin, the tingling in his palms, the heat and light that emanated from them…it all happened just as it always did, though it took a little longer, and he seemed to have to dig more deeply for the energy.

He felt Rhiannon and Roland watching him, but he paid no attention to them. His entire focus was on the woman, on her spirit, on restoring its connection to her physical body, on healing the damage done by twenty-four hours without oxygen or blood flow, and by the water in her lungs.

His muscles tensed as the energy moved through him and into her. And then they tensed more. And then, suddenly, there was a release. A rush shot from his core and out through his palms with so much force that he felt a slight recoil effect pushing him away. He stumbled back a step or two, and then Roland caught him from behind. He felt drained, as if the energy he'd pushed into the corpse had come directly from him instead of just through him.

And then he opened his eyes and stared at the table.

The woman was stirring, her eyes moving beneath her closed lids. Her body began to tremble, her head to thrash and then her eyes flew open and she blinked in stunned terror.

Stumbling close to her again, James put a hand on her shoulder. "It's okay. You're okay. You're safe now. You're perfectly safe. Do you know who you are?"

She blinked blankly a few times and then said, "I'm…Ellen. Ellen Gainsboro." She looked around the darkened room. "Where are my boys? Where's my husband? Who are you?"

James smiled in relief and nodded at Roland.

The cloaked vampire moved closer. "You're going to sleep now, Ellen," he said, his voice melodic, hypnotic, irresistible. "And when you wake, you'll be with your family again. You'll rest easily until you hear their voices, and that's when you'll awake, relaxed and happy. You will not remember me, nor anyone you've seen in this room, nor the room itself. You'll sleep until you hear those beloved voices, and then you'll awake to the most blissful joy you've ever known. Do you understand?"

Her eyes were already closing as she whispered, "Yes."

And that would have been comforting to James, if Rhiannon hadn't immediately said, "We're going to need more bodies, Roland. You can't put it off any longer now."

"On my way, love," Roland replied, clapping James on the shoulder as he left the basement, carrying the sleeping woman in his arms.

James staggered a few steps backward, stunned by what he'd just managed to do. He leaned against the wall and wished this task had fallen to anyone else but him.

8

After Brigit left, list in hand, Lucy worked on the translation for the better part of two hours, until her eyes were beginning to glaze over and water from the strain. She longed for her glasses. Her nerves were jumping with frustration. She was as curious about what the tablet had to say as any of them—though not because she thought it would prevent the extinction of their species, admittedly. Still, a new tablet was always a cause for excited anticipation. And yet there was very little she could do without her books and her notes. Oh, she knew several of the more common words, but it was almost always the uncommon ones that told the story, and without those, there was no context for the bits and pieces she knew by sight.

Eventually, she felt sure, she would fall asleep there at the table if she didn't get up and move around at least a bit. She decided to explore the rest of the house. Not the entire house, of course, just the hidden, secret section—behind the walls, beneath the stairs. It was all very much like something out of a Nancy Drew mystery.

Still, Brigit had told her to make herself at home, to look around freely, but not to emerge from the secret depths of the crumbling old mansion, and she'd decided she had nothing to lose by obeying. She didn't want to rock the boat or do anything to anger these people. She didn't want to defy them or fight with them. She wasn't a rebel plotting a coup. She just wanted to go home. And the simplest path to that goal, as far as she could see, was to just do what they wanted, and hope they would keep their promise when she finished and send her on her way.

Beyond the big room, with the computer and conference table, the room she thought of as the office, other rooms led into each other like a long railroad flat. No hallway in between. There wasn't room for one. The rooms were all shaped the same, long and narrow, and they followed the outline of the house all the way around two sides, as nearly as she could figure. The room beside the office was a kitchen of sorts. It held a fridge and some cupboards, a microwave, but no range. There was a sink, too, with running water. Relief flooded her at the sight of the fridge. She was hungry—Brigit's offering had filled her briefly, but she craved something more solid than fruit. Tummy rumbling, she opened the refrigerator to see what was inside, then gasped and slammed it shut again.

Bags of blood with the Red Cross logo on the front. Deep red fluid within. God.

Her hunger pangs turned into queasiness, and she didn't explore the kitchen any further. She left it behind, going to the room after it, which was a bedroom. Tall false windows with glass one couldn't see through. She noticed the big locks on the doors between the rooms and, although they were unlocked at the moment, she shuddered at the implication.

Next in line was another bedroom. There were four of them, all told, each one arranged the same way, each one with locks on both its doors.

The final room's door was closed, but as she approached it, the door swung open, revealing a bathroom and James, who paused in the act of exiting it, spotting her and going still.

He looked…tired. Tired enough that she had to wonder what could have happened to him in the two hours since she'd seen him last. Not to mention how he'd gotten into the secret section of the house without walking past her. There must be another entrance somewhere, she realized, and filed that knowledge away for future use. His hair was tousled and damp, as was his face, as if he'd been splashing water on it in an effort to wake himself up.

"Lucy," he said with a nod. "Sorry if you've been waiting."

"I haven't been." She tipped her head to one side. "Are you all right?"

"What?" He blinked at her, his expression distracted, and then seemed to digest her question. "Oh. Yeah. Why?"

"You look...worn out."

He didn't meet her eyes. "No, I'm good. I was just leaving you a note, actually."

"A note?"

He stepped aside, to let her enter the bathroom. It was almost as big as the bedrooms, and painted a minty shade of green. There was a huge tub with clawed feet and brass fixtures, including a tall, old-fashioned showerhead and a wrap-around rod for the curtain. There was a matching toilet and sink, both ivory colored, with those same brass faucets. An antique stand with a green and black swirling marble top stood beside the lav, and it was littered with bottles. Shampoos and conditioners, soaps and soaks, lotions and perfumes.

"Looks like the best-stocked room in the house," she said softly. "And you said something about a note?"

He nodded past her toward a brown wicker hamper with a pile of clothing stacked on it and a note lying on top. A single sheet of unlined vellum, folded once, with her name on the outside.

Frowning, she turned back toward him, curious, but just as she did, his knees seemed to buckle and he grabbed hold of the door frame to keep from falling. Lucy found herself reaching for him before she could stop herself. She slid her arms beneath his and held him to her. "Easy," she said. "God, what has Rhiannon been making you do?"

"Only what's necessary." His hands closed on her shoulders, and he pulled away slightly, but at that moment she lifted her head and he lowered his. Their eyes met, locked. Her arms were around his waist, and it felt for all the world as if they were embracing.

For a moment, just one breathless moment, she thought maybe he was going to kiss her. It felt like a kiss in the making. Not that she'd experienced many of those. And unbelievably, she was craving it, already feeling his mouth, tasting his lips, in her mind.

And then he straightened and the moment was broken.

"I'm...well, there's the note."

"Yes, I..." Silence was better than stammering. She let her arms fall to her sides and stepped away from his warmth, picking up the note, unfolding and reading it.

> Lucy,
>
> I've left a change of clothes for you. Please use anything you find here freely, and be as relaxed and at ease as you can in this situation. I intend to make your stay here as brief and as painless as possible. And although you were given no choice, your help is deeply appreciated.
>
> —James

Lucy nodded, and felt her heart soften toward James Poe. She thought he really meant those words.

She thought he was truly torn by what he was being asked to do, pushed to do, by his family. She supposed she could understand that.

"Thank you. That was…most considerate." She lifted her head to meet his eyes, but he was gone. She leaned through the doorway, looking back the way she'd come, but there was no sign of him. He must move like a ninja, she thought.

More like a vampire, her mind whispered. Don't forget what he is—part monster. And a kidnapper, too. Don't trust him for a minute, Lucy.

She disliked the voice in her head, because it made utter sense, and she would have preferred not to hear it at all. She could easily believe the others were monsters, driven by their own sense of self-preservation. Especially the vampire queen, if that was indeed what Rhiannon was. Lucy disliked her intensely, distrusted her utterly and feared her more than both together.

But she wasn't sure just yet what she thought of James. He seemed to be a decent man, pressed into a bad situation. He seemed different from the others. Even from his sister. And maybe he'd been trying to break away from them, to lead a normal life, given the fact that he'd been living away from them and had been out of touch, much to their dismay, for quite some time. Trying to exist as a human? To pass? she wondered. Trying to embrace his humanity and shun his inner beast?

Not that it mattered to her. Not in the least.

Still, she availed herself of his apparent kindness

and took a long, hot shower, which eased her aching muscles and cleared her still-foggy head. And then she got out, wrapped herself up in a decadently soft, cushy towel and took a look at the clothes he had left for her.

Jeans. Low-rise jeans that fit far more snugly than the waist-high, relaxed-fit style she wore at home, when she wore jeans at all. A tiny black T-shirt, with its sleeves and collar ripped out. It had been cut off, too, so that it revealed most of her midriff when she pulled it on. It was as far as possible from anything she would have found in her own closet at home. There were socks, and a pair of what could only be described as high-heeled army boots. The four-inch heels were thick and chunky, but there was a good two-inch platform, too, so the angle of her foot remained fairly comfortable. The boots laced up over most of her calf and had buckles besides.

These had to have been taken from Brigit's wardrobe. Lucy felt so uncomfortable it was ridiculous.

No mirror. Of course there were no mirrors. It was just as well, she probably looked awful. She wound her damp hair up into its customary bun and walked back through the secret rooms, past the blood-filled fridge, to the office, wobbling on the high heels and tugging constantly on the shirt.

God, she wanted to go home.

Well, then, she supposed, the best thing was to get back to work. She took a seat at the table, opened the notepad, squinting without her glasses, and got busy.

An hour later Brigit was back, tossing Lucy's long-lost satchel onto the table.

"Nice try," the sweet-looking blonde with the dominatrix wardrobe said. Then she dropped the book Mr. Folsom had given Lucy right beside the satchel. "I presume this is what you really wanted?"

What she really wanted, Lucy thought, setting her pencil carefully on the table, was whatever smelled so good in the white takeout bag Brigit still held.

And to read that book.

"I thought I'd like to know a little more about the race I'm being forced to help save."

"Yeah, well, you'd better get on it, or there won't be a race left to need your help. The existence of vampires is the hottest topic going right now, thanks to the bits and pieces of this book that have leaked. At least from what I heard on the car radio on the way back here. Vigilante groups are popping up all over the country, and innocent people are dying."

"Innocent vampire people or innocent ordinary people?" Lucy asked.

"Innocent is innocent, bookworm. But to answer your question, both."

"I'm sorry if that sounded…bigoted. I didn't mean it to. And I'm sorry your people are suffering."

"Your people, too."

Sighing, Lucy eyed the book again. "Maybe there are some answers in here." She reached for it, but Brigit snatched it before she could pick it up.

"Not so fast. Let's see what Rhiannon has to say

about this. Besides, anything you want to know, you can just ask. And you don't have time for leisure reading right now, anyway. We need that prophecy translated ASAP. Understand?"

Lucy frowned, tilting her head to one side. "You seem upset."

"You think?" Brigit sighed, shook her head, then dropped the fast food bag on the table at last. "Figured you'd be as starved as I am. My relatives may have the house well stocked with sustenance for them, but I doubt there's much food fit for human consumption around here."

"True enough. I've heard they never drink… wine."

Brigit went stone silent, staring at her for a long moment before asking, "Did you just make a Dracula joke?"

Lucy nodded. The smells emanating from that bag were making her mouth water and her brain senselessly joyful. "I think so, yes." She opened the bag, grabbing the fries first. The colder they got, the more they tasted like salty cardboard.

"He's real, you know," Brigit said while Lucy ate.

"Who is?"

"Dracula."

Lucy stopped with a French fry between her teeth and stared at Brigit, wide-eyed.

"Vlad Tepish. Of course, that wasn't his original name." Brigit bit her lip. "And I'm telling you more secrets than Folsom's book probably will." She looked

Lucy up and down. "I see you did as I suggested and took a look around the place while I was gone."

Lucy nodded. "I took a shower. The clean clothes are…appreciated. I presume they're yours."

"*De nada*. I told J.W. to take whatever he thought you could use. The rest of the stuff you asked for should be arriving shortly. I sent someone who could move a little faster than I can, and I asked them to bring back some of your own clothes, as well." She grinned. "Though you really do have a bod under all your starch and tweed. You should show it off more."

Lucy thought she should say thanks, but she was too busy blushing. Since when did women talk that way to one another?

"Shit, you think that's bad, wait till my brother gets a load of you in that getup." Brigit nodded at the bag. "Go on, eat your junk food."

"Um…did you bring some for…your brother?"

Brigit frowned, tilting her head to one side. "Yeah. Sure I did. Why do you ask?"

Lucy shook her head, averting her eyes, not wanting to reply and not sure why. She shouldn't be concerned about the well-being of her captor. Was this the beginning of Stockholm Syndrome? No, it was far too soon, and yet… She wanted to like him. She wanted this odd and inexplicable—yet entirely undeniable—attraction she felt for him to be…okay. He'd seemed exhausted, worn out, run down, after only a few hours with Rhiannon and her notion of his "training," whatever that entailed. But she couldn't tell Brigit she was worried about him, not without giving herself away.

She prayed he was good and not evil. She wanted to think of him as her hero again.

"I just…figured he'd be hungry, too," she finally said, and it was lame, but it was the best she could do.

Brigit was eyeing her curiously. "Nothing to worry about. I brought him a ton."

Time for a subject change, Lucy decided. "I've, um—I've actually already begun translating. Just a word here and there, the ones I recognize without my notes."

Brigit looked at the notebook where Lucy had been copying the cuneiform line for line, leaving blank lines in between for her translation. A few simple words already occupied those blanks. Simple conjunctions like *and, to, with, the,* and a few more meaningful words like *ancient, death, murder,* and the names *Utanapishtim* and *Ziasudra.*

Brigit looked at Lucy again. "You really know your shit, don't you? I mean, you've already got a lot, and you didn't even have your reference books or notes or anything."

"Or my glasses," Lucy added, fishing them from their designated pocket in the bag and putting them on. "It's what I've been doing all my life. What my parents did. I grew up with this." She thought Brigit looked as if she admired her just for a moment, before the other woman shielded her expression. Lucy decided to try again for more information. She'd really been counting on that book to tell her what she wanted to know about the vampires. "It would help a lot if I knew what you were looking for. Specifically, I mean. That way I could let you know the minute I find it."

Brigit studied her face. "It's a reasonable request. I'll ask and get back to you. Meanwhile, the rest of your stuff is in your satchel. Phone included. There's no reception in here, and the wireless connection for the computer is password protected. God knows 3G hasn't made it out here yet. So there's no risk you'll do anything stupid, like calling for help."

"I wasn't going to do that."

"Better safe than sorry," Brigit said, and then she nodded at Lucy's cleavage. "That's pretty," she observed.

Lucy's hand rose, and she felt the necklace she'd forgotten all about, the jade Kwan Yin Mr. Folsom had been using as a bookmark. And as she fingered it, she detected for the first time what felt like a seam in the jade.

"Thank you. It was…a gift," she said, keeping her hand closed around it so Brigit wouldn't spot that telltale rift, surprised that Brigit seemed to be making an effort to be friendly.

"Suits you," Brigit said. "Kwan Yin. Mercy and compassion and all that soft-ass shit. I'd probably be more in tune with a Kali pendant. You know, with her necklace of skulls and every arm wielding a weapon or a severed body part."

"Destruction and creation go hand in hand. Kali has her purpose."

Brigit frowned. "You're the second person today to use that word to me. Purpose. Interesting. I gotta run. The world's going to hell out there. You get back to work, okay?"

"Thank you. For the food, the clothes."

"You're welcome." Brigit left the room, taking Mr. Folsom's book with her.

Lucy fingered the jade Kwan Yin, prying at the very fine seam along her graceful neck. As she tugged, Kwan Yin's head popped off to reveal that this was more than a necklace.

It was a flash drive.

She dug through her bag until she found her state-of-the-art cell phone—the brand-new Cyborg 4G. She'd been teased over it when she'd bought it, but she was a geek on many levels, including technology, and she'd had to have it. And now she was glad. How many phones had a USB port built in?

Not many. Yet. It was the one thing they lacked, she'd often said.

And then she'd bought the one model that did have one.

She turned her phone on, noting that Brigit had been right—the words *No Signal* floated in the upper left corner of the screen. Quickly, Lucy plugged Kwan

Yin into the side, and when the icon popped up, she tapped it.

And got a Truth-Eyes Only Version pdf.

Luckily her ereading program could handle pdf files. She quickly opened it, imported the file and then disconnected the flash drive. After putting Kwan Yin's head back on, she draped the charm around her neck again, tucking it beneath her shirt, out of sight and, hopefully, out of mind.

Finally she sat back down and began reading the "Eyes Only" version of Folsom's book. She guessed that meant that there were secrets here even the public version of the book didn't contain. And when she saw how he depicted the vampires as soulless, bloodthirsty beasts, she hoped to God that part was one of those secrets. But given what Brigit had told her—the vigilantes, the murders—she guessed not.

9

Lucy knew she was supposed to be sleeping, and she certainly needed some sleep.

She'd worked throughout the night on the transcripts, usually with someone present to watch over her, either Brigit or Roland, the dark, soft-spoken Frenchman who dressed and spoke as formally as if he'd stepped off the pages of a historical novel. His accent had eluded her at first, it was so faint. Barely noticeable, but there all the same. And his manners were flawless. He seemed too gentle to be—a vampire, not to mention—Rhiannon's partner or husband or whatever they called their better halves.

Roland was definitely that. Rhiannon's better half, though Lucy would never say so aloud for fear of eliciting the vamp queen's rage. She found herself liking Roland, though, in spite of what he was.

She'd seen little of James tonight. He'd been off with Rhiannon doing more of that training. Training for what? she wondered.

And then she wondered why she couldn't get him out of her mind. Their encounter earlier had left her shaken and feeling things she…didn't like feeling. Attraction. A dangerous attraction, and a stupid one. She'd never thought she would be one of those women who fell for dark, dangerous men—men who would hurt them. She'd always thought herself too smart to do something so self-destructive.

And yet, all she could think about was James and how it had seemed, for one blazing moment, as if he'd been about to kiss her.

What would have happened if he had?

She bit her lip and hoped the vampires weren't reading her thoughts. No, they couldn't be. It was daytime. James could, but she suspected he was either too busy or too exhausted or both. As for Brigit, Lucy didn't think that one gave a damn *what* she might be thinking.

And she *was* tired, despite the fact that it was daylight outside. Kismet, she supposed. Her sleep patterns had been changing gradually over the last three months or so. Enough that she'd asked her doctor for a prescription to counter her tendency to lie awake with her mind racing by night, then fall asleep at her desk by day. She hadn't brought the pills to New York City with her, though, and wished now that she'd added them to the list she'd given to Brigit.

Still, tired though she was, she didn't allow herself to fall asleep. Not yet. Instead, she waited, lying silently in the bedroom nearest the bathroom, at the very end of the row of secret chambers, waiting until she thought the others must all be down for the count. Surely James and Brigit would sleep by day, too, since they'd both been up all night. The house was silent and utterly dark. And there was a certain change in the air when everyone else was asleep. A heaviness that was palpable. A peaceful resonance that was broken as soon as one individual stirred. She'd noticed it as a child, while sleeping in her parents' tent in the Northern Iraqi desert on that last dig. She remembered sliding out of her bed and stepping outside, staring up at the stars and feeling that heavy silence.

The same heaviness had blanketed the dig site after everyone was dead, except that it had been even weightier, even more palpable. But just as peaceful, just as silent, as she'd hidden in the dunes, afraid to come out. She'd tried to trust that feeling that no one remained in the camp. That none of the keening gunmen were there. There was no feeling of consciousness. It had fled, just as it did when one slept. Everyone who remained, she'd told herself, was sleeping. Permanently, peacefully, sleeping.

And yet, she'd been unable to move. Maybe she'd known it would be too much to see her parents' bullet-riddled bodies. That was one memory she was glad she didn't have.

Sighing, she tugged her mind out of the past and focused on the task at hand: learning as much as she could about her captors. Not so that she could defeat them or even try. Just to satisfy her ever-curious mind, to educate her knowledge-ravenous brain, and to give her an edge in staying alive.

She moved carefully, trying not to make a sound, and got her cell phone and glasses from her satchel, which she'd hung on the bedpost. Then, sitting silently for a moment and listening, hearing no movement and sensing no consciousness from elsewhere in the house, she pulled the covers up over her head and turned the phone on, quickly hitting the Mute button as it powered up. She'd been sneaking in a page of Mr. Folsom's book here and there whenever possible during the night—any time she could think of an excuse to get away from them for a few minutes. And what she had read so far fascinated her. The last time she'd had to stop, he'd been talking about the Belladonna Antigen—the rare element in her blood that was going to ensure that she died young. Before her time. It had honestly never bothered her much, knowing that. She'd always felt she had been meant to die on that dig with her family.

But she was curious to know what her blood type had to do with all of this. With vampires and government agencies and crazy old men who wrote tell-all books that got them shot.

She opened the file, found the spot where she'd left off after her last bathroom break, and began reading voraciously.

The Belladonna Antigen is a rarely occurring one, found in exceedingly few human subjects. Exact numbers are hard to come by, as a great many carriers may go undiagnosed. The antigen doesn't show up in typical type and cross-matching but requires more in-depth screening to detect. Belladonna sufferers do develop symptoms, but they mimic many other conditions. Carriers lack sufficient clotting factor and therefore bleed excessively, much as hemophiliacs do. Until adulthood, that's the main and only known common symptom. Upon reaching their mid-to-late-thirties, however, other symptoms occur. A decrease in energy levels, and a general feeling of malaise and lethargy, set in. A tendency to sleep more by day and suffer from insomnia by night is an often reported but far from universal occurrence. The weakness increases, and the health of the individual continues to wane, until death ensues. Individuals with the antigen rarely live into their forties.

However, there are a few rare exceptions.

You may be wondering by now why information about a rare human condition is being included in this book about the undead. There is, in fact, a very good reason. Only those humans with the Belladonna Antigen can become vampires. Every vampire in existence today possessed this antigen as a human being.

"What?" she whispered, stunned. "My God." She blinked in shock, before her eyes resumed speeding over the lines.

Moreover, vampires know this and have always known, even before they had a name for the condition. They sense the humans who possess the antigen with an animalistic sixth sense that allows them to recognize their own kind, or at least their own kin. They refer to these humans as the Chosen. DPI research has shown that vampires are unwilling—perhaps even unable—to harm members of this rare human caste and in fact tend to act as guardians, stepping in to offer aid when such humans face trouble or danger.

Many of the Chosen, those who have been told none of this, have revealed, under hypnosis, suppressed memories of dark strangers intervening in times of peril and vanishing again when the individual is safe. Some have encountered the same stranger at multiple times throughout their lives. The similarities in these reports are these: The stranger always appeared by night. The memory of the victim was erased through a means that is apparently similar to post-hypnotic suggestion, though in an extremely powerful form. And the victim nearly always felt a sense of connection, of ease, with the stranger. Other similarities, though these are not universal, are reports that the stranger exhibited superhuman strength, could speak and apparently hear the victim's replies mentally—that is, without words—and that the stranger appeared able to teleport, i.e.: move from point A to point B instantaneously. DPI research has found that this teleportation is an illusion. It is simply that vampires can move at speeds too fast for the human eye to detect. (See the actual recovered memories and session transcripts in the Case Studies Section, Appendix 2.)

She was scrolling toward the specified appendix

when there was a tap on her door that nearly made her jump right out of her skin. She swallowed hard and closed the file, shut off her cell phone and quickly dropped it back into her satchel.

"Who is it?" she called, removing her glasses, setting them on the nightstand.

"It's James."

"Oh." She got up, glancing down at herself. She removed the Kwan Yin pendant, draping it from the opposite bedpost and then hanging her bathrobe over it. Brigit's minions, whoever they were, had returned with all the things on her list and then some, including that robe and several sets of pajamas. She tended to gravitate toward high thread count cotton in various pastel colors. They were cool and felt good against her skin. And yet she suddenly felt ridiculous in them.

Dumb. He was not only her captor, he wasn't even her species.

Not according to what I just read, though. Folsom said I'm related. I have the antigen. That's why they can't hurt me.

"Lucy?"

So he knew, then. He knew she had the antigen, and he knew that meant she would die young. Maybe within the next eight years or so. Maybe less—since her new sleep patterns were apparently symptoms of the antigen beginning to turn active. So maybe her life expectancy was shorter than she had ever guessed. Unless, of course, she became a vampire.

She rolled her eyes at the ludicrous thought. That

couldn't possibly be true. Sighing, she pushed the disturbing thoughts of death—and undeath—from her mind and opened her bedroom door, then looked up at James. His eyes were puffy, his lids heavy. He wasn't standing up as straight as he had before, and his hair was tousled, as if he'd been pushing his hands through it repeatedly.

"Can I come in?"

She nodded, stepping aside. He pulled a large white box from behind his back, and the smell finally hit her. Her eyes widened. "Pizza?"

"I hope you like ham and pineapple."

Her stomach answered for her, growling in anticipation as he walked inside, looking around for a place to set it down. She hurried to the bed and straightened the covers, then sat near the headboard, legs crossed, and patted the spot in front of her. "Right here is good."

James stood beside the bed, opened the box and held it out. She took a big slice and bit into it. The flavors exploded in her mouth, and she closed her eyes. "Oh, this is so good," she said. And then she realized he was still standing there, just watching her. "Aren't you going to have some?"

"Uh—right. That was the plan." He helped himself to a slice, set the box aside and then sat on the edge of the bed and ate.

There was no more talking until they'd both finished—she'd managed to down two full slices, and he'd had three. It reassured her that her appetite was still healthy. And honestly, she felt fine. Maybe that old man was a little bit crazy after all, even if he'd been right about the existence of vampires.

"I'll put the rest in the fridge," James told her. "We can have it for breakfast."

She made a face, then tried to hide it.

"What?" he asked.

Sighing, she said, "I don't think I could eat anything that had been in that fridge."

He rolled his eyes. "The blood is in sealed bags, Lucy. It's not like it's going to get on the pizza."

"It's still disgusting."

"I guess you get used to it."

"I hope I'm not here long enough for that."

James lowered his head.

She pressed him, though. "You're going to let me go, just like you promised, right? As soon as I've translated the tablet?"

"Yes."

"And yet Brigit's minions brought me enough clothes to last a couple of weeks. Why is that?"

He lifted his head, met her eyes, looked amused. "Minions?"

"Well, whoever she sent to get my things. Those dark beings who were lurking by the gate after we arrived, I presume."

"Family, Lucy. They were family. She sent some of our relatives to get your things."

She didn't quite know what to say. "I'm sorry. I didn't mean to be offensive. I'm just not quite up on the political correctness of discussing a species I didn't know existed. Probably using any of the old clichés is bad form. But then again, I don't even know which ones are myths and which ones are true."

He shrugged. "I don't suppose I can blame you for being impatient with us."

"No, you can't. You broke your word to me once already when you let me believe you were taking me home, only to bring me here instead, so I'm not sure how I'm supposed to trust you to keep your promise now. Clearly you intend to keep me here for as long as you need me, regardless of how badly it interferes with my life and my career. But I need to know you'll keep your promise to let me go once I've translated the tablet."

He nodded and seemed to be deep in thought for so long that she felt compelled to speak again.

"Aren't you even going to promise me that much?"

"That was my first inclination. But the thing is, a week ago, I would have sworn I would never do anything like this. Bring you here against your will, keep you here when all you want to do is leave, force you to help us in a struggle that has very little to do with you." He closed his eyes. "I don't want to make a promise I may not be able to keep. I'm doing a lot of things I never would have thought myself capable of, Lucy. I don't expect you to believe that, but I swear it's true. I've always considered myself one of the good guys."

"Then why are you behaving like one of the bad guys?"

Lifting his head, he looked her in the eye, and she saw him searching for an answer. He got up, paced away from her, seemed to gather his thoughts. Lucy closed the pizza box and set it on the floor beside the bed. Then she made herself comfortable and watched him.

"I was born with the gift of healing," he said. "But I never knew why."

She thought about that. "Does there have to be a reason?"

"Doesn't there?"

"I don't think so. I was born with brown hair and eyes. There's no reason for it. It just is."

He nodded. "Lots of people are born with brown hair and brown eyes. But I'm the only one of my kind."

"You're a twin."

"Brigit's...entirely different from me."

"I see." But she didn't. Not really. "So she doesn't have the healing touch, then?"

"No."

She sensed there was more, but she didn't press. He was in a talkative mood. She sensed it would be best to let him run with it, see where it led, rather than risk making him clam up again.

"Go on," she said. "Please."

He nodded. "I don't really know where I was going."

"You have the healing gift. You believe it's for a reason. You've been wondering what that reason is for your entire life. What else have you been doing while you were wondering?" she asked. "I take it you've been…estranged from your family?"

He nodded. "They see it that way. I haven't been out of touch with them, I just chose not to live among them. I've been trying to lead a more…normal life, in constant search of a raison d'être."

"So do you have…a job?"

"Lots of them. Mundane ones, though. Jobs where I can be largely anonymous, and come and go at will. Nothing like a career, the way you have. I do whatever is necessary to earn enough money to keep me going. My real vocation has been healing."

"You just…go around putting your hands on people?"

He nodded and got a faraway look in his eye. "Huts in HIV-ravaged villages in Africa. Cancer wards at children's hospitals. Refugee camps in Darfur. I slip in while the mortals sleep, and I put my hands on them. The little ones, usually. And then I try to slip away without being caught." He shook his head in self-deprecation. "Brigit says I'm like some oversized tooth fairy."

She sat there, stunned to her core. Of all the things he could have told her he'd spent his time doing, saving dying children was not one of them. Not even close. She found herself starting to see him as angelic again.

"You're just like a vampire," Lucy whispered. "Only instead of taking life, you're giving it."

He smiled softly. "Vampires don't take lives, Lucy. Not anymore. Not unless it's a life sorely in need of taking."

She thought about that, fascinated. "But...they need blood. I mean, do most of them really subsist by robbing blood banks?"

"Not entirely. But they don't need to kill in order to feed. They can drink from the living without taking enough to do harm and even remove any memory of the experience. It can be...quite pleasurable, actually."

"Do you...?"

"No." He looked away. "Yes."

Lifting her brows, Lucy said, "Which is it?"

"I...I can extend my incisors—vamp up, as Brigit calls it. I can pierce a jugular, imbibe human blood. But I've only tasted it once, and not from the living. And it wasn't my choice—I was a child."

She wrinkled her nose. "Was it...horrible?"

"It was...wonderful."

Her face went lax, brows rising, stomach clenching. And yet, even while being repulsed, she found herself wondering why he was being so honest with her, so open. He had to know it would disgust her to think of him feeding on blood.

"But I'm not a blood drinker," he said quickly. "I don't need to be, so I've chosen not to be. I eat normal food, drink normal beverages and keep my fangs firmly retracted." He smiled to show her.

For one brief moment she got lost in that smile, in those eyes, in the man who was…once again convincing her that he was some sort of a hero. Her kidnapper. Damn, what was wrong with her?

"And what about Brigit?" she asked, to change both the subject and the line of her thoughts.

He averted his eyes again. "I believe she imbibes on a regular basis. It increases any vampire's strength, their power. She thrives on it."

"What sorts of powers does your sister have?" Lucy asked.

He shook his head. "That's for her to tell you, should she choose to."

She couldn't help but want to continue the discussion, her curiosity more powerful than her fear. "So vampires, and half vampires, can drink and make the victim forget?"

"Three-quarters, not half. And yes," he said.

"And what about the…the marks?" She touched her own neck as she asked.

His eyes followed the motion of her hand and then lingered there on her throat. It seemed to Lucy that his gaze heated while it rested there. "The punctures heal at the first touch of sunlight. So the mortals rarely even see even a hint of a mark."

She was quiet, contemplating.

"It's a lot to absorb, isn't it?"

"It's an entire world I never even knew existed."

"Most people don't know. At least—they didn't. Until now."

She lowered her eyes. "Can I ask about the clichés without offending you?"

"Of course."

"Is it true about the garlic and the crucifixes?"

"No. And no."

"And the holy water? It doesn't burn?"

"No."

"And what about you and Brigit? Are you really... immortal?"

"We don't know."

She frowned, puzzled. "You don't know?"

"How can we? There have never been children born to vampires before—until our mother. She stopped aging, as near as anyone's been able to figure out, the first time the DPI killed her."

She blinked in shock. "The...the government... *killed* your mother?"

"My mother was their most sought-after captive for a time. Half vampire, half human, bred in a DPI experiment just to see if it could be done. Vampires are supposed to be sterile, you know. Turns out the males are. In females, though, it takes a few months for all the viable eggs to leave their ovaries. They fertilized one in a female prisoner right after she was turned, using semen from...from a mortal who hadn't yet been turned. Then they implanted the fertilized ovum and held the female captive until she gave birth. That baby was my mother."

"And the parents were…your grandparents?"

"Yes."

"What happened to them?"

"They escaped, along with their child. Jameson and Angelica—they're still alive today, still look as young as they did then and they're still together and deeply in love."

"And your mother?"

"The DPI found her again as a young woman, captured her, then experimented on her, killing her in various ways to see if she was immortal or not. Reviving her and killing her again. Over and over, until her family managed to rescue her. She, too, is still alive, as is my father."

"Good God," she whispered. "And she conceived—why? How?"

"There seemed to be some healing properties in her blood, that restored my father's seed." He looked at her quickly. "I'm sorry. Our nightmarish family history isn't something you really needed to know about."

"I had no idea."

"How could you? But maybe it'll help you to see why Rhiannon is so…hostile toward humankind."

"And yet she once was. Human, I mean."

"That's the irony, isn't it?"

"And you go around saving them. Healing them. Us." Lucy drew a deep breath and put a hand on his chest. "And you don't even know…if you're immortal or not?"

"I've never been sick a day in my life. Nor has my sister. We aged normally into adulthood, and since then I've been waiting for years, searching the mirror for signs of my first gray hair or crow's feet to appear."

"How old *are* you?"

He smiled. "Old enough that I should have seen some of those signs by now."

"Do you have other—you know—powers?"

He shrugged. "You already know I can read your thoughts."

"It's very disconcerting, you know," she admitted.

"It's considered bad manners to go probing around in someone's head without their consent or knowledge. I don't do it. I only heard you before because your thoughts were so...well, vehement. They were projectiles, in a way. You were sort of sending them."

"I see."

"Everyday thinking, I wouldn't hear unless I was listening in. And I'm not. I promise."

"Okay."

"You can block them, shield yourself from eavesdropping vampires, if it makes you feel less...violated."

"Really? How?"

"Visualization. Picture an invisible helmet, impermeable, no thoughts can escape it. See it strongly, and often. Design it. See its colors, feel its weight. Then just don it whenever you have thoughts you want to keep to yourself."

She nodded. "So you…you communicate with each other that way? Is that one of your powers, too?"

"It's so natural to us it doesn't seem like a power, exactly. I mean, maybe anyone raised by adults who communicate telepathically would pick it up, you know? And a lot of mortal twins seem to have a bit of that ability. Beyond that, we're very strong, far stronger than any ordinary human being. We can run faster, jump higher and we see well in the dark. None of those things are as strong in us as they are in our vampiric relatives, but they're far stronger than in humankind."

He sighed, looking at her again, and this time he covered her hand with his. "I'm going on and on, and you need to get some rest so your mind will be fresh come sundown. I just…I wanted to talk to you. I wanted to show you that I'm not bad, not evil. And to tell you how sorry I am that I had to drag you into this drama."

"Why?" she asked softly, her eyes on his hand, where it rested on top of hers.

His gaze was there, too. "I care what you think of me."

She lifted her head just as he raised his. Their eyes met. "I'm fascinated by you, James." Maybe that was too much. She blinked and said, "By all of you, I mean. And by your history and your abilities and your family. Thank you for telling me a little more about you. I think…I think I understand a bit better now."

"I hope so." He reached out with his other hand,

as if he were going to brush it through her hair, then stopped himself and blinked at it as if in surprise. "I'm overtired. I need to get some rest, too," he said, lowering his hand to his side. "If you can think of anything that would make this time a bit easier on you, please don't hesitate to let me know."

She nodded. "This…training they have you doing. Is it pretty grueling?"

"It drains me. Physically as well as spiritually. But it has to be done." He moved toward the door. "Oh, before I forget, Brigit said you thought you could work faster if you knew exactly what you were looking for."

She nodded. "I can't see what harm telling me might do. I mean, I'm going to know what that tablet contains anyway, once it's translated."

"That was the argument I made to Rhiannon. She forbade me from telling you anything, of course."

"Of course."

"I've decided to tell you anyway."

She lifted her brows in surprise. "You're defying her?"

He shrugged. "The faster I'm finished with this, the better. She'll see that it did no harm in the long run."

"So…?"

"According to legend, that tablet contains the entire account of the death of Utanapishtim. It is our hope that it also contains some clue that will lead us to his remains. As well as telling us how he can help us prevent this so-called vampire Armageddon."

She frowned. "The original tablet didn't actually say he could prevent it," she told him. "It did seem to be about to say that, but then the rest of the segment was missing."

"I know. Those missing segments are another piece of the puzzle. Translating what we have here might fill in the blanks. We desperately need to know everything we can, everything that prophecy has to say, especially about Utanapishtim."

She frowned hard. "I think you take these things far too literally."

"I think you're going to change your mind about that."

That, she realized, was entirely possible. "Then again," she said, "a week ago I'd have said there was no chance, not even a remote one, that vampires could exist, and now I'm surrounded by them." She rubbed her arms as a chill ran up her spine. "Just saying it out loud still feels so…surreal. It's like my entire world-view has been demolished. I don't know what's real anymore."

"Nothing has changed from when you felt secure and serene, not really."

She shrugged, not agreeing with him at all. From her perspective, everything had changed. "What do you want with Utanapishtim's remains?"

He shifted his eyes away from hers. "There's a ritual. It's complicated, and also sort of oathbound."

"Oathbound?"

"It's something we don't share."

"I see. And are you going to tell Rhiannon that you told me all this?"

He got to his feet and stood beside the bed. "Not unless I have to. Good rest, Lucy. I'll see you at sundown."

"Good night—I mean, good rest, James." She got up, as well, and there was an awkward moment when she tipped her head up to stare into his eyes and he stared right back. The air between them actually seemed to snap and spark. But only for a moment. Then he turned away, moved to the door and was gone, and Lucy wanted to stomp her feet in frustration.

She closed her eyes tightly, wishing she could control this desire, fight this magnetism of his that drew her like a moth to a flame. And then she lifted her hand to the doorknob, intending to turn the lock—but stopped with her hand in midair. What if he wanted to come back in later?

What the hell was she thinking? She was in a den of vampires, for God's sake!

She turned the lock, firmly and decisively, and then she went back to her bed and tried to get some sleep.

10

At sundown, James once again found himself in the hidden basement room with Rhiannon by his side, giving orders as if she had some inherent right to do so. He resented it but didn't say so aloud. She was older than he, more powerful. An elder among the undead. A leader. And besides that, she was family and he loved her. So he tended to give her more leeway than he would have given anyone else.

Before him lay five corpses, and the stench that filled the room was almost unbearable.

"Dab some of this beneath your nostrils," Rhiannon said, handing him a jar of menthol rub. "Brigit said it would help."

"Brigit watches too much television," he muttered, but he obeyed, and the vapors did indeed mitigate the stench of rotting flesh. "You really expect me to…to try to resurrect these?"

"No, I don't expect you to try. I expect you to do it. Start with this one." She moved to a table and yanked a dusty sheet, probably one that had been covering old furniture upstairs, from the face of a corpse. "He's only a few days dead."

He thinned his lips. "Does he have a story? Is there going to be a way to explain his return to his family?"

"If you insist on a full biography of every stinking bag of flesh you work on, we'll be extinct before you get to the bony ones. Now do it."

He balked at being ordered around, but he knew she had a point. "I'm just trying to make this okay in my mind. In my soul, Rhiannon."

"That's the trouble with having a soul."

"Oh, don't be ridiculous. You have a soul and you know it." Still, he approached the corpse, which was blue but mostly intact. He suspected its closed but sunken eyes and shriveled lips, and the peeling skin here and there, were not quite as pronounced as in the other bodies that lined the room.

"Fortunately," Rhiannon said, "I don't let my soul dictate my actions as if I'm a slave to it."

"You mean the way I'm letting you dictate mine?"

"Revive the corpse, J.W."

He sighed and held his hands over the stinking body, not touching it, but very close. Far closer than he wanted to be. The light began to emanate from his hands, to beam into the body on the table, and within a few minutes the corpse's peeling flesh began to smooth itself out again. The sunken eyes seemed to plump themselves, and the flesh to lose its gray-blue cast. He felt it when the heart began beating, felt it echoing in his own chest. The rib cage expanded as the cracked lips healed, then parted, and when the being on the table exhaled, the stench made James sway backward, pulling his hands away.

But the eyes did not open.

"Very good. Very good!" Rhiannon clapped her hands several times. Applause, for making a half-rotten corpse breathe. Go figure. "On to the next one, then," she said.

"But we don't know how this one is going to turn out yet." He frowned, then faced her, trying hard to read her thoughts. "What's going on, Rhiannon? Why are you in such a rush all of a sudden?"

She lowered her head, and he found her mind completely blocked.

He probed, but she was stronger. "Where is Roland? And Pandora? Where's Pandora?"

"I couldn't have the cat in here. She would have made snacks of our experiments. And then how would I have borne her breath?"

"Rhiannon. Something's going on, isn't it?"

She wasn't letting him read her thoughts at all. But she did lower her eyes, guilt showing in them. "Things out there have...taken a bad turn."

"Out where? What things?"

Rhiannon lifted her head and moved her long dark hair behind one ear. She met his eyes, her regal bearing wavering very slightly. "The vigilante movement has exploded all over the nation, and it's spreading overseas. We've lost even more of our own, J.W."

He felt the knowledge hit him squarely in the chest. "Who?"

"Hundreds. During the day, while we rested, they set fire to countless homes. Anyplace they suspected might house a vampire. They were wrong as often as not, idiots that they are. Uneducated, ignorant bigots who don't know the first thing about our kind. They killed as many of their own as they did of ours, and—"

"My parents? Where is my mother?"

"We don't know. We can't contact anyone mentally—"

"The hell we can't!" James closed his eyes, began beaming his thoughts out to his family.

"James, no!" Rhiannon's shout stopped him dead. It was the first time she had ever called him James, and it got his attention. "You know as well as I do that there are humans with the power of telepathy. ESP, they call it. They're able to tap into our thoughts if we do not block them carefully. Your mother knows that, too, so she would be blocking. We *cannot* risk communicating by telepathy right now. It might only lead them straight to us—or to your parents."

"I have to find her. All of them. And—"

"Roland has gone to check on them. He intends to gather up everyone still alive and take them to a safe haven."

"No. *I* have to go. I have to be with them and—"

She clapped a hand on his shoulder. "You, James, are the only one who can end this madness. This is exactly what the prophecy foretold. We should have expected it—*did* expect it—but it's unfolding far more rapidly than any of us could have imagined." Rhiannon spoke softly, but there was power in her voice. "This is what you were chosen to do. This is why you have the power you have. The prophecy foretold this war. We need Utanapishtim to end it. If your family is still alive, they will only survive if you stay here and do the job you were born to do. That's how you will save them. It's the only way you can."

He stared into her eyes for a long moment, and then he sensed his sister behind him in the doorway and whirled, wondering how much she had heard.

She met his eyes. There was absolute fury in hers. "I, on the other hand, was born with a power that hasn't been much use at all," she said. "Until now."

"Brigit, we need you here," Rhiannon said.

Brigit shook her head, backing away slowly. "I love you, Aunt Rhi, but I have to do this. And you know damn well I can protect our family better than anyone else."

Rhiannon couldn't seem to drum up an argument for that. She nodded and said, "Go and pack some things. I'll contact Roland as discreetly as possible—he deigned to take a cell phone with him, and you know how he hates technology. I'll call and hope he can figure out how to answer. I'll find out where he's decided to take the survivors."

Brigit nodded once, patting her pocket. "You have my number." Then she sent James a long look that spoke volumes, turned and ran from the basement.

James nodded firmly and made himself face corpse number one, which was still lying on the table, twitching every now and then, as if in the grip of a restless sleep. Time would tell whether it would return to full lucidity or remain a mindless animated bag of meat. But time was something he didn't have. He moved to corpse number two and held his hands over it.

Lucy knew something drastic was going on when Brigit came slamming into the office, practically emanating rage from her pores. Lucy looked up from the tablet, where she'd been right in the middle of something major—then froze as she saw what appeared to be a light glowing from behind Brigit's eyes.

Lucy found herself caught off guard. She'd seen a glow behind James's eyes, but this one was different. His glowed the way she would expect an…well, an angel's eyes to glow. His sister's seemed to gleam the way a demon's would. The light from within had a redness to it. And it felt…angry.

"Brigit? What's wrong?"

"Later." The blonde with the angelic face sped into the next room—the little kitchen, and on through it to the first of the bedrooms.

Lucy got up, about to follow, but she stopped after only a single step. She felt an instinctive fear that she didn't dare ignore. The hair on her forearms was standing upright, and the nape of her neck was tingling. Every cell in her body was warning her away from Brigit, and she decided she would do well to listen.

Swallowing hard, Lucy sat back down at the table and bent over the passage she'd been working on. It wasn't hard to focus her attention on the job at hand, because it was fascinating beyond all reason. In all her years of studying the tales and texts and legends of ancient Sumer, she had never seen this one—this account of the death of Utanapishtim. And what stunned her most of all was that the story matched what the vampires had told her—of how he had been punished by the gods for sharing the gift of immortality with the great king, Gilgamesh, and how Gilgamesh's sworn enemy, Anthar, had forced the old man to share immortality with him, as well, to better enable him to fight the king. And how Anthar had then beheaded the ancient one, and abducted his young servant and taken him as a slave. She picked up her smart phone, hit the digital recorder and began reciting her translation of the text into it. She had written it down, as well, but felt compelled to have more than one record of this vital piece of history.

"'Thirteen days passed, thirteen nights, as Ziasudra lay there. Dead, but not. Eternal and imprisoned. Until the old woman, the one they called Desert Witch, came upon him there, as if asleep. No maggots, nor flies, nor stench of decay, did she find upon him. And it was she who burned his body. With fire and with herbs, with chanting and with dance, did she burn him, to break the curse that could not be broken, to free the spirit that could not be freed.

"'His ashes she took to the artisan of Uruk, that he might make for her a likeness of the man himself, with his remains secreted within, and to engrave upon it his secret name, Utanapishtim, that the gods might never find him and curse him again.

"'And so the craftsman formed the limestone into the likeness of the priest-king Ziasudra, although he knew it not. The length of his forearm, he formed it, in a pose of submission, and obsidian eyes he gave to him, that he might see. Ziasudra, who had been made like a god, given the breath of life by the gods and cursed to suffer by the gods, now, he was ash and dust, hidden within the statue. But his curse was not to be broken, not until he reversed his sin against the gods.'"

Lucy lifted her head. "I think I know where he is," she whispered. "Oh, my God, I think I know where he is!" She jumped to her feet just as Brigit came surging back into the room, a leather biker bag over her shoulder.

"Brigit, I—"

"Not now." Brigit stomped through the secret passage into the crumbling bedroom of the main house, but Lucy ran right behind her, grabbing her handbag and slinging it over her shoulder as she dropped the phone into it, her notebook still in her other hand. It was only as Brigit turned to close the panel in the wall that she realized Lucy was still behind her. "What the hell? You're supposed to stay—"

"I think I know where he is!" Lucy said.

"Where *who* is?"

"Utanapishtim. I think I've found him." She frowned, seeing how distracted the girl was. "God, what's wrong with you?"

Brigit seemed to bank the fire behind her eyes. "Hundreds of vampires were burned alive in their sleep while we rested safe and sound here. That's what's wrong. Mortal idiocy, moral bankruptcy, murderous pigs who think thou shalt not kill only applies to their own kind, right down to species, race, creed and color. I'm surprised they don't annihilate according to age and gender. Humans suck, and I intend to start exercising some old school justice. One of theirs for one of ours. Eye for eye, tooth for tooth. That's right up your alley, isn't it?"

"Straight from the Code of Hammurabi," Lucy replied.

Brigit was surging through the house as she spoke, into the hallway, down the stairs, with Lucy rushing to keep up. They crossed what had once been the glorious foyer, raced down a long vaulted corridor, and then Brigit flung open what appeared to be a basement door, with a dark stairway vanishing beneath it. She turned back, seeming to finally realize that Lucy was still with her. But she only paused for a moment, then shrugged and kept on walking. Down the cellar stairs, across the basement. When she reached a closed door, she said, "Wait out here."

And then there was a crash, followed by Rhiannon's voice screaming, "Kill them, for the love of the gods!"

Brigit yanked the door open, and the stench that wafted from within the room beyond nearly knocked Lucy to her knees. She stared in paralyzed shock as what she saw inside the room delivered a second, even more debilitating, blow to her psyche.

There were…corpses…or zombies or something— half-rotted bodies—stumbling around what looked like a demolished laboratory. One of them had Rhiannon by the throat. Its flesh was falling off its bones as its bony hand clutched the beautiful vampiress. Three more of them, one no more than a bleached white skeleton that looked like a Halloween decoration, were surrounding James, yanking at his limbs, his hair, his face.

Brigit started to hum. No, she wasn't humming, but there *was* a hum coming from her, and as Lucy watched, unable to speak or move more than her eyes, she saw Brigit lift both hands, palms up, fingers lightly touching her thumbs. Her eyes were glowing red, and then, as she flicked one hand open, a beam of white light with a reddish tint—flashed like a laser from her eyes. It shot from her to the creature that had Rhiannon, and the corpse exploded.

Lucy jerked away in reaction, falling on her backside on the floor as scraps of rotting meat rained down on her. Even before her stomach could heave, Brigit's other hand flicked open and her killer gaze was blasting another corpse to bits. And then another, and another, with pinpoint accuracy and deadly results.

Within two seconds there were no more walking corpses. No more bleached white bones, grasping... But Lucy's mind felt as if it had been hit by one of Brigit's beams. She stared at the mess, at the gore, at James moving slowly toward her. He was speaking, but she was still hearing that hum in her brain, or maybe that was the reverberation left behind from the explosions. She only knew she was terrified, unable to think coherently and wanting nothing more than to crawl into a hole and then pull the hole in after her.

James moved toward her, and she scrambled away across the basement floor like a panicked crab.

"It's okay. It's all right, Lucy, it's all right."

There was a long purple vein dangling from his hair. She lifted a trembling hand, pointed. "What... why...you... *How?*"

"It's okay, it's all okay." He shot Brigit a look. "Why the hell did you bring her down here?"

"She's figured out where to find Utanapishtim. And I'm out of here." Brigit looked at Rhiannon. "Are you both okay?"

"I would have gotten the better of them momentarily," Rhiannon said, batting at the muck in her hair in irritation. And then she frowned. "What is that sound?"

Rhiannon turned her attention upward, toward the floor above, but Lucy heard nothing.

"I want to go home," she said. "I want to go home *now*. I did what you asked, and I'm finished here. I really am. This is not my problem, and I want to go home."

"Yes, yes, I know." James bent to grip her elbow and help her to her feet. "It's okay, you're safe."

"What were they? What did you do?"

"What was necessary, Lucy. What I had to do."

"But…but they looked like…like the dead. Did you bring them back from the grave? Is that what you— God, James, how could you? That's so wrong. That's just so *wrong*."

"Is it wrong to try to save my family?" He met her eyes, then looked away, his attention turning upward, too. "I hear it now."

"Mortals. A lot of them," Rhiannon said.

And then even Lucy heard the roar, the shouting, the motors and squealing tires. Right on their heels came the sounds of shattering glass, and the smell of smoke and burning wood.

"They're torching the house!" Brigit shouted.

"Oh, God, and we're in the basement." Lucy looked around frantically. "We're trapped!"

11

James took Lucy by the hand and tugged her back into the lab. She resisted, pulling against his grip, but he couldn't let her go, and he couldn't wait for her to get over her current state of shock and fear, or try to reason with her. He had to move her now, or they would all die.

He didn't blame her for being traumatized by what she had seen. He understood why she didn't want to walk through the gore that Brigit's zombie blasting had left behind. But again, no choice.

He yanked her arm when she tried to pull away, enough so that it hurt, because the pain would be the fastest way to cut through the haze of panic in her eyes. He could tell he'd reached her.

"There's another way out, Lucy. Come with me. If you don't, you'll die."

She stared at him as if she'd never seen him before and said, "Forgive me if I have to think about which option I prefer."

Angry words, delivered in a voice that was thick with unshed tears. He narrowed his eyes, impatient and remorseful and determined. Pulling her close, he hauled her up and over his shoulder, then strode through the lab. His feet slapped down into the remnants of the bodies, fat and flesh and parts of organs, and plenty of fluids. He heard her gag, whether at the sight or on the choking, cloying smells, he couldn't be sure. He was close to gagging himself. But he hurried onward, to a shelf along the rear wall. And then, holding her with one arm, he pulled on a hidden catch and the shelf swung inward, revealing itself as a door in disguise.

Once it was open, he stepped aside, and let Rhiannon and Brigit race through ahead of him. As Rhiannon hurried past, Lucy spoke.

"Pandora?" she asked. "Where's Pandora?"

Rhiannon stopped in her tracks, looking back at the woman hanging over James's shoulder. Then at James. He saw what was in her eyes. Surprise, and appreciation that Lucy, their captive, would be concerned about Rhiannon's unconventional pet. "I sent her away with Roland earlier. I...was afraid something like this might happen." Then she nodded at James. "Put her down, for God's sake. She can walk."

And then they hurried through the wall and down into the darkness.

"The tablet," Lucy whispered, as James set her on her feet and she peered into the deep gloom ahead of them.

"It's too late." He took her arm and led her down into the sloping, earthen passage, pulling the door back into place behind him. And then he led her onward, through utter darkness.

A moment later she stopped walking and turned to stare at him, though it was pointless, with no light to see by.

"Don't do anything stupid, Lucy," he said, wondering what she was up to.

"You mean like trying to reanimate rotting corpses, for example?"

"That wasn't stupid. That was necessary. This way." He took her hand to lead the way, holding it too tightly for her to try wriggling free and running back to those murderous mortals.

"Necessary? You're playing God, James. With human lives. What could possibly justify that?"

"The need to prevent the extermination of my people."

"No. No, those were human beings, with souls. What if they were in some kind of afterlife or—"

"I was given this ability for a reason, Lucy. I'm meant to use it."

"How can you possibly be sure of that?"

He refused to answer, because she was asking the same questions he'd asked himself. And yet, he'd been overwhelmed by amazement that his healing ability was so much more powerful than he'd ever realized. More than he could even have imagined. He wasn't just a healer. He had the power of restoring life to the dead. No one had that, no mortal, no vampire. Surely he had been given that power for a reason.

"I know my calling now," he told her. "I was born with a power normally reserved for the gods themselves. It's a power no one, mortal or vampire, has ever possessed. The power of life over death." He shook his head as she stared at him with horror in her eyes. He could see her quite clearly. He doubted she could see him much at all, aside, perhaps, from the outline of his form in the darkness. "I don't expect you to understand. You're just a human."

"Right. I'm not a god, like you, with this ever so useful ability to make rotting corpses do bodily harm. That wasn't exactly a resurrection back there, James. You're fooling yourself if you think it was."

"They might have improved with time."

"They were mindless, animated sides of beef."

"You can't know that."

"I *saw* that. And so did you."

He shook his head. The ground was sloping upward now, and he dearly wanted to change the subject. "Rhiannon has a car parked in a cave at the far end of this tunnel. Roland borrowed Brigit's T-Bird, leaving the bigger Lincoln in case we needed it."

"What if they've already found it? What if they're waiting for us?" she asked.

She sounded terrified, and he felt a little sorry. "I'm scanning for their presence, and so are Rhiannon and Brigit. We would sense them out there."

"What if you don't? What if someone told them how to…how to block?"

It was, he thought, a very good question. What did he expect? The woman likely had a higher IQ than anyone he knew.

"If there's anyone out there—and there won't be—then we'll back off and take another fork. This tunnel has several. One leads out to the Sound, where there's always a boat or two nearby. Another leads deep into the forest, where we can go on foot."

"This place is like a fortress."

"My people are used to being hated, feared and hunted," he explained. "Though this latest uprising is above and beyond anything in our history—at least as far as I know."

"That's why you're wishing you had…some god-like ability to fix it, then. Isn't it, James? But you don't. You're a man, not a god. Part vampire, yes. Able to heal, yes. But not a god. You can't restore life to the dead—"

"I can. Or did you not see that for yourself back there?"

"I meant can't in the sense of shouldn't. Just because you're capable of doing something doesn't mean you should. Nothing good can come of working in complete opposition to nature itself, James."

"I have no choice," he said.

She blinked then, planting her feet quite suddenly, tugging him to a stop. "My God, is that why you want to find Utanapishtim's resting place? Are you planning to try to reanimate a man who's been dead for more than five thousand years?"

He faced her slowly. "You know where he is, don't you?"

"Yes. I think I do. And you're out of luck, thank God. According to your own tablet, back at the house, he was cremated, James. There's nothing left of him but ash."

Up ahead, Brigit called back in a harsh whisper, "It's all clear. Hurry up, you two."

Nodding, he pulled his captive into motion again. "I have to try."

"You're out of your mind."

"Look, I'm supposed to do this. I wouldn't have been chosen as the one to save my people if I couldn't make it work. It's not supposed to be easy. But I've got to try. It's what I was born to do."

"You are so full of yourself I can hardly believe you're the same man who was sneaking in and out of hospital rooms trying to cure dying children."

"Not trying to, doing it. And we're done discussing this. I didn't ask your opinion."

"I didn't ask to be kidnapped!"

"I get that. You would rather have run away and let everyone else fend for themselves. You told me you were a coward, and I guess I should have believed you. But get this. Just because running and covering your own ass are the things you would do in this situation, that doesn't mean they're the things *I* should do, Lucy. I will *die* for my people, if that's what it takes."

She yanked her hand from his and stomped past him, and for one brief instant, as she walked by, he distinctly felt that his words had torn open a deep, deadly wound in her heart, and left it wide and bleeding.

He'd hit a nerve. He didn't know why. And he regretted it, but he didn't know how to make it better. There was too much else going on for him to worry about the professor's hurt feelings at the moment.

She emerged from the tunnel into a cave, the mouth opening to the darkness of the night, and as predicted, a large black Lincoln Continental was parked there waiting for them. Rhiannon and Brigit were already sitting in the backseat, so Lucy yanked open the passenger door and got into the front.

James smelled the smoke and saw the glow coming from the direction of the house, though the woods blocked the mansion itself. He went around and got behind the wheel, then drove out of the cave and across the rough ground. He pulled the car onto the road a half mile from the mansion and headed away from it. A look in the rearview mirror showed him a night sky alight with an angry red-orange halo, and arrow-sharp flames licking at the very stars.

Lucy didn't speak again that night. Not to anyone. Not even to demand he let her go. He supposed she had figured out that he still couldn't do that. For one thing, she hadn't told him where to find the remains of Utanapishtim. And once she did, she would know where he was going next. He couldn't risk her telling anyone what he was up to until it was done.

And even with all that, all the worry and the remorse and the anguish of having lost friends, relatives, in this war…he still couldn't quite quell the thrill of challenging his powers to the ultimate extent. Restoring life to a pile of five-thousand-year-old ash.

It was almost dawn when they arrived at a gorgeous—but normal-gorgeous, nothing out of a period fantasy—house on a jutting peninsula that thrust itself into Salem Harbor like a forefinger pointing out to sea.

It looked to Lucy like the kind of place a presidential family would go for a weekend summer break. And yet it was filled with vampires, she was sure of that. She didn't know how many, but she knew there must be a den of them.

Brigit and Rhiannon hurried inside as soon as the car came to a stop in the curving driveway. Lucy saw Roland in the doorway, as he flung it open to greet them, and she could tell there were others beyond him, though she barely glimpsed them.

"This is Will and Sarafina's place. They're friends," James said softly.

"I don't care." She sat in the car, hugging herself, staring at the sea.

"She's a Gypsy—and a vampire, of course—and he's mortal. You won't have to be the only human around anymore."

"I told you, I don't care."

He sighed. "Please come inside, Lucy. I need to find out if there's any word from my family and—"

"Then go. I'm not setting foot in that house until the sun comes up and the undead freak show closes down for the day, all right?"

He was wounded. She felt it, and she didn't care about that, either. His words had really hurt her earlier.

"I can't leave you alone."

"If you don't, I'll never tell you where to find Utanapishtim."

He blinked at her. She saw, but refused to meet his eyes.

"I want some time to myself. I'm going to go down to that beach, and I'm going to sit there and watch the sunrise, and I don't want you to bother me. I'm not going to run away. If I did, you'd only find me anyway. But I want this time alone, and if you don't give it to me, I swear to you, James, I will refuse to help you even if Rhiannon kills me for it."

And with that she opened the car door, hefted her bag up onto her shoulder, got out and walked away from him. She walked into the darkness, onto the white sand, down toward the water's edge. And that was where she would stay, she decided. She would wait for the sun to rise, when they would all—most of them, anyway—finally, fall silent and asleep....

Like the dead.

God, it was all just too much.

She sat in the sand, drew her knees up to her chest,

lowered her head and let the tears flow. She heard James open and close the car door, and then his footsteps crossing the large wooden deck, the door opening, then shutting behind him. Finally, she thought. Solitude.

And so she sat there, weeping and wondering how the hell it was that she had been dragged into a war that was not her own. And how it was that she had let herself begin to care what some half-breed demon angel thought of her.

Because she *did* care. He thought she was a coward. And it probably wouldn't hurt so much if it wasn't quite so true.

She was still weeping when, a few minutes later, a large hand landed on her shoulder from behind. She lifted her head, dashed away her tears and tried to pretend she hadn't been crying. "Sorry. I'm just so… stupid."

"That's not quite the way I've heard it."

It wasn't James's voice.

She turned at last and found herself face-to-face with an imposingly handsome man, large, broad, with raven hair and eyes and skin that seemed dark for a vampire. And yet she had no doubt that was what he was. And, in fact, an old one. He exuded power. The glow in his eyes was almost constant, and his skin was even more flawless than the others' were.

"I'm not going to hurt you, Professor. I actually…I came out to thank you. And to introduce myself."

She blinked, staring up at him, not moving. He

should have seemed ordinary. He wore jeans and a forest-green knit pullover sweater with the collar of a white T-shirt showing at the neck. But he wasn't ordinary at all. She got chills, he was so far from ordinary.

"We share some interests, I understand."

"D-do we?"

"Ancient Sumer. You study it…and I lived in it. Ruled it, actually." He extended his large, powerful hand. "I'm Damien Namtar, but you'd be more familiar with my earlier name. Gilgamesh."

Her eyes widened, and her heart tried to pound a hole straight through her chest.

"You…can't be…"

He smiled gently. *"Idib balazu nam hé-ébtarre."*

"'When you cross the threshold, it is a blessing,'" she translated, blushing at the compliment. "Thank you." Then she shook her head in awe and quickly scrambled to her feet, brushing the sand from the front of her khaki cargo pants and pressing her palms together in front of her body, then bowing slightly to him. "It's…it's an amazing honor, great king, to meet you. And a bit of a miracle. And I feel like I might faint, so I'll apologize in advance if—"

"I should be the one bowing to you, Lucy. I understand that you're the translator of the prophecy. And that now you've located Ziasudra's remains?"

She shook her head. "It won't do any good, your high—"

"Damien. Really, I'm just a man. I make my living

as a magician, entertaining the masses in Vegas when I'm not on tour. Though I imagine my onstage vampire persona will be seen through now. They'll know it's for real, and I'll be hunted, like the rest of us."

She lifted her head, met his eyes. "You never found him again, did you? Your beloved friend, Enkidu?"

His eyes shifted toward the sea, maybe to hide the reaction she'd glimpsed at the mention of his friend's name. "I like to think he's in a better place."

"All of this, all of it, this entire race began, because of your search to restore life to your best friend. And now James is going to try the same thing. He's going to try to bring life back to a pile of ash. Don't you see how futile that is?"

He met her eyes and stared deeply into them. "You're very wise for a mortal possessed of only a few decades. And I said much the same thing, only an hour ago, to James. He's hearing none of it."

"But surely you have the authority to tell him to let this go?" she asked.

He shook his head. "I might. But I'm not convinced that, futile or not, it isn't worth a try." He sighed and glanced out toward the sea again. "Sunrise approaches, and I must go inside. But I had to meet you. If we both survive this, I would love to spend some time in conversation with you, if you would permit it."

Part of her wanted to say that she hoped beyond hope never to set eyes on any vampire ever again, once this was over. If she lived through it. But the rest of her was in awe at having a real time conversation with a legendary historical figure she'd studied all her life. And she heard herself saying, "I truly hope we have the chance to do that."

He lowered his head in a semi-bow to her. "Thank you for helping us."

"I wasn't given a choice. But in your case, you're welcome."

He reached for her hand, brought it to his lips, kissed the back of it gently. And when he straightened, he smiled and without turning said, "I fear you've been treating this gem with less than the tenderness and reverence she deserves, James. It's a situation I would strongly advise you to remedy."

"Fuck you, Damien."

She gasped and clapped a hand to her mouth, but the great king only grinned, gave her a wink and then spun around and vanished right before her eyes, leaving only a sand-whirlwind to mark the spot where he'd been standing.

She stared at James, still stunned. "Do you have any idea who he is?" she asked.

He made a face, as if to say, duh.

"Of course you do. Well, that was just stupid. And rude. And uncalled for. And—"

"Several of my relatives have just finished reading me the riot act. Rhiannon, of all people, reported our entire conversation in the cave, and then Brigit took it upon herself to fill me in on the parts of your background that I didn't yet know."

She blinked twice, then averted her face. "You know about my family?"

"That they were murdered in the desert. That you were the only survivor. Yes. I know, and I can't tell you how sorry I am, nor how much I regret what I said to you. You're not a coward. You've been very brave, and I keep forgetting just how frightening this must be for you and—"

"Oh, please shut up." She turned away, shaking her head.

"I mean it."

"No, you don't. You thought I was a coward a few hours ago, and nothing has changed, other than that you've found out where I learned to be so good at running away from danger, hiding while the people I love die, doing absolutely nothing to try to help them. I learned my lessons very well. And I'm alive today because of them."

"You were a child. There was nothing you could have done."

"I'll never know, since I didn't try. But the last thing I want or need is absolution from you, a man with no moral compass whatsoever."

"I have a moral compass, it's just not pointing to the same true north as yours does. That doesn't make it wrong."

"Interfering with life and death is wrong. I don't care who you are or what your reasons."

"Right. Tell me now that if you could go back, hold your hands over some corpse and, by doing so, prevent your parents being shot down in that desert, you wouldn't do it."

"I already told you, I did nothing to try to help them. What part of that do you not get?"

He was speechless, staring at her. "Where is he?" he asked. "Where is Ziasudra? Utanapishtim?"

"He was Ziasudra all his life, and Utanapishtim in death. It was how the Babylonians referred to him, and now I know where they got it. The tablet called it his secret name, and said it was carved into the statue that is his urn. It's one of three similar figures of priest-kings, male, nude, about nine and a half inches tall. Look for engravings of water, waves, the flood or a boat on it. If there aren't any, you'll just have to take all three."

"From where?"

"Normally they're in the Louvre. But you're in luck. The Sumerian exhibit is currently on tour. Last I knew it was spending a month at the Metropolitan Museum of Art, in New York."

"How the hell am I going to get it out of there?"

She shrugged. "I'm sure you'll think of something."

He pressed his lips together.

"I'm going home now."

"You can't."

"Oh, yes, I can. I kept my word, and now I'm holding you to yours. And if necessary, I think I could get King Gilgamesh to back me up on this."

He sighed, clearly angry and getting angrier. "He has a wife, you know."

"Who?"

"The great king."

She frowned at his retreating back and wondered if there was any chance in the world that he was actually jealous. And for some reason, that notion banked her anger just slightly.

He'd been stomping away, or doing the closest thing he could do to stomping in the shifting white sand, but he turned back to face her again after only a few steps. "You can't go home—because you're wanted by the FBI."

"What?"

"They've named you a person of interest in the murders of Lester Folsom and Will Waters. It's all over the news. That's how Brigit learned about your past. They're saying the trauma of seeing your parents and their entire party murdered in front of your eyes did something to your mind, setting a time bomb in your sanity that finally went off. You snapped, and murdered Folsom and Waters, then ran for your life and have been in hiding ever since. Your face is being plastered everywhere. They're offering a reward."

She could barely raise her voice above a whisper to ask, "How much?"

"One million dollars."

All the life seemed to go out of her at once. She sank down to her knees on the beach.

"I'm sorry, Lucy." He was trudging toward her

again. "I promise you, once my people are safe, I'll find some way to make all of this up to you."

Her lips parted to ask how on earth he thought he could possibly do that, but no sound emerged. Her throat was sealed, her stomach empty, her head pounding, her energy utterly gone. She sank down farther, covering her face with her hands. "You've ruined everything. God, you've ruined my life!"

"Me? How have I—"

"By involving me in your disaster! My career is over. My reputation destroyed. Even my freedom is hanging by a thread."

"Look, I'm not the one who publicly executed an author and a talk show host, nor am I the one who set you up to take the fall for it."

"You dragged me into all this! And now there's no way out for me."

"There's one way out." He sank into the sand in front of her, his hands on her shoulders. "There's only one way out as far as I can see, Lucy. You're in this now. You have to see it through to the end. Help me find Utanapishtim. He's the key to everything, according to the very prophecy you translated. That has to mean something, doesn't it? That you're the one who found it, and you're the one here with me now? I think *you* were chosen, too. I think you were meant to help us survive."

She lifted her head slowly. "I think you'd say anything right now to ensure my continued cooperation. And I don't believe you anymore. You've lied to me.

Broken promises to me. Abused and insulted me. Kept secrets from me—and I sense you still are."

He blinked, perhaps surprised by her accuracy.

"Only one thing you've said to me rings true right now, James."

"And which thing is that?" he asked, sounding morose, almost bitter.

"That I have no other way out. So why don't you just go on inside and leave me alone? I certainly won't run now that I know I have nowhere else to go."

"I'm sorry," he said. "I am, but I'm not going to grovel. Have it your way."

He got up and walked back toward the house, and she couldn't help but watch him go.

Standing on the deck, looking out at them, was a woman she'd never seen before. A beautiful woman, tall and curvy, with long masses of raven-wing curls so black they appeared blue in the moonlight. She wore flowing skirts and scarves, an off-the-shoulder peasant blouse and more jewelry than Lucy even owned. She had to be Sarafina, the Gypsy. Yet another vampire.

Hell, Lucy thought, *just shoot me now.*

12

Lucy slept on the beach, refusing to go into the house with James, though he cajoled. In the end she'd insisted, and also insisted that he leave her alone. She wasn't going to run. Where could she go? And how could she hope to escape with a dozen vampires hot on her trail come sundown? No, she would stay. But she wasn't going to pretend to be happy about it.

She slept until midafternoon, when hunger pangs hit, and then and only then did she come slowly awake. There was an umbrella stabbed deeply into the sand beside her, providing shade, and she wondered who had taken the time to put it there, even as she stood up, stretched and brushed the sand from her jeans. Staring out at the ocean, smelling the sea breeze that fingered her hair, she wondered how she could be in the middle of such utter beauty and perfect tranquility, and yet at the same time in the midst of chaos.

"Good afternoon."

Lucy turned around, not having heard anyone's

approach. The man couldn't be a vampire, because it was daylight and he was standing right in the sun. So he must be—

"Willem Stone," he said. "Sarafina's husband. This is our place."

Frowning, Lucy studied him more closely. "You… you really aren't one of them, are you?"

"No, I'm human. And they're all dead to the world at the moment." He winked when he made the lame joke. "Except for Brigit and J.W., of course. They're out running some errands. Won't be back for at least a couple of hours. And in the meantime, I have coffee, a dozen doughnuts and one of the most luxurious bathrooms you could ever want to see. And you're welcome to all of them."

She sighed. "It does sound tempting."

"I promise, it'll just be you and me in the house. Awake, anyway. And I'll leave, if you want."

"I wouldn't throw you out of your own home." She looked at the place, with its giant deck. Seagulls perched on the roof, a few more coming in, a few others taking off. Constant motion, like the ocean itself, with its waves rolling up onto the beach and hissing as they fled again, leaving foam and shells in their wake.

"Come on. I'm a great cook. I'll make whatever you want, if you don't want doughnuts for breakfast. Or you can do both, real food and empty calories."

She smiled. "A doughnut and a cup of that coffee

will do nicely. And thank you. I need a little normalcy more than you know."

"Oh, believe me, I know."

He walked her into the house, and just as he'd promised, the place seemed entirely empty. "Bathroom's upstairs, first door on the right. And I put a change of clothes in there for you, too. They're Fina's, and her style doesn't suit everybody. I hope they'll be okay."

Lucy felt a pang of regret for the things she'd left behind in the house the vigilantes had burned. Especially for the Kwan Yin pendant she'd left hanging on the bedpost. Thank God she'd imported the file to her phone. It was now the only copy of Folsom's "eyes only" version of the book in existence, as far as she knew.

"Are you sure she won't mind me borrowing her clothes?"

"She's the one who picked them out."

She lowered her head, sighing. "Thank you. I won't be long."

Lucy went up, half afraid of stumbling over sleeping corpselike bodies on the way, but she didn't. She imagined there was probably a suite of darkened rooms hidden in the bowels of the basement somewhere, with emergency exits and secret passageways, and big locks on the doors.

The bathroom was every bit as luxurious as Willem had promised, and Lucy allowed herself to relish a very long, very hot shower that would have been even longer, had it not been for the siren's call of coffee and doughnuts. The clothes were a decent fit, a long, broomstick type skirt of russet and orange, and a frilly white off-the-shoulder blouse with a gathered waist and short puffy sleeves. There were high-heeled black boots, as well.

She combed her hair and left it to dry naturally. She couldn't find a rubber band or a scrunchie, so she was forced to hold it in place with a pretty silk scarf, which she knotted at her nape, its ends trailing down her back. Finally she headed down the stairs. The smell of coffee greeted her as she entered the kitchen.

She accepted the mug Willem held out and took a grateful sip.

"Feel a little more human now?" he asked.

"A lot more."

"Good. Fina's clothes look lovely on you, by the way. She'll be pleased. And the doughnuts should complete the transformation." He waved a hand toward the table, where a familiar pink-and-white box stood open, an assortment of doughnuts, éclairs and muffins awaiting her selection.

She took a powdered sugar-coated jelly doughnut and told herself she would have the chocolate frosted éclair next. She'd earned at least two goodies today. Then she sank onto a tall stool in front of the breakfast counter, took her first bite, washed it down with more coffee and dabbed her mouth with a napkin. "Now that's heaven," she muttered.

Willem nodded, taking a huge bite of his own glazed sourdough doughnut. "I agree."

"Where are the others?" she asked, then added, "I don't even know who's here. Sarafina, Roland and Rhiannon, and...Gilgamesh—I mean, Damien. Anyone else?"

"Shannon. Damien's wife. You'll like her, she's... from this century." He made a sheepish face. "Well, you know what I mean. Anyway, they're all safely tucked away in the basement."

"I figured as much. Is it full of secret passages and hidden exits?"

"Just the one—there's a tunnel straight out to the cliffs above the ocean, but we've never needed to use it. It's just a precaution. And Pandora's down there, too, on guard duty, with a bowlful of food and a velvet cushion. But truly, we're safe. No one bothers us out here."

"Even now? I mean, the locals must...notice that they see you, but not her, by day."

"We say she works in Boston. It's a bit of a commute. Gone before daylight, home after dark. It seems to work."

"And how long have you been here?"

"You think they'll wonder why she hasn't aged. But really, women seem to find aging optional these days."

She laughed. "Well, some do."

"Either way, I'm sure no one suspects we're anything unusual. Even with the madness going on in the world right now. Still, better safe than sorry."

"Speaking of what's happening out there—what sort of errands are James and Brigit running? I mean, if it's all right for me to ask."

He blinked rapidly. "Why wouldn't it be all right? You're family, Lucy."

She averted her eyes. "Because I have the Belladonna Antigen, you mean."

He nodded. "Yes. That, and the fact that you're turning your life upside down to help us."

Shaking her head, she said, "I didn't have a choice about the helping part. And as for the Belladonna thing, I don't really know what that means—I mean, to them. I know what it means to me. I've known for years now. And I'm okay with it. But other than that they all had it, too, when they were human, and that they can sense those of us who have it now, I know next to nothing."

"No one's talked to you about this?" he asked.

"No. I found that much out…on my own."

"I see." He nodded, but he looked slightly pissed off. "I suppose James is distracted."

"I'd say obsessed is a better word. And maybe starting to get a little bit drunk on his own power lately, but I think he means well."

"The antigen makes you prone to being a night owl, sleeping during the day. It makes you grow more and more sensitive to sunlight, and eventually it starts to cause some physical problems. Some weakness, dizzy spells. Are you having any of those yet?"

"No."

"Then you've got time before you really need to know any more about that."

But she already knew. The effects of the antigen would kill her before she hit forty. That was a lot to contend with. She frowned. "Do you have it?"

"No. I can never become what they are. We have ways around that, and I can fill you in as much as you want later on. Right now you're probably more interested in knowing about you. About how this thing impacts you. Do you know they can't harm you?"

"I…heard that somewhere."

"Well, it's true. Vampires are compelled to protect the Chosen—that's what they call people with the antigen. Sometimes they risk their own lives trying to protect them, and sometimes they do it in spite of themselves. They're driven. It's like a genetic imperative."

"I see." She was riveted.

"You don't need to fear them, Lucy."

"I guess not." She took another bite, then asked, "Do I get any other…you know, extra abilities with the antigen? I mean, like being able to read thoughts, the way they do?"

"You might. Mainly, though, that tends to happen with only one of them."

"Only one?"

He nodded. "*The* one. You see, for every vampire,

there's one of the Chosen with whom the psychic bond is far stronger than with any other. It's a powerful connection. An unbreakable link. And it remains, even after that human becomes one of the undead, if indeed they do." Tilting his head to one side, he asked, "Why do you ask? Have you experienced telepathy with anyone?"

"No."

"Well, when you do, that one will protect you with his or her life, if necessary. More than likely you'll be compelled to do the same in return."

"That would be a switch. I'm not exactly the protective type."

He smiled at her as she finished her doughnut, then pushed the box closer. She took her éclair, reached for the pot in the center of the table and refilled her mug.

"You asked what the twins were up to. They got a few hours sleep, of course, and then headed out separately. They're trying to see if they can find their relatives. Their parents, grandparents. If they find them, they intend to stand guard until nightfall, then bring them back here."

"And then what?" she asked. "It sounds as if it's not safe for any vampire out there right now."

"We have a plan, a place to go. An island. We're spreading the information by word of mouth, vampire to vampire. Many are already on the way. I could actually use an extra pair of hands today, to help me get our yacht stocked with supplies, so we're ready to head out ourselves. Are you game?"

She felt herself smile just a little bit. "I have no other plans for the afternoon," she said. "And as long as you keep using such lovely bribes as hot showers, fresh clothes, delicious coffee and gooey doughnuts, you'll probably find me quite helpful."

"I thought so."

James stood outside his parents' home, a beautiful Appalachian Mountain cabin.

Or at least it had been. Now it was a pile of rapidly cooling ash. And there was nothing left. Nothing. Not a stick of furniture, like the antique rocking chair where his mother had cradled him as a baby. Not a scrap of clothing, like the long leather coat that had become his father's trademark.

Nothing.

And he didn't know whether his beautiful parents had been at rest when the place had been burned and now lay, no more than ashes themselves, amid the ruins or not. He tipped his head toward the sky, whispering "Why?" as he dropped to his knees. Tears burned his skin, and his face twisted into a painful grimace as his fangs extended and his fury raged.

Finally his rage subsided, pushed out of the way by another thought. He wondered if he could find his parents' remains among all this ash. And if he did, whether he could restore them. Heal them. Bring them back.

Rising, scrubbing his knuckles across his cheeks, retracting his fangs, he stumbled into the still warm ashes of his childhood home and bent to press his hands to the charred remains, then closed his eyes and willed the light to come. Willed the power of life to beam from his hands. When it didn't, he moved to another spot and tried again, and then again and again. For hours he knelt in the wreckage, trying to restore life to ash.

But either his parents weren't there or their deaths were beyond his ability to undo.

It killed him to give up. But when it became obvious that staying was useless, he forced himself to get to his feet, to move on.

And he prayed with everything in him that his family had made it to safety before the humans—his other family—had attacked.

He was ashamed that he'd turned his back on his own kind in favor of trying to live as a human. That he'd been repulsed at the thought of living as a vampire. It was clear to him now who the real beasts were. And they were not the undead.

Two hours later, Lucy found herself standing on the deck of one of the most luxurious yachts she'd ever seen, not that she'd seen many. The *Nightshade* had four cabins, two Jacuzzis, a galley and a dining room, living room and wet bar. It was like a floating five-star hotel. She'd never been onboard a yacht before, but she seriously doubted most were this high end.

Willem piloted it expertly through the waves. They'd taken it from the marina, and were speeding toward the harbor and the house. The shoreline was on their left—port, she corrected mentally. As she watched it speeding past, thinking this was actually a pleasant way to spend an afternoon, she suddenly caught a whiff of something that wasn't so pleasant.

"Willem, what is that?" she asked, pointing.

At the helm, he followed her gaze to where smoke and flames were licking up toward the sky. And then he swore. "God, that's my house!"

Lucy's jaw dropped, and she sent him a look of stunned horror. His wife was in there.

And not just her. They'd left five vampires asleep and defenseless in a home that was now ablaze. Rhiannon and her cat, and gentle Roland. The great king Gilgamesh himself!

Tears brimmed in her eyes as she willed the boat to go faster.

Willem pushed the throttle all the way forward, and the front end of the boat lifted above the water as it picked up speed. She could feel the immense power of the engines propelling it, and the ocean wind in her face kept her tears from spilling over.

As they drew nearer, they could see fire trucks rolling into the driveway, sirens wailing, lights strobing in the late afternoon sun. By the time Willem had guided the massive vessel up to its deep water pier, dropped anchor, jumped off and raced toward the house, the firefighters were manning their hoses, sending rivers of cooling water onto the place.

Racing up to them, a man in a heavy yellow coat and helmet, shouted, "Was anyone inside?"

Lucy opened her mouth, but Willem's hand closed on her forearm, making her bite off the words she'd been about to shout. "No," he said. "The house is empty."

Nodding, the man returned to his work.

Lucy sent Willem a searching look.

"They're either all right or they're not," he said. "If the flames reached them, they're already gone." His voice broke when he said it. "And if they didn't, then they'll be okay. The smoke won't harm them. This is the work of vigilantes. Hate groups. We can't risk revealing the presence of vampires to those bastards."

Just then a familiar blue vehicle came bounding to a stop on the roadside, blocked from getting any closer by the fire trucks. James got out, and one look at his face told Lucy of his horror. Forgetting everything else, everything bad that had passed between them, she ran to him, stopping herself just short of flinging herself into his arms.

"Rhiannon?" he asked. "Fina?"

"They're still inside—as far as we know."

He gazed down into her eyes; then, his arm anchoring her to his side as if she belonged there, he strode up to the nearest firefighter. "Who's responsible for this?"

The man shouted to be heard above the roar of the

flames and hoses and trucks and pumps. "Rednecks trying to burn vampires while they sleep. Damn fools buying into all this hype on the TV. Press don't know what harm they're doing, playing into it the way they are. It's sensationalism, is what it is. They need to get a handle on things—and fast. This is our fifth call today. Every last one of them arson."

James turned, his eyes scanning the road in both directions, then the beach. Lucy noticed that his clothes were covered in ash and soot, and his hands were gray with it.

"You won't find 'em hanging around," the fireman said. "They throw their damned Molotov cocktails and run like hell. Cowards."

"Oh, I'll find them. Believe me, I'll find them."

James's voice trembled as he spoke, and he held himself in check. But Lucy could feel the pent-up rage in him, and it frightened her.

"Any word on your family, James?" she asked softly.

He met her eyes, and his were bereft. "My parents' home was burned. No sign of them. I don't know if they left before…or if they…" He swallowed, cleared his throat, started over. "The others' homes were empty. I just…I don't know. I don't know."

For the first time she saw tears well up in his eyes. And for the first time, she realized, she saw him as he was. Not as a heroic angel or as a savior, not as a demon, but as a man. A man who didn't know if his loved ones were dead or alive. A man in anguish.

She did not stop herself any longer. She slid her arms around his waist, laid her head on his chest and just held him. "I pray they're all right," she whispered. "All of them."

James had still been having doubts about his actions, mostly due to Lucy's obvious disapproval of what he was doing, and why. He'd never been a man who believed a worthy end justified the use of immoral means. And yet he'd been employing just that: immoral means. He wasn't kidding himself. He knew it was wrong to dabble in matters of life and death, matters that belonged to the discretion of the gods themselves, or to fate, or to whatever higher power was in charge of the world and its inhabitants. He knew it was wrong of him to try to take charge of life and death. But he'd believed he had no choice if he wanted to save his people. He'd felt he had been born to do this, right or wrong. He'd chosen to proceed on a morally questionable path for the greater good.

But now that he saw what the world of man was capable of firsthand, he no longer had any question about the rightness or wrongness of his actions. This was war. His people needed a champion, and he'd been chosen to be the one. If this wasn't proof positive of that fact, he didn't know what was.

Any people who could try to annihilate innocents while they slept, completely helpless to fight back, had long since tossed morality to the winds. And one couldn't fight that kind of evil by following the rules.

He was going to do whatever it took to raise Utanapishtim from the dead, and then he was going to fight by that ancient immortal's side to preserve his race.

Lucy's arms around him, her head on his chest, finally drew his eyes to hers. She was shaken right to the core, and hot tears were burning streaks down her face as she tipped it up to his. "I don't see Willem anymore. Where did he…?"

Alarm clamored in his veins, and he looked toward the sea. "He's gone inside, after them. Thank God."

"But…he's just a mortal."

"And as such, he'll have a better chance against the flames than they have." He met her puzzled frown and went on. "Vampires are highly flammable. Fire is one of the few things that can kill them."

"But—how did he get in? How did he get past the firefighters, and—wait. The tunnel. He told me there's a tunnel."

"Yes," James said, nodding, and wondering just what else Lucy and Willem—the man his middle name had been chosen to honor—had spent the day discussing. "There's a tunnel that leads from the basement to an opening in the cliffs, above the sea."

"Where?" she asked, stepping away from him, shielding her eyes with one hand and staring out toward the water.

For the first time he noticed the skirt she wore. Full and whipping in the wind. And the blouse, baring her shoulders, hinting at the breasts beneath. And then her hair, long and loose, satin sable-brown locks he wanted to bury his hands in.

"James?" she asked.

He met her eyes and realized that he was falling for this woman. In spite of everything else going on, he was falling for her. And he was being forced to make her his enemy.

"It's right there." He nodded toward a spot farther along the shoreline. "Where the sand turns to stone and the beach rises."

"I see where you mean."

"Don't stare too long or you'll draw attention," he said.

She sighed as if relieved.

"Vampires have a penchant for escape hatches," he said.

"I can see why they would. But there are too many of them for him to move by himself," she whispered. "Can't we try to sneak away, too?"

"We?" he asked.

"I can't stand the thought of all those people…" New tears flowed down her cheeks, and then she blinked rapidly, as she processed a new idea. "Can you talk to Rhiannon? You know, with your mind, to find out if she's okay?"

"Not while she's asleep, no. And believe me, it's killing me not to rush into the flames myself, but we'd definitely draw the notice of those firefighters. We'd have to pass them all to get to the shore. Look, they've already noticed Will's absence. And if they follow him and find—"

"I'll distract them," she said. "And when I do, you go. All right? Go help Will get them out."

"And how do you intend to distract them?"

"I...spent some time in the drama club in high school," she said. "Trust me, I've got a lot of angst to draw from right now. You can move fast, right?"

"Very fast."

"Then do it."

And before he could guess what she was even intending, Lucy lifted her voice in a scream that sounded as if it came straight out of a horror film and went running straight toward the burning house. It looked for all the world as if she planned to rush inside, despite the flames, and three firefighters dropped their hoses to race after her. All the others were entirely focused on the little drama she'd instigated as she shouted about having to try to save her cat.

Shaking his head in admiration, James poured on the speed. Three seconds later he was at the top of the cliff, and a moment after that he was diving over the side. He hit the water, plunging deeply, knowing exactly where to knife through it without cracking his skull on hidden rocks. Hell, he'd played here often throughout his childhood. He knew the beach like he knew his own sister.

That thought brought another as he broke surface again and began swimming toward the tunnel's hidden exit. Trails of weeds and brush covered the gaping maw, but he knew where it was. And as he neared it, he thought again of Brigit. She was on the warpath already, and this was only going to solidify the choices she was making. Hell, he wasn't even sure anymore that her notion to put together a resistance force and go head to head with the mortal vigilante groups was all that misguided.

Wipe the bastards out, she'd said. And why not? That was what the humans were trying to do to them.

He bounced out of the water high enough to grip a stone outcropping, then pulled himself up and, with a quick glance behind him to be sure he was still unobserved, pushed through the weedy entrance and moved into the cool darkness of a stone passage.

It smelled of smoke, and that worried him. He wouldn't die from smoke inhalation, as far as he knew. But Will might. Covering his face with one arm, James moved farther in, shouting Will's name as loudly as he dared. And then he tripped over something soft and, kneeling, realized it was Sarafina, Will's Gypsy bride. Her body was still and limp and lifeless, just as it should be by day. It was too dark to tell if she'd been burned. Bending, James scooped her into his arms and carried her closer to the entrance, where he laid her on the cool stone floor, far enough from the mouth to ensure no sunlight touched her.

He raced deeper again, stopping at the sound of a rasping cough. "Will?"

The coughing continued, and James followed it, the

smell of smoke becoming stronger as he neared the basement. And then he met Will, carrying Rhiannon in his arms and coughing as if he were about to collapse at any moment.

"Is she...?"

"Don't know. But she's not burned." Will choked out the words, dropping to his knees.

James took Rhiannon's still body from the other man, anchoring her over his shoulder and then helping Will with his free hand. Arm around the man, he assisted him to the place where he'd left Sarafina, then set the beautiful Egyptian princess down beside the Gypsy. Then he put his hands on the other man and felt them begin to heat.

Will's coughing eased, his breathing becoming less raspy. But he pushed James away before the healing had taken full effect. "Leave me. Get the others. Shannon, then—Roland and Damien."

Nodding, James rushed back through the cave at full speed. At the end, a large steel door blocked entry into the basement. Will had taken the time to close it behind him to keep the tunnel from being flooded with smoke. Wise. Opening the door, James was stunned at what he saw. The sky, for one thing, beyond a crisscrossing web of charred beams. Piles of smoldering rubbish. A partial ceiling, still intact over two-thirds of the basement—including, thank the gods, the part where he stood and where his beloved ones rested beyond yet another door. He made his way through the smoky basement, opened that door and saw them there, laid out in their custom-made beds. And beside them, Rhiannon's cat, lying still and lifeless on the floor.

"God, no. Pandora." He knelt beside the cat, feeling its body, which was already beginning to cool.

"Dammit!" But there was no time. Not just then. He left the cat where it was—dead on the floor, near Rhiannon's empty bed—and began carrying bodies out to the entrance, one by one. Shannon first, then Roland, and finally Gilgamesh. He was choking and his eyes burning when he went back in one last time to gather the limp and unresponsive body of Rhiannon's beloved panther, who, unlike her owner, had not been immortal.

The firefighters captured Lucy bodily as she shouted about her cat still being inside, and she fought them, just to keep them busy, until James was out of sight. Praying he would be able to save the others, she finally surrendered, and allowed the firemen to wrap her in a blanket and lead her a safe distance from the house. She perched on the tailgate of a rescue truck, watching them douse the flames.

Finally the flow of the hoses trickled to a stop.

Firemen stood nearby, shaking their heads sadly. The far end of the house still had two walls standing upright, but burned halfway down. The rest was gutted, nothing but blackened beams and piles of charred rubble. The smell was like nothing else. A house fire, Lucy thought, had an extremely distinct aroma to it. Not the comforting smell of a campfire, a hearth or a wood-burning stove. No. A house fire smelled evil. It had a bite to it, a sourness that was hard to describe but impossible to forget.

The fire chief came over, and looked her up and down. "Do you know where the owner went?"

"To a friend's," she said. "It was too much for him. This was his dream house, you know."

"Well, tell him for me that no one's allowed anywhere near the place. We'll have an arson investigator out here tomorrow, when it's cooled down enough to poke around safely. The police are on their way now, but—"

"The police?" She was wanted by the FBI. She had to remember that.

"They'll be a while. As I said, those vigilantes are keeping us pretty busy today. They probably won't be able to do much for now besides tape off the scene, anyway. But they're going to want to talk to the owner. Please pass along my regrets," he added. "I'm sorry we couldn't do more. These damned idiots with their minds set on wiping out vampires, are making our lives hell. And the worst of it is, most of the people they're burning out are just ordinary human beings, for cryin' out loud."

"Are you saying it would be all right if they were vampires?" she asked, and then wondered why she'd bristled in defense of the very people who'd ruined her life.

"Yeah, right," he muttered. "Vampires. Like that's for real." He shook his head slowly.

"Shoot, boss, I know they're real. I've seen 'em!" one of his men put in, overhearing as he passed by with a rolled-up fire hose over his shoulder.

The chief rolled his eyes. "You have somewhere to go, miss? You gonna be all right?"

"Fine. I'll call someone to pick me up. Thank you."

He nodded, then frowned. "Do I know you from somewhere?"

She shook her head. "I have one of those faces," she said, wishing he would just leave. The others were winding up hoses, stowing equipment. A couple of the trucks had already pulled away.

"Are you sure? 'Cause I could swear—"

His radio crackled, and he yanked it from his belt. "Hell, this better not be another freakin' arson. C'mon, boys! Let's move it!"

Already the voice on the radio was speaking in a feminine monotone. Structure fire, possibly multiple victims inside, 2938 Oak Tree Lane…

The rest was beyond Lucy's hearing as the fire-fighter dove into his truck and pulled away. His siren started wailing a second later.

She watched them all the way out of sight, then ran toward the spot where she'd seen James vanish. "Please, let them be all right. Please, please, please." She got to the edge and looked down. Rocks and frothy water were all she saw. If there was a secret passage, she didn't see it. And then suddenly a head poked out through the weedy vines that clung to the stone face, just above the spot where the waves were crashing in.

It was James! Relief flooded through her.

He looked up and saw her there, and she could have sworn he looked as relieved as she had felt at the sight of him.

"Are they gone?"

"Yes, but the police will be here next. Is everyone okay?"

"We won't know for sure until nightfall, but I think so. Meet me by the boat."

Nodding, she raced back along the shore to the end of the long, slender pier, then began untying the ropes that held the vessel in place and tossing them onto the deck.

James swam up to the pier as she worked, and she bent over, extended a hand and helped him up out of the water.

And then, without any warning at all, he pulled her right into his arms and kissed her on the mouth. It wasn't a long kiss, or a passionate one. But it was firm and powerful. And when he stepped back, he looked her in the eyes and said, "You were wonderful. Thank you, Lucy. Thank you for helping me save them."

She held his gaze, stunned, not by his gratitude but by that kiss. And as his eyes searched hers, he must have realized it, because he lowered his head again, and this time, he kissed her as if he meant it. It was long and slow, a soul-deep kiss. And when he stepped away, she wasn't sure she would ever be the same again.

13

"Quickly, now."

James had maneuvered the yacht as near the rocky cliff face as possible, but he couldn't get it any closer than twenty-five feet from the shore. The water was too shallow, the rocks too dangerous. Then he'd filled the attached dinghy with every blanket he could find on board and rowed to shore, leaving Lucy aboard the yacht to keep a lookout.

It was still daylight. This was a dangerous mission, moving the undead beneath the blazing sun. But none of them dared wait. If the police arrived…if they found the vampires—or her, Lucy realized—it would be over.

Lucy gave her head a shake in an effort to free it of such dire thoughts and gazed up the shoreline toward the sandy beach beyond. She couldn't see the smoldering wet remains of Will and Sarafina's beautiful home from here, and that was just as well.

A few yards away, in the mouth of that hidden

passage, James and Will carefully wrapped each of
the bodies—and that was what the sleeping vampires
were, really. Just bodies. Dead weight. Conscious of
utterly nothing. Defenseless. And Lucy couldn't help
but wonder, as she watched the men load the first
three mummylike bundles into the dinghy, what the
other vampires in the world were doing to stay alive.
With humans trying to burn them while they slept,
how could they protect themselves by day? Not all
of them had a mortal lover like Will, or mixed-blood
relations like Brigit and James.

And where the hell was Brigit, anyway?

Lucy lowered her eyes and realized that she was
genuinely worried about the hot-tempered but cou-
rageous blonde. And about the vampires she hadn't
even met. She was beginning to care about these
people. And it surprised her. And yet, at the same
time, it didn't. She'd always been one to root for the
underdog; she just never would have imagined she
would see a group of powerful immortals with su-
percharged strength and speed, and enhanced senses
and telepathic abilities, as the underdog in a war with
humans.

She should have. Humans were by far the most
dangerous creatures Planet Earth had ever evolved.

James rowed the dinghy closer to the yacht. It
rocked precariously on the waves as he anchored the
first bundled body over one shoulder, holding it there
as best he could while climbing a rope ladder up to
the deck. Lucy leaned over to try to help him, holding

the ladder as steady as she could. As he came level with the rail, he eased the body off his back and it fell heavily onto the deck.

Lucy jumped, emitting a squeak of alarm, and quickly bent to tighten a loose fold in the blanket. "Try not to break their skulls," she told him.

"They can't feel a thing," he reminded her.

"But when they wake—"

"The day sleep heals and regenerates. Any injuries they receive by night are completely mended while they rest, so long as they make it past sunrise alive. An injury received during the day sleep would heal instantly. As long as it wasn't fatal."

"Like the fire would have been."

He nodded. "Now you're getting it." Then he vanished back down the ladder. Lucy gripped the body and dragged it across the deck to the open hatch that led below, and then down the steps, wincing every time the legs and feet banged a stair, and they banged every one of them, all the way down.

Before long all three women, Rhiannon, Sarafina and Shannon, were loaded onto the yacht and tucked away in the cabins below, where they would be safe. When that was done, James went back for the men, Roland and Gilgamesh, and also Will, who was waiting in the tunnel with them.

In a few minutes Will came up the ladder with one body, James with the other. And then James climbed back down the rope ladder one last time to retrieve a final body. Pandora.

The cat was limp, lifeless, as James laid her body on the deck of the boat.

"Oh, no. Oh, no no no," Lucy said. She knelt beside the cat, stroking her silken, blue-black fur, but feeling by the coolness of her body that there was no life left in the animal.

Lifting her head, she met James's eyes. And then suddenly, she realized… "James? Can you…?"

He was kneeling opposite her before she finished the question, placing his palms on the innocent animal, closing his eyes. Lucy sat there, keeping her own hands on the cat, as well, and in a moment she felt James move. He lifted his hands and laid them on top of hers, which still rested on the cat.

"But I—"

"Shh. Just feel."

She closed her eyes and opened her mind, her heart. And soon it felt as if warm honey were somehow passing from his hands straight through hers and sinking into Pandora. It was an amazing sensation. But that was just the beginning. There was more. She felt as if some kind of soul-sunroof opened in the top of her head, as if there were a light source that was unlike any light she'd ever seen or felt—an energy source, really—and heat, and sizzling crackling electricity and…love. Yes. Love. It moved from wherever such things originated, or from everywhere all at once, into her. And through her into…it. The cosmos. The universe. It was all one thing. All one thing, and she was a part of it, and so was James, and so was Pandora. And the boat, and the ocean, and the planet.

One.

One.

One.

It was the most serene sort of knowingness she had ever felt, or ever even imagined. And then it blinked out, and she was herself again, an individual, and James's hands were on hers. She opened her eyes, found his locked with them. He leaned a little closer, and so did she and his lips brushed hers very briefly....

And then the cat squirmed out from beneath their joined hands, knocking them apart as she bounded across the deck. Three leaps, then she stopped and turned, staring accusingly at the two of them, ears laid back, tail twitching angrily. Her green eyes seemed to be asking just what the hell they had done to her, in a voice that sounded, in Lucy's head, a lot like Rhiannon's.

Lucy smiled, then laughed, and when James laughed with her, she knew in that moment that there was something powerful between them. Something that went beyond attraction or any of the craziness that had thrown them together. There was a connection, and she'd felt it from the moment when she'd first opened her eyes to find him leaning over her as she lay with the very lifeblood seeping out of her and soaking into a New York City sidewalk. She'd known it. She'd felt it. She'd questioned and doubted and ignored that feeling, because it didn't make any sense to her. It wasn't logical.

But now she had to wonder just what good logic was anyway. She was on a boat full of vampires with a man who could heal the sick and raise the dead. The Jesus of the Damned, he was. Their savior. Was it any wonder he thought anything he did was justified? With a power like his, how he could not develop a bit of a god complex?

"I'm going to need your help!" Will called from the helm.

Looking up quickly, Lucy realized he'd already piloted the yacht away from shore, while the two of them had been preoccupied, James with the cat and Lucy with James.

"On my way," James replied. Then he met her eyes, and his had a lot going on in their blue depths. An entire universe swirling within them, and all of it focused on her in that moment. She felt…admired, approved of, complimented and appreciated by him, though he hadn't spoken a single word. It was all there in his eyes.

"Why don't you check on our passengers, Lucy? They ought to be coming around soon."

She nodded and got to her feet, turning to jog across the deck and down the hatch to the cabins below. But as she paused outside the first door, she sensed a presence behind her and turned slowly. Rhiannon's black panther was slinking down from above, her nose twitching as she searched for her mistress.

Pandora's eyes, like black marbles, met Lucy's, and the cat went still, crouching a little lower.

Lucy swallowed hard and didn't dare move as the cat growled low in its throat. She felt the sound reverberating in her solar plexus. Her fear made her want to run. It was what she did, after all. When danger threatened, Lucy fled.

And she could have run then. She could have opened the door to the first cabin, right there at her back, and slipped quickly inside. But something made her stiffen her spine instead. And instead of backing away, she focused on a point just to the right of the panther's head, because wasn't looking them in the eye supposed to be challenging behavior? And then she crouched low, and in a very strong, steady, but calm tone she said, "Easy now, Pandora. I'm a friend."

The growl ceased, and the cat's ears rose slightly. Her nose twitched, as if sniffing Lucy's essence, so Lucy opened a hand, palm up, and extended it just a little. "Friend," she said again. It crossed her mind that up until today she hadn't even known for sure whose side she was on. But she did now. She felt anger toward those who'd tried to murder the vampires who slept beneath the decks of this massive yacht. She hoped beyond hope that they were all right and would rise with the sunset. She prayed that Brigit and the rest of James's family were safe. She was indeed a friend to these people. And to this cat. The tears she'd shed when she'd seen it, fallen and lifeless, had been real, and had welled up from the depths of her soul.

Pandora touched her cool nose to the tips of Lucy's fingers, pulled back slightly, then touched again. And then the cat's eyes closed slowly, regally, and she lowered her head, tipping it nearly upside down, to nudge Lucy's hand into petting her. Lucy stroked Pandora's head, and the cat pressed upward against her palm.

"Oh, my God." Lucy continued to stroke the animal, which made a chuffing sound, a lot like a purr. "Oh, my God, I'm petting a panther. I'm on a yachtful of vampires, and I'm petting a black panther."

"Life takes some weird turns, doesn't it?" James said, drawing her gaze as she wondered when he'd arrived.

She met his eyes, still stroking the cat and smiling. "I've always had a weak spot for cats."

"Really? Do you have any of your own?"

"Just one. A fat spoiled Persian."

"She's safe?" he asked.

"He. And yes, he's perfectly safe. I left him with a cat-worshipping colleague. Well, Marcus is more of a mentor, really. He worked with my father, back in the day. Should have been on that dig with us, but he'd gotten sick and had to leave for the hospital only the day before."

"That was kismet."

"He's the only friend I have from those times. The only person who knew me then who remains in my life today. He was the one who came to find me in the dunes, who took me home."

"Did he raise you, after that?"

"No, from there I went to an elderly aunt who tolerated me as long as I didn't make her life inconvenient. I spent six years with her, living like a boarder in her home, and then I went off to college. But Marcus checked in, stayed in touch, never missed a birthday phone call or a holiday gift. He cared for me as much as anyone ever has, I suppose."

"And your cat—he won't mind keeping it longer than expected?"

She rolled her eyes. "Poor Marcus. It was only supposed to be overnight, but he's a lonely, aging intellectual without a pet or a wife to keep him company. I'm sure he's glad of the extra time with Huwawa."

"Huwawa?"

She lowered her head, embarrassed. "In Sumerian lore, Huwawa was the monster that guarded the sacred cedar. Supposedly he was slain by Gilgamesh and Enkidu on their final adventure together. In fact, that was the battle where Enkidu received the wound that led to his death. Which is the event that sent the king in search of immortality."

"In search of Utanapishtim." James shook his head slowly. "A search that resulted in the creation of my race. Do you have any idea how ironic that is?"

"It hasn't escaped my notice." She couldn't quite bear the scrutiny of his eyes. She wanted to ask if he was feeling what she was—that their coming together in this quest was somehow fated. Preordained. But no, that was reaching, and she was not a believer in fairy tales. She was a scientist, for heaven's sake. "Where are we going?"

"Will knows of an island offshore. It was once used by…" He looked at her, and his eyes sparkled just a bit. "You're going to love this. Dracula."

"No."

He nodded. "It's a long story. I'll tell you when we have time. Meanwhile, 'The Man Himself' has a knack for hiding things. He lived on the island for years, keeping it masked by a veil of mist. If we can get him out there to repeat the trick—" He stopped there, looking at something behind Lucy, and she realized by the prickly sensation along her nape that the vampires were rising. Pandora abandoned Lucy's stroking hand, for the one she'd been seeking. Lucy turned all the way around as she followed the big cat's progress.

Rhiannon stood there in a less than modest floor-length black nightgown with bloodred lace trim, petting her cat, her long red nails scratching Pandora's head gently. "A first-degree adept could mask an island with mist," she said slowly. "It's little more than a twist on a simple glamoury. The question is, why is it necessary? And what are we doing on this pathetic excuse for a yacht?"

"According to Will, it's a forty-six-meter Mystic, Rhiannon," James informed her. "One of the most luxurious yachts there is. Not that I couldn't tell just by looking around."

"Pssht. It's a rowboat with a motor. Now tell me what's happened. And…" She wrinkled her nose. "What is that pungent aroma? Is that coming from my peignoir?"

Behind her, through the open doorway that led into what looked like a suite at a five-star hotel—king-size bed, gleaming hardwood everywhere, brass fixtures— Roland was rising, too. He gave a brief look around him and then came into the hallway to stand protectively beside the vampire queen, though she needed no protection.

Directly across the hall from them another door opened, revealing a nearly identical room, where Damien and a beautiful, willowy blonde stood arm in arm.

Lucy saw that there were two more cabins, one on each side, and at the end, a wide living-type room, its door standing open.

Willem came down the steps then, taking them all in with a sweeping glance. Lucy shivered, realizing that the Gypsy vampiress, his beloved Sarafina, hadn't yet risen. Did that mean she was…?

Then a third door opened, and Sarafina stood there, looking puzzled in her satin robe. "Will?"

She caught the scent of smoke that clung to them all, wrinkling her nose, and widening her eyes. "Will, what's happened? Why are we on the *Nightshade?*"

Will opened his arms, and she moved into his embrace. "The house is gone," he said softly.

Rhiannon gasped.

Sarafina seemed to wobble in Will's embrace. "How?"

"They burned it, didn't they?" Rhiannon demanded, lifting a long lock of her own hair and bringing it to her nose to sniff. "With us inside. Those putrid mortal weaklings tried to murder us in our sleep."

"Not just us," James said softly. As he spoke, he moved, sliding an arm around Lucy's shoulders to bring her to his side. Then he led her past the four cabins, one with its door still closed, and into the room at the end, which turned out to be a sitting room carpeted in pure white, with elegant brown and butterscotch furnishings that included a three-piece modular sofa and a two-piece love seat that sat at a right angle to each other, glass-topped tables, a wet bar and a huge flat-screen TV.

James picked up the remote from a holder mounted to the wall and flicked on the TV. Its satellite system took a moment to come online, and then he scanned through the channels, finally stopping on one of the twenty-four-hour news networks.

"There were fires all over the nation today," he said, and the images on the screen backed up his words, as did the ticker running beneath it.

They all read the words scrolling there. *The so-called Human League, a group of anti-vampire vigilantes who describe themselves as humanity's only hope, have organized themselves in a stunningly short time. Their website has already logged more than 2 million hits. They're claiming 300,000 members, and say they're attracting more all the time. This group advocates the use of violence, and claims that only by wiping the vampire race from existence do humans stand a chance of surviving.*

"The Human League?" Rhiannon looked from one face to the next. "And I suppose they think that's clever? Sick, murderous animals is what they are. I've always said their kind ought to be wiped from existence. Maybe now the rest of you will finally believe me."

"Shit, Rhiannon, you think just like they do," James said.

She glared at him. Lucy put a hand on his forearm. "James is one of their kind," she said softly. "So is Brigit, and so is Will. And I'm one of their kind, too."

"And so were you once, Rhiannon," James reminded her.

"I was never one of them. My father was a god."

"A Pharaoh, love," Roland said gently. "And I think all the young ones are saying is that there is good and evil in all of us. In humans, as well as in our kind. You know this is true. We've encountered rogue vampires."

"Yes, and when we do, we destroy them. We police ourselves, unlike these weak-willed, morally bankrupt beasts who seek to destroy whatever they do not understand." She shot Roland a glare, but he only winked at her, which had the effect of softening her expression immediately. Rhiannon sighed, and looked again at Lucy, then at Will and finally at James. "I assume it was the three of you who saved us from a fiery death?"

James nodded. "Not bad for a trio of filthy mortals, huh?"

"So we annihilate all but the good ones," she hissed. "That will leave a dozen or so left breathing."

"We're in your debt," Roland said, with a deep and formal bow toward James and Lucy. "What is the plan, James? Where are we going?"

"More importantly," Rhiannon asked, "where is your sister? Tell me we didn't leave her behind with this kind of mayhem—" she waved an arm toward the TV "—breaking out in the world of man."

Brigit waited until sundown to send out a mental call. Not a spoken message, no words went out from her mind. No directions. There were a handful of mortals in the world who could pick up on telepathic exchanges, and she didn't want to give her location away. At ten minutes past dusk she simply closed her eyes and imagined a beam of light shooting from her to them. The vampires. To any and all of them who might pick up on it. It was a brief flash, a beacon. Long enough, and strong enough, she prayed, for the undead to recognize it as legitimate and to home in on its source. Assuming there were any on the mainland who were still alive to pick it up.

She waited a half hour, and then she did it once again.

By the third time Brigit sent out her invisible call, her beacon, she was able to feel them gathering in the shadows just beyond the isolated stretch of beach where she stood. As the moon began to rise at her back, she felt no hint of mortals nearby, and so she lifted her arms to get the vampires' attention—in case she didn't have it already.

"I'm Brigit Poe," she said. "I am one of the so-called mongrel twins. The children of Amber Lily and Edge. And I have summoned you here because we need to organize, to band together, or else we're going to be wiped out. Our kind faces annihilation. It is up to us to fight back."

She paused there, hearing the muttering, seeing the pale faces in the darkness nodding in agreement.

"First, please, I must ask, have any of you had word of my family? The Poes, the Bryants, the Marquands?"

Someone shouted out, "I saw Eric and Tamara Marquand last eve. They were heading to some island they'd heard was a refuge. Urged me to go, but I wanted to wait, to find my family." That pale face lowered, head shaking slowly side to side. "I found them too late. Burned while they slept."

Brigit sighed. "I'm so sorry."

"Is it true? Is there an island refuge?"

"Yes," Brigit said. "There is. If you begin heading north by northeast, and scan continuously, you'll pick up on the energy of others. But they won't be transmitting mentally, you'll just have to use your senses to locate them. Trust your abilities. Do not use your telepathy, or you run the risk of leading the murderous mortals straight to them."

Again there was muttering. Brigit looked around them as they drew closer, and she found herself stunned by how few there were. Thirty, perhaps thirty-five. This couldn't be all that remained, could it? There had to be more.

She cleared her throat, tried to refocus on her mission. "It must be obvious to all of you by now that the mortal world has learned of our existence. Vigilante groups have formed with the purpose of murdering vampires. They're burning our homes, not to mention the homes of ordinary mortals with nocturnal tendencies. You are no longer safe where you live."

There was muttering in the ranks, and she gave it a moment before going on. "I have two options to offer you now, tonight. First, my brother and the elders—Rhiannon, Roland, even Gilgamesh himself—are creating a safe haven on the island of which we've been speaking. It was formerly known as the Isle of the Impaler. Those of you who do not know of it, speak to those who do. Quietly, and not telepathically. Or simply do as I said and head north by northeast, opening your senses until you feel others of our kind are near. You'll be safe there. It's well-stocked with supplies, and its existence will be concealed. That's your first option."

"And what's the second?" someone shouted.

She blinked and looked into those white, ghostlike faces appearing like stars in the darkness. "Join me. Join the resistance. Fight back. Wipe them out before they can exterminate us."

14

Lucy stood at the bow as the island came into view, and not for the first time, was struck by the contrast between where she was and where she was going. The yacht was modern and luxurious. The bridge contained every possible modern navigational marvel. The staterooms were the equal of anything a posh hotel could offer. The bathroom was as luxurious as the one in Will and Fina's home, and each of the vampires had taken a turn using it to wash away the smell of the fire, before donning clothes chosen from the shipboard collection.

And ahead of them…? Ahead was the island, looming dark and foreboding, with a half-burned-out castle rising against the midnight stars like something straight out of a movie set. The sky was black velvet, and foamy froth sizzled with every wave that broke against the rocky shore. It couldn't have been more evocative. More clichéd. And yet the sight of it made Lucy's heart race. Part of her was dying to explore, to hear the history of the place, to poke around the crumbling ruins. But there was too much to be done for any of that. And already there were people on the island. A large campfire danced against the darkness, and around it, shadows moved.

As soon as they anchored the yacht in a deep harbor near the shoreline and deployed a gangplank onto the rocks, they all hurried to debark. Lucy knew that James was eager for news of his family. Hell, everyone onboard had friends, relatives and loved ones who were missing and unaccounted for. And the ban on using their minds to search must be driving them all to the brink of madness, she thought.

But even then, they paused as they gathered on the shore to look back to where Rhiannon stood alone. She'd stepped up onto a boulder that jutted out over the ocean waves, and stood there with the blue-black sea heaving before her. Slowly she lifted her slender arms over her head. The wind blew against the long black dress she wore, snapping the draping points of its long sleeves just as it snapped her raven hair. She closed her eyes. And Lucy watched, James at her side, as a thick fog began rolling from the very surface of the ocean, swirling and rising and thickening, boiling higher and higher, until it reached into the sky like a mountain, entirely blocking any view of the island from the mainland.

Rhiannon lowered her arms, opened her eyes, looked around and gave a brief, sharp nod. "That's better."

And then, even as Lucy was staring, awestruck, at the woman, there was a joyous shout. Everyone turned to see other vampires come running toward the shore. A woman with bloodred hair and the face of an angel slammed into James so hard she nearly knocked him over. He caught her up in his arms and spun her in a circle, then kissed her face over and over.

And just when Lucy was starting to feel the rising tides of a jealousy that was as fierce as it was irrational, he set the woman on her feet again and said, "Lucy, come and meet my mother, Amber Lily."

Lucy spent the entire night surrounded by them, and it was nothing like she would have imagined. She met James's family, all of them young, strong, beautiful couples who appeared to be in their thirties or even younger. He introduced them as his parents, Amber Lily and Edge Poe, and his grandparents, Angelica and Jameson Bryant, and as "the closest thing to great grandparents I could have," Eric and Tamara Marquand. And yet it was as if she were meeting her peers—hell, Tamara could have been one of her students.

This entire new society, with its web of relationships and its nonexistent aging process, was going to take some getting used to.

And then she realized that no, it wouldn't. Not for her. She wasn't going to be around them much longer, anyway. James had promised to return her to her life as soon as possible, and that time was rapidly approaching.

She didn't know if he would triumph, or how he could possibly hope to save them. But she did know they couldn't remain on this island forever, and that if they were to survive, they would have to find a safer place, one farther away from man, where no one could ever find them again. And though he had once turned his back on this way of life, this society of the undead, it was very clear to her that he would not—and probably *could not*—do so again. They were looking to him as a leader now. Not to Damien, the onetime king, as would seem logical. Not even to Rhiannon, the queenlike Egyptian high priestess of Isis, with the power to control nature.

No, it was James they all looked to for salvation. For leadership. It was as if he were their king.

And while Lucy was bursting with pride to see him assume the mantle and the heavy burden that came with it, she also knew it meant there was no future for the two of them. She was no vampire queen. Nor did she want to be. And wherever these people ended up, James was going with them.

And *she* was not. She was going to return to her mundane little house, her job and her dusty lab in the university basement, with her bits of clay and her notebooks. And her cat, Huwawa.

She decided to put all that from her mind for the night. Because there was true joy around her, and it was difficult not to let it in. There were happy reunions, families finding each other, old friends re-united. Over and over, all night long.

But though touching, those were not the events that rocked her most deeply. Those came later, as other vampires began arriving. They came mostly by twos and threes, or even all alone, in tiny rowboats, motor-boats, canoes. They came with terror-filled eyes and scalding tears, having lost the ones they loved most.

Lucy had withdrawn from the intimacy of the fire-side reunions. She was an outsider, knowing little about their conversations, their reminiscences, the names of friends still unheard from. Like a stranger at a huge family reunion where everyone knew and loved everyone else, she'd felt out of place and awk-ward. So she'd left James to the throng of loved ones demanding his attention and wandered back to the beach alone. There she'd begun meeting the incom-ing refugees, directing them to where the others were setting up campsites and shelters in the shadow of the hulking, hollow castle.

And then a small canoe wobbled onto shore, and a man—a boy, really—jumped out, gathering a girl into his arms. Lucy ran forward into the surf to help.

He was young. So was the girl he held, though you could barely tell, with most of her hair burned down to the scalp and the skin of her face looking like a melted crayon. Her clothes hung in blackened tatters.

The young man looked up, his face streaked in soot. "Please, please, I need help. She can't die, she can't—"

The girl opened one eye, the one she still could, and somehow Lucy felt her pain. It was pouring out of her in telepathic waves, probably because it was too much for one person—even a vampire—to contain.

"Lay her down—over here, in the cool grass," Lucy instructed, and then she turned to shout for James at the top of her voice. When he didn't respond immediately, she turned to the young man. God, he couldn't have been more than eighteen. "Stay with her. I'm going to get help."

"No one can help," he whispered. "And I don't think she's going to make it until dawn." He lowered his head, tears streaming, sobs wracking his shoulders. "God, Ellie, what will I do without you? Why did they do this to us? Why? We never hurt anyone. Never."

"James!" Lucy shouted, and this time she ran in the direction of the camp.

He met her halfway, nearly bowling her over. She gripped his hand, and tugged him with her. "Hurry!"

They ran side by side, then came to a stop. The boy was holding the young woman in his arms again, rocking her and sobbing. "She was on fire. I threw her into the water. I thought I could save her, but…"

Lucy lowered her head as her tears spilled like waterfalls. She couldn't contain a gulping sob that drew James's eye, but he looked away quickly, going to the boy, putting a hand on his shoulder. "Lay her back down and step away. Let me take a look."

"It's t-t-too late. She's…"

"Please," James urged. "Let me try."

The boy stilled and lifted his head slowly, staring at James and perhaps finally sensing that he was different. Not vampire, not mortal, not one of the Chosen, as Lucy was. He was something else altogether.

"Who are you?" he asked.

"James Poe. You?"

"Jeremy," the kid said. "Why is your name familiar?"

"I'll tell you later," James said. "Lay her back down. I think I can save her, if you just let me try."

The boy frowned, but he obeyed, lowering the girl's body to the grass once more. He remained kneeling beside her.

James knelt on her other side and pressed his hands to her body. And in spite of herself, Lucy moved closer, dropping to her knees right next to James, riveted as she watched the light begin to pulse from his hands. That soft white-gold glow that was unlike any light she'd ever seen, natural or manmade. It suffused the young body, the poor ravaged, charred body.

"Please, let it work. Let it work. Let it work," she whispered, not even aware she was saying the words aloud. The boy was looking at her, and then at James again and then his eyes returned to his beloved.

It seemed to Lucy that the girl's charred skin began to smooth itself out, the blackened parts to fade to brown. Difficult to be sure in the darkness. Surely she was wishing for it hard enough to play tricks on her mind. But no, it was happening. The burns grew even lighter, gold, then orange, and then slowly muting into pink. The hair on the girl's scalp came twisting and writhing from within, and it was like watching time-lapse footage. Only it wasn't. It was real. This was real.

And not for the first time since she'd been lying on that sidewalk, watching her life bleed from her body, Lucy saw the pure beauty of James Poe, and of his gift. He became, once again, an angel in her eyes.

The girl's body was restored and whole. Her eyes blinked open, then widened. And then Jeremy yanked her upright and into his arms, and the two clung, sobbing and crying and laughing and holding each other as if they would never let go.

James rose to his feet, moving away from them, and before she knew what she was about to do, Lucy rushed to him and wrapped her arms around his neck, hugging him hard to her. He grasped her around the waist as she buried her tear-damp face against his neck and whispered, "You're amazing. You're a miracle, James. You are so incredibly special."

One of his hands stroked her hair, and he bent his head to whisper back, "We're not alone, Lucy."

Sniffling, she pulled back from him just far enough to wipe her eyes dry and take note of her surroundings. The rest of the vampires had gathered, every one currently on the island, and they were standing around in a semicircle, apparently alerted by her earlier shouting. They'd seen it all. And they looked at

James now in such intense awe that she thought they might all be about to take a knee. To genuflect.

She didn't blame them, but she felt instinctively that adoration like that was the last thing James needed. She tugged on his arm. "We need to talk, James."

"We will. On the way back to the mainland."

She blinked in shock. "James, you can't leave them. They need you, don't you see that?"

"They need me to go do what I'm supposed to do."

She stared up at him, her rejuvenated hero-worship already beginning to fracture, a tiny hairline crack opening in its formerly crystalline surface. "To find Utanapishtim? To try to raise a man from the dead after five thousand years?"

"It's my purpose."

"No," she whispered. "*This* is your purpose. Don't you see that now? This, these people, they're your true calling. You need to be here, to heal the innocent, to save the wounded, to ease their pain and, where it's still possible, restore life to those who've had it snuffed out unfairly and before their time. Not to try breathing life into a tiny mound of ash and bone."

"Look at them," he said to her.

Unwillingly, she turned her gaze to the sea of faces, all of them looking to James as if he were their only hope. And she realized that there *was* hope in those faces now, where before there had been only devastation and despair. He'd put it there, that hope.

And now he was determined to fulfill it.

"We have to go back and end this madness. It's time to find Utanapishtim. It's time I fulfilled my life's purpose."

15

"Back in a Manhattan hotel room," Lucy said softly. "I sure have come full circle. I was in a room just like this only—what? Less than a week ago? And yet my entire life has changed since then."

James backed away from the window, letting the curtain fall back into place. The hotel had a direct line of sight to the Metropolitan Museum of Art, where Lucy thought Utanapishtim's ashes were secreted in an old and unremarkable statue. He couldn't seem to stop himself from looking out at the museum every time he walked past the window. Talk about lives changing... Now that he knew his purpose, it was burning in him, driving him. But he knew she was going through as much as he was. Her life, too, had been turned upside down. And unlike him, it wasn't her destiny.

He looked at her then. She had been on the computer they'd managed to borrow from the concierge, with a little power of suggestion. Just like they'd checked in with a nonexistent credit card and phony names. Lucy had also been on the phone, though he thought that was a very bad idea. She was on hold now, the cordless receiver anchored between her ear and her shoulder. The television set was on, the volume low. It was showing continuous footage of various conflagrations, weeping family members, burned bodies—human ones. Vampire bodies turned to ash when they burst into flames. They burned hot and fast. It was a miracle the girl on the island—Ellie—hadn't just exploded in a flash when her skin had begun to burn. Her boyfriend, Jeremy, must have dumped her into the water almost instantly, or there would have been nothing left of her.

And she was young. Vampires' weaknesses, their vulnerabilities, grew larger with age, just as their powers and strengths did. For most, fire would end them. There would be no remains for hype-hungry reporters to parade in front of a national audience. None to be confiscated for study by government scientists, either. No "alien autopsy" video, with a vampire playing the role of the little green man, would be showing up online anytime soon. Thank God.

And he was thinking all of that because it kept him from thinking about what was front and center in his mind. Lucy. Himself and Lucy.

He had no business focusing on that when his people were on the brink of extinction.

"I still think we should just break into the Met tonight and take the statue," he said, hoping to distract himself. But it did little good. She was wearing clothes she'd found on the yacht. A pair of skinny black jeans, with high-heeled black boots that covered them all the way to her knees. A tank top that hugged her slender body closely. A button-down shirt of army green, heavy with military insignia on the breast pocket, over that. Her hair was in a ponytail that rode high on her head, and her tortoiseshell glasses were perched on her nose as she stared at the computer screen.

His bookish professor had taken a turn toward *Tomb Raider,* and he could barely keep himself from acting on the impulses that were burning through his body every time he looked at her. So he looked over her shoulder at the computer instead and saw what she was examining so closely: a live satellite shot of the Met. She was scrolling up and down, left and right, noticing windows, exits and the landscaping around the museum.

"They have state-of-the-art security. We'd never get away with it. We need to come up with some fake credentials, and then you can use your powers to get them to hand it to us."

"Can we at least go look at the statue?"

"Statues. There are three. But I'm ninety-nine percent certain I'll know which it is as soon as I see it. And we'll go soon," she said. "James, this is my area. Museums, collections, artifacts. These are my people, curators and translators. You need to trust me on this. I'll get us in there. Okay?"

He met her eyes, beyond those glasses of hers, and nodded. "I know you will."

She looked at him again, and there was worry in her eyes this time. "You look like a wreck. You didn't sleep last night, or all day today. You must be exhausted."

"I couldn't sleep if I wanted to." He paced to the bed nearest him, sat on the edge, bounced up again. "Too much on my mind."

"That's an understatement. The weight of the world is riding right on your broad shoulders," she said softly. "I don't know how you're even holding up under all of this—" She held up a hand as, apparently, someone came back on the telephone line. Then, nodding, she said, "Have him call me at this number as soon as possible, please." And then, "Yes, it's very urgent. The name? Ms. Enheduanna. That's e-n-h-e-d-u-a-n-n-a." There was a pause. "Within thirty minutes? That would be perfect. Thank you so much for your time."

She hung up the phone.

"En-who-whatta?" he asked, teasing just a little. "You couldn't have gone with 'Smith'?"

She smiled, as he had hoped she would. She had the most beautiful smile. It seemed healing to him, for some reason.

"Enheduanna was a Sumerian high priestess and the first author credited by name for her work. I'm her biggest living fan. Marcus will know it's me."

"And what's to stop him from calling the authorities and giving them the number instead?"

"Loyalty," she said. And then she shrugged. "And curiosity. He'll at least phone me first to find out what's going on and then decide how to proceed."

James nodded slowly and felt a bit of jealousy that he told himself was entirely misplaced. Marcus had been a friend and colleague of her father's, he reminded himself. So he must be at least fifteen or twenty years older than she was. "This guy—is he some…Indiana Jones type?"

Her smile was bright and wide, and it took his breath away for a moment, and then he wondered when he'd started reacting that way to her. Not only the breathless desire, not only looking at her and then getting stuck, unable to look away, but also this jealousy. What the hell was that about?

But he knew when. He knew exactly when. It had been on the yacht, when she'd sat across from him as he'd healed Pandora. It had been when he'd seen her crying over that damned cat, and when they'd shared in healing her. And it had intensified on the island, when she'd been weeping for Ellie, and then after the healing, when she'd looked at him as if she wanted to kiss him, as if he were some kind of a hero, or a god, and flung her arms around him and whispered in his ear that he was special. He'd realized then that he'd been dying for her to feel that way about him ever since he'd met her.

And now maybe he was starting to get why. He was falling for this bookish little mortal.

"A retired Indy, maybe," she said, and laughed. "He's almost seventy. He's one of the few friends I've allowed myself in my life. But more importantly, he has a lot of influence in the antiquities community. And I have no doubt that a phone call from him will get us permission to take a closer look at those statues."

"That doesn't get the one we want out of the museum."

"Well, if it gets it out of the case, into a quiet, private room and into my hands, we'll be ahead of the game. Won't we?" Then she tapped the computer screen, and he saw that she'd switched to the page for the museum's gift shop. She clicked on a thumbnail of one of the items for sale, enlarging it, and he saw a small, rather crude statue of a nude man with his arms held close to his chest, elbows at his sides, thumbs pointing upward. Beneath the statue were the words, Sumerian Priest-King Replica—Actual Size. Gypsum Stone. $149.99.

He nodded. "You're one smart woman, Lucy Lanfair."

She tapped her head. "Professor, remember?" But then her smile died, and she frowned past him at the television screen.

And no wonder. A photo of her filled the screen, with the caption *Professor Lucy Lanfair. Wanted in connection with the Waters/Folsom Murders.*

He reached for the remote to shut the thing off, but she grabbed it first and cranked up the volume.

"...I think the government is reaching, here," said one of the journalists seated on the set of a popular Sunday morning news program.

"The woman's family was murdered in front of her," said another.

"Family and the entire team on that dig in Iraq." The camera went close on the man on the far right, close-cropped black curls and thick glasses. A caption read Dr. Jarod Cunningham, Clinical Psychologist. "She was the sole survivor. That's going to leave some scars."

"So then you think it's possible this book of Folsom's—meeting him by chance in that greenroom—somehow triggered a violent break with reality?" asked the host.

"It's entirely possible. All this vampire stuff, all wound up with Sumerian legend, the very thing her parents were studying. It has to be connected," said the shrink.

"Right. But the question remains, where'd she get the gun?"

A third man broke in, identified as a congressman. "None of that is relevant right now. What we need is for Professor Lanfair to come in and talk to us. And in the meantime, I must reiterate my call for calm. People are panicking—"

"People are dying, Congressman," the host interrupted.

The politician nodded and looked right at the camera. "These vigilante groups are murdering their own out of fear and ignorance. People, there's no such thing as vampires. No such thing. This violence needs to stop, and the sooner this professor comes in and tells the truth about what happened in that studio that night, the faster that will happen. There is more blood on this woman's hands than just that of the two people she shot in Studio Three."

"Allegedly shot," said the host.

The congressman went on as if he hadn't been interrupted. "This was not a government sponsored execution, as some fringe internet sites are claiming. There is no conspiracy here. There's no more than one deluded old man, one irresponsible publisher looking to exploit his delusions and one mentally scarred genius who suffered a break with reality."

James took the remote control away from her and turned the television set off. Lucy looked...stricken. And stunned and horrified and...

He went to stand between her and the TV set, because she was still staring at it. "You and I both know that's all bull."

She met his eyes then. Hers were wet. "But what we know is irrelevant. Most people are going to believe it. I'm a reclusive brainiac. I have no family, almost no friends. If they ask my neighbors about me, they'll say, 'She keeps to herself.' God, they couldn't have picked a better scapegoat."

"Lucy, we're going to fix this."

"How? *How* are we going to fix this?" She lowered her head and shook it slowly. "My career is over. My credibility is destroyed. And I know, James—believe me, I know—this isn't anywhere near as devastating as the possible extermination of an entire race. If I had to pick one or the other, I'd choose helping to save your people over my own career—I hope you believe that."

That was the thing. He *did* believe it.

"But it's still devastating. Because I can't go back home again. My life as I knew it…it's over. It's *over*." Blinking back tears, she looked at the telephone. "My God, I don't know if even Marcus will believe me now. What must he be thinking?"

The telephone rang, and she nearly jumped out of her skin. James was all too aware of her turmoil, her fear, her uncertainty about her own future, and he wished he could make things right, but he would be damned if he knew how.

The phone was still ringing. Lucy stared at it, and then, reluctantly, she picked it up. "Hello?"

James leaned close to her, so he could hear. She tipped the phone toward him slightly.

"Lucy, is it you?" said an urgent male voice. "Please, for the love of God, tell me it's you."

"It's me. Hello, Marcus. Your phone's not tapped or anything, is it?"

"Of course not! Lucy, are you all right?"

"Yes. But I didn't do what they're saying I did. I didn't—"

"I know. It never even crossed my mind. Mental break? You're the sanest person I know. Lucy, where are you? Are you all right? Can I do anything to help you?"

"Yes, actually. I need to get my hands on the three priest-king statues from that traveling Sumerian exhibit that's at the Met right now. I just need to examine them. Can you get me through the red tape?"

"The Met? Yes, I think I can do that. You can't go as yourself, though, not with all the press you've been getting. Could you…manage a disguise of some sort? I know it sounds over the top, but given the situation…"

"I was already thinking that, myself."

"All right, give me some time."

"I'm afraid we don't have much time, Marcus."

"We?"

"Yes, I'm, um…with a colleague. He's helping me."

"But you're safe, yes?"

"I'm as safe as I can be, given the circumstances."

The older man sighed. "I'm just glad you're not alone. Can you hold off for an hour? I'll call you back then—sooner, if I can manage it."

"An hour. All right, Marcus. Thank you." She hung up the phone, lifted her eyes to meet James's.

"An hour, Lucy?" James asked. "You do realize that's more than enough time for him to give the authorities this number, and for them to trace it and surround this place. Are you sure you trust him?"

"Yes. I do trust him. But I don't trust them. They know I know him, so they could be tapping his phone and he wouldn't even know it. Let's see how far down the hall this cordless phone will work, shall we?"

He lowered his head, amazed yet again at her ingenuity. "All right."

She turned to begin gathering up their things, not that there were many.

Reaching behind her head, he snapped off the scrunchie that held her hair in place, and as she spun to face him, surprised, the long strands flew around her shoulders. Smiling, he took off her glasses. "You look nothing like that buttoned-up professor in that shot they were showing on TV. Not now."

"I feel nothing like that buttoned-up professor," she said. "My entire worldview has been turned inside out, James. Everything I thought was real is on shaky ground. And so many things I thought were just fantasy are walking around in my reality now."

"The good guys turned out to be the villains, and the monsters turned into victims."

"Heroes. Not victims. Heroes." She lowered her eyes. "Especially you, James."

He felt blood heating his face and averted it to hide the reaction. "If it doesn't work…"

"If it doesn't work, you'll know you did your very best."

Lifting his gaze again, he asked her, "Do you still think it's a mistake to try?"

"To try to raise the ashes of a man who's been dead for five thousand years? Yes, I do. But I don't believe it's a mistake to try whatever you have to, to save your people. And I also think that if you do any less and your people die, you'll never forgive yourself. And in case you haven't noticed, I've completely changed sides in this. I'm helping you now because I want to. Not because I have to."

He couldn't take his eyes off her face. There was something more there. Or maybe he was only seeing what he wanted to see, because of his newly awakened—or at least newly acknowledged—feelings for her. But maybe not. Maybe she really did look as if she wanted him to kiss her.

Maybe he'd better find out.

"I'm sorry I ruined your life," he said.

"You saved my life first," she replied. "That kind of makes up for it."

He took a step closer. "Let me make up for it a little bit more, hmm?"

"How?" she whispered.

"Close your beautiful eyes, Professor."

She did. And he laid his hands over them, so that his fingertips extended upward, into her silky mink-colored hair, while the heels of his hands rested on her cheeks. He willed the light to come, and it did. It glowed, and gleamed and he heard her suck in a breath.

And then the light faded, and he lowered his hands. "Okay. Open them now."

She opened her eyes and frowned. "What did you…?"

He picked up her glasses and tossed them into the wastebasket.

She blinked. "Oh, my God, you fixed my eyesight."

"I would have done it sooner, if I'd thought of it."

"James, you didn't have to—"

Before she could finish, he swept her into his arms and kissed her, unable to hold in the desire any longer.

She opened her mouth to him, let him probe with his tongue, taste her. And as she fed from his mouth in return, he moved her across the room and then fell with her onto the bed, arching his hips against her, sliding his hands beneath her to pull her hard against his grinding hips.

Her eyes flashed open, and she stared into his. And he knew her answer to his unspoken question was a resounding yes.

His hands were trembling, as if he were a teenager and this was his first time, as he pushed her top upward and out of his way.

He bared one small perfect breast and lowered his head to nuzzle at its peak.

And then the phone rang, shattering the moment.

He closed his eyes. "Dammit."

"We have to answer it," she told him.

"I know. And I love that you know it, too." He raised himself up off her body, gently righting her top in the process.

Pressing a hand to her chest as if to calm her racing heart, Lucy reached for the phone and answered. "Yes?"

"It's me, Marcus. I thought it best to act with haste—you mustn't stay in the city any longer than you absolutely have to. So you're in. You are Professor Sandra Duncan. Your colleague is Dr. Winston Marlboro."

"I'm an actress from the seventies and he's two packs of cigarettes?"

"I had to think fast," Marcus said with a self-deprecating sigh. "Mr. Scofield Danforth will be expecting you. He'll bring the pieces to you for examination. He's been told this is a matter of national security, that he mustn't tell anyone else. I didn't say it had to do with the current issue dominating the news, but I said enough that he no doubt drew that very conclusion. So he'll cooperate. Please stay safe, my dear."

"I'll do my best. You've been a good friend to me, Marcus. I'll never forget it."

"Nonsense. Go now, do what you must. Whatever it is, I know it's the right thing."

The phone went dead, and she hung up, smoothed her hair and lifted her eyes. "We can go now."

He didn't want to go now. He wanted to follow up on what had almost happened between them. And

yet, that was ridiculous, wasn't it? The survival of
his race was at stake, and he wanted to put off saving
them for the sake of making love to this goddess of a
woman?

Yeah. He did. He wouldn't act on that desire, but
deep down, that was exactly what he wanted. Chuck
it all for an hour in her arms. Buried in her body. Two
hours. An entire afternoon.

Hell. Wrong time. Wrong place. And probably, he
knew, the wrong woman. And yet the thought lingered, playing out in his mind in vivid Technicolor
and making his lips tingle at the thought of hers beneath them.

They left the hotel. In a strained and nervous silence, they walked side by side, but not touching, to
the museum.

After their brief visit to the museum's gift shop and
the purchase that would enable them to pull this thing
off, followed by a quick stop at the rest room, they
went to their appointment with the twitchy little man
with the pretentious and unlikely name of Scofield
Danforth who was in charge of the traveling exhibit.
They waited at a table in a private room in the glass-
lined administrative section. They were on the north
side of the breathtaking building, and the office windows were unprotected, as far as she could tell. Not
that anyone could get out via those windows, with or
without any valuable artifact, painting or jewel. They
didn't open, and there was nothing outside them to

use as an escape route. No trees, no fire escape on that side of the building. Only an uninterrupted, albeit brief, drop to the manicured lawns of Central Park below.

No way out. Hell.

The curator returned with the requested items, three nine-inch-tall limestone sculptures of a nude man. He set the pieces on the table and stepped out of the room.

Lucy took the pieces in her hands one by one, reveling, as she always did, in the miracle of holding, of touching, something that had been held, touched, fashioned, by the hands of people who'd lived more than five thousand years ago. The three pieces were similar, with rough surfaces and an overall weathered appearance, gray-white in color, with varying striations of rust and darker grays. Holding the first one, she noted that the priest king's body was almost cylindrical, his legs one blocklike unit, with an incised line to differentiate one from the other and hash marks to separate the toes. The figure flared from the hips into the upper body. The arms were bent at the elbows and held close to the body, fists at the chest, and like the legs, they were only roughly delineated. The round face featured expanded cheeks and full lips, a disc-shaped beard and a band around the hair. The genitals were carved in more realistic detail than any other part of the body.

"He left us alone with them. Not very nervous about us taking off with them, is he?" James asked softly, interrupting Lucy's reverent contemplation of the artifact.

"Why should he be? There's no way out of here other than the way we came in. And besides, we're under constant surveillance." She nodded at the video camera mounted in a corner of the room.

"We need to figure out which one it is and get it out of here," he said, lowering his voice.

"It's this one."

"You've barely looked at the others. Are you sure?"

She sent him a scowl, her fingertip almost caressing a series of lines, carved in the stone. "His name is on it. And here are the wavy lines I told you to look for, as well."

He held up a hand in surrender. "Okay, it's that one."

She shook the piece, frowning. "It doesn't feel hollow, though."

"Do you have the replacement ready?" he asked.

She nodded, glancing down at her jacket. Her handbag had been searched before she'd come in, but she hadn't been patted down. The replacement statue, bought in the gift shop downstairs, was taped to her side and hidden there by her jacket.

James got to his feet and leaned over her with his back to the camera, as if in intense contemplation of the artifact. Lucy quickly hiked up her top and gently freed the replica from the duct tape holding it to her side. Then she set the fake on the table and taped the real statue to her skin, righted the shirt and straightened the jacket. The entire exchange took all of twenty seconds.

"He's going to know it's not the real one, James," she said worriedly. "The size isn't even a perfect match. I should have had some kind of a Plan B ready."

James nodded. "You let me take care of that part, okay?" He tapped his head. "Vampire, remember?"

Smiling, she said, "Right." She rose from the table and went to the door, opened it and smiled at the man who stood outside. "We're all finished, Mr. Danforth. Thank you so much for your cooperation."

The man nodded, entering the room, his eager eyes shooting straight to the items on the table. Then his eyes narrowed on the fake statue. "Wait, there's something…"

"There's nothing wrong," James said, lowering a hand to the man's shoulder. "There's nothing wrong at all. The piece is exactly as you last saw it, precisely as you remember it to be, to the tiniest detail. You are supremely confident that all is well. You have no question whatsoever about that. Do you?"

"Of course not," the man said, his voice oddly soft. He blinked, as if shaking off a stupor, and hurried to the table, picking up the artifact in gloved hands, handling it as reverently as Lucy had done. "You'll let me know what this was all about when you can?"

"Of course we will," Lucy said. "Your help is very much appreciated."

He nodded, said goodbye and Lucy and James walked out into the public part of the museum and down to the ground floor. As they approached the main entrance, she tried to conceal her nerves. God, she was walking right out of the Met with a stolen artifact taped to her waist! This was so not typical Lucy Lanfair behavior.

Just the opposite, in fact.

And yet, they were doing it. They were getting away with it. They were almost to the massive, beautiful doors. They were—

James grabbed her arm. "Don't freak out on me."

"What?"

He nodded toward the door. "Police. Outside."

"For us?" She blinked, staring at the door.

"Stop looking."

She looked away. He lifted an arm, pointing to the left, and she followed his gaze. "Try to look like a tourist admiring the place."

She made a face at him as he steered her toward the nonexistent thing he was allegedly pointing at. "Do you think the curator...?"

"No. He has no clue. I messed with his mind...just a little, but enough. No, this has to have come from your friend, Doctor Jones."

"Marcus Payne. And he wouldn't have ratted us out, James. Not Marcus."

"Then maybe they really did tap his phone. Who the hell knows?"

He picked up the pace, heading for an elevator. "How are we going to get out of here?"

She looked around, saw a group of tourists being led by a college-age tour guide, swallowed hard and said, "Follow my lead. Blend in with the group."

"What?" He frowned at her, but she rushed over to the group, tapped the young girl on the shoulder and, with a quick glance at her name badge, said, "Sarah?"

"Yeah, that's me."

"Hi. I'm Molly. I'm new. Um, listen, the boss told me to take over. You're wanted upstairs. Something about a special project."

"Really?"

"Yeah. Do you know what it's about?"

"No idea."

"Well, will you tell me when you come back? I'm dying of curiosity." Then Lucy turned to face the group. "Hi, all. I'm Molly, and I'll be taking over the tour for Sarah. Did she tell you about the architectural history of this place?"

Heads shook slowly, as Sarah hurried away.

"Oh, then you're in for a treat. Follow me outside the building, if you will—just a brief external tour. You're going to love this."

She led the group out the front doors, talking all the way, pointing, explaining, elaborating, even making things up from whole cloth. They walked right past the police, one of whom even nodded hello. She led the group around a corner of the building, toward the park that bordered it, and then she said, "Oh, no! I forgot your free gifts. Wait right here. You," she added, with a nod toward James. "You can come help me carry them."

He nodded, and the two of them raced off into the park, leaving the puzzled tour group alone and confused as to what had just happened.

"Now what?" Lucy asked, when they were in the clear, pausing on one of the winding footpaths that meandered through Central Park. She located a bench, sat on it, then gave a quick look around before reaching under the shirt to pull the tape off her side. She winced. "I'm not going to have any skin left there."

"We can't go back to the hotel," James said, sitting down beside her. "If they were bugging Marcus's phone, they'll know that's where we were calling from." He took her bag from her shoulder. Then he eased the statue from her hands and tucked it inside.

"No reason to go back there anyway," she said. "We didn't leave anything. We need to get out of the city, James."

He nodded. "This would be a bad place to resurrect old Utanapishtim anyway. Can you imagine a man who's been dead for five thousand years waking up in the middle of Manhattan?"

"I can't imagine him waking up anywhere," she said. "And it's Utana."

"What is?"

"His name. The one he used, his familiar name." She reached into the bag and pulled the statue out, but only far enough to see the lines engraved on its base. "I've read these same lines on that stone tablet of yours. Utana. Called Ziasudra. Called Utanapish-tim. Called the Flood Survivor. Called the Servant of the Gods. Then cursed by them. And hidden here by my hand, hidden from the Divine wrath of the Anunaki."

"Anu-what?"

"The gods."

He frowned at her. "Are you going to be able to communicate with him? When we raise him, I mean."

She opened her mouth, then snapped it closed again and lowered her head, shaking it slowly.

"What?" he asked.

Drawing a breath, Lucy chose her words with care. "James, I don't want you to do this. It's not a good idea. And it probably won't work anyway. It didn't work with those...those corpses," she whispered. "Back at the mansion."

"It did work. They were up and walking around. How is that not working?"

"They were pieces of animated meat. Not think-ing, sentient beings. It's not going to do any good to raise a zombie, is it? Besides, this isn't even a body. It's ash."

"You don't think I can do this. After all you've

seen." He got to his feet, walking away from her and shaking his head.

She hiked the bag onto her shoulder, got up and went to him. Standing close behind him, she said, "Maybe it's that I'm afraid you can do it. I wouldn't be so worried if I thought you were going to hold your magical, glow-in-the-dark hands over a pile of ash and nothing was going to happen, would I?"

He lowered his head with a sigh and turned to face her. "That's what happened at my parents' house," he said softly. "I ran around holding my hands over one pile of ashes after another. Trying to…"

"Oh, James… But they weren't there, so it's no wonder you couldn't—"

"I know. They're okay. But see, they won't be if I fail. No one will. I have to try. You've seen what's been happening. You've read the prophecy."

"The prophecy was incomplete. We still don't know the details of what it is that Utanapishtim's supposed to do, if and when you bring him back."

"If and when I do," he asked again, "will you be able to communicate with him?"

She shook her head slowly. "I don't know. We're guessing, at best, as far as what the language sounded like. I could write—maybe—basic things. But…it's going to be a challenge. No one alive has ever heard the Sumerian language spoken." She bit her lip, raised her head. "Wait a minute, someone has."

"Yeah. Damien."

"Gilgamesh," she whispered.

"Vlad, too."

"Vlad…you mean Dracula?" she whispered the name.

"Yeah. He's far older than his legend would lead you to believe. He took on the role of Prince Vlad Dracul, but he'd already been alive for thousands of years by then. But it's a long story, and we don't have time."

"You're right. But I'm fascinated, James."

He met her eyes, and she stared into them. They almost kissed, but she bit her lip and drew away.

James tried to focus. "Okay, so we'll have people who can talk to him. We think. So we just need to raise him in a safe place. A place where we'll have privacy, where we won't be interrupted, and where nothing's going to pop up and scare the hell out of the poor guy, like a truck or a bus or a plane or—"

"The island?" she asked.

He met her eyes, considering it, then shook his head. "Too many people wanting to talk to him, with good reason for impatience. We need to bring him up to speed, explain how it is he's been returned to life and what's been happening in the world since he was last a part of it."

"It boggles my mind that this might actually be about to happen, James."

He nodded. "Let's take him out on the *Nightshade*. Get him out on the ocean, try to do it there."

"Kind of close quarters, don't you think?" she asked. "What if something goes wrong?"

"I won't let anything go wrong."

She closed her eyes and wished the phrase *famous last words* hadn't chosen that moment to run through her mind. "Fine. The *Nightshade* it is."

16

James ended his phone call, then powered his cell phone down and replaced it in the belt clip attached to his khaki trousers. "Brigit's fine," he said, moving across the foredeck to join Lucy. She was leaning on the rail, looking out at the expanse of ocean and twilight. The sun had set behind them, and the purple sky and blue sea were equally placid. Unlike the rest of the world.

"Where is she?" Lucy leaned down to the nearby table, anchored to the deck and surrounded by several lounge chairs, and picked up the two dewy glasses that were sitting there, offering him one.

"Outside Boston, with a group of vampires she's gathered together. The Resistance, she calls them." He took the glass from her. "What's this?"

"Seven-and-Seven. I thought we could both use one."

He took a sip and nodded. "Good idea."

"So what are they up to? This resistance group of hers?"

He sighed, turning his back to the sea, looking at her instead. "Surveilling the houses of vampires who've fled. Waiting for the mortal vigilantes to try to torch one, and then…" He shook his head, then took another swig from the glass. Swallowed, baring his teeth at the strength of the drink. "Killing them."

"…Killing them?"

He met her eyes, nodded. "I didn't say I approved. But that's what she's doing, yeah."

"But that's…murder."

"She says it's war."

"What do *you* say?" She watched his eyes as he formed his answer, and she saw his inward search, his quest for understanding.

"I think it would only be justified if she were defending innocent vampires, asleep inside. But if there's no one there to be harmed, this is just an ambush attack against members of a species who can't hope to defend themselves against something as powerful as Brigit and her vampire gang."

"And yet they've been doing the same thing, these mortals. Attacking the helpless while they're unable to fight back."

"Yeah." He shook his head. "That's what Brigit said."

"She's putting herself at risk. Those vampires with her, as well."

"I told her that, and added that with most of our

kind either already dead or in hiding, these battles she's waging are based on nothing more than a hunger for vengeance."

"What did she say to that?"

"She hung up on me."

Lucy closed her eyes, one hand automatically going to his shoulder. "I'm sorry, James."

"She'll come around once she gets it out of her system. But God knows how much more her acts will fuel mortal hatred and fear of our kind first." He tossed back the remainder of his drink and set the glass on the table. "Are you ready to try this thing?"

She stared into his eyes and thought that this insane experiment he was about to try wasn't going to work.

It couldn't possibly work.

They'd dropped anchor far from shore, in calm seas, away from shipping lanes, and an equal distance from the mainland and Haven Island, as they were calling it. She supposed it had a better ring to it than "the Isle of the Impaler," as she'd heard James refer to it.

"I'm not sure I'll ever be ready for this," she said, and she kept drinking as if there was strength in the bottom of the glass, even while walking beside him back across the deck and down the steps to lower level. They moved along the narrow hallway, past closed cabin doors and into the sitting room at the end. James had cleared off an oblong, gleaming hardwood table and set it in the center of the room. They couldn't have done this deed outside, where an errant sea breeze could blow the ashes of the great Utanapishtim away forever.

He laid the sculpture on the table and stood looking down at it, troubled. Lucy still wished she could convince him—or even herself—that this madness wasn't necessary. But she knew she couldn't. She'd tried. He was a man on a mission, and he believed the ends justified the means. He wouldn't go ahead with it otherwise, and she had to respect him for that.

Right then, he was torn. She could see it and wished she could ease his mind, so she decided a change of subject might be in order.

"I wonder how things are going on the island?"

He looked up from the statue and into her eyes, then past her, through a large porthole at the glittering starlit night sky and the rippling sodalite sea. "I'm worried about that, too. It's not that big an island, and there are a lot of vampires there."

"So many I couldn't keep all their names straight. Except the really unusual names, like that guy Reaper. And Briar. And Vixen."

"Many vampires take on new names once they've been made over. And many, if not most, use only one. It's the name by which they are known among their own kind, even while having to live under one false identity after another to escape detection in the world of man. One is supposed to grow old, to age, to die, after all."

She smiled, lowering her head. "So your father's name isn't really Edge?"

"It's Edgar," he said with a slow smile.

Her eyes rounded. "Edgar Poe?"

"He says his human parents had a warped sense of humor."

She laughed softly, sipping her drink again, knowing they were only putting off the inevitable: the moment when he would try to bring Utanapishtim, the first Noah, back to life. He was probably afraid he would fail. Just as she was afraid he would succeed. "How many do you suppose are on the island by now?"

He met her eyes again. "I don't know. A lot. And the more there are, the more supplies are needed. And the more often they have to make a run to the mainland, the more likely they are to be discovered, or even followed." Shaking his head slowly, he gazed out to sea again, opening the porthole to let the fresh air waft in. "They would be sitting ducks out there, if the vigilantes found them."

"They won't. Not with that fog trick of Rhiannon's."

He nodded. "I hope not. But even so, it's not a permanent solution."

Lucy stared out over the water, and the breeze lifted her hair from her shoulders. She turned to look at him beside her, only to find his eyes on her face, intense, searching. "What?" she asked.

"You're very beautiful. I haven't told you that, have I?"

Lowering her head, she said, "No."

"I've been so wrapped up in…in all of this," he said, with a wave of his hand toward the table. "I haven't even bothered…to thank you. Or to tell you that I…well, I like having you around. With me, I mean."

She lifted her gaze and her brows as one. "You do?"

"I've been thinking about how close we might be to…to finishing our work together. You've done everything I've asked you to do, and once we have Utanapishtim up and running and back on the island, with Damien to help us communicate with him, you'll be free to go. If that's what you want."

She looked away. "I don't have anywhere to go anymore, James."

"We can fix that. It's not even that big a challenge. We find out who did the shooting, we exercise some mind control to make him confess, we create an alibi for you, whatever it takes. We can give you back your life."

"You have been giving this some thought," she said, surprised to her core. "I appreciate that."

He nodded. "But the more thought I give it, the more I realize…I don't want you to go."

Blinking in shock, her eyes flew back to his, and she tried with everything in her to read them. The whiskey was warming her blood just a little, but not enough to make her see something that wasn't there. And she *did* see…something.

"I'll miss you, Lucy."

Warmth flooded her, right to her toes. "I'll…miss you, too," she whispered.

He curved his hand around the back of her neck, spread his fingers over her nape and drew her head closer to his, bending until his lips brushed over hers. And then he kissed her.

Feelings she had never known until she met this man—sizzling, electrical, yearning feelings—rushed through her veins like pure liquid fire. She let him kiss her, opening to him like a flower to the sunlight. This was primal, and this was right, and they would not be interrupted this time. She knew it, and she rejoiced in it. This had been a long time coming. There was no pretense of shyness or propriety, no hesitation. It was what they both wanted, and she wasn't going to pollute it with anything false. Whatever was coming to life between the two of them was pure, and it was real. And there was no way she would deny it, nor did she believe she could have, even if she'd wanted to.

She twisted her arms around his neck and kissed him back, letting herself be swept away by passion. James continued to cup the back of her head with one hand as their tongues tangled. He slid the other hand down over her back to her bottom, pulling her hips to his as he arched into her. Her stomach knotted in need and anticipation.

The boat's gentle rocking, the soft sounds of the sea water lapping against the hull, and the scent of salt water and fresh sea air, seemed to work as aphrodisiacs on her. It was all too beautiful, too perfect, and as they began tugging at each other's clothes and tossing them to the soft white carpeting beneath their feet, she knew life would never be this perfect again.

Tonight was once in a lifetime. Their lives were entirely different—opposite, really. Hers was the existence of a bookish, timid intellectual. His was the constant adventure of a true hero to his people. She'd done all right, she thought, in surviving for a short while in his world. But she'd managed only because she hadn't been given a choice.

She was a coward and would truly be far more comfortable in a dusty basement, studying cuneiform carvings on a jagged piece of ancient clay than running from enemies, saving lives, stealing artifacts and raising the dead.

"Lucy," he whispered, while kissing her neck and earlobe. "Stop thinking."

She smiled to herself. "I'm sorry. There's just so much—"

"Just feel. Just shut your mind off and feel, Lucy. Feel my touch. Feel what's happening to your body."

She closed her eyes and refocused, this time on sensation. His breath, warm on her neck, and the way it sent shivers of pleasure up her spine. His palm on the flat of her back, sliding beneath the tank top she wore, so it was skin on skin, his rough, hers smooth.

"That's it," he whispered. "That's all. Just feel."

He pushed her back against the wall and tugged the tank top up over her head, and she raised her arms to let him. The bra came next. And then he was pushing her jeans down, every movement of his hands a caress as he undressed her. His knuckles dragging over her hips, his fingertips trailing over her thighs, pausing to dance in the hollows behind her knees and making her suck in a breath. And then he stood staring at her naked breasts, his eyes raking them before his hands covered them. Rough palms on sensitive nipples. She tipped her head back and bit her lip.

"Oh, Lucy. My beautiful Lucy." He replaced his hands with his lips, and the sensations rippling through her made her gasp aloud. When he scraped his teeth over those yearning peaks, her knees nearly buckled.

But he didn't let them. He was right there, holding her upright as he sucked her breasts. She barely noticed him standing on the legs of her jeans to help her step out of them. Or pushing down her panties until they fell at her feet and she felt his hard, strong hands closing on her bare buttocks.

Then he slid one hand down between her thighs, parting and probing her there, while she gasped for air.

She clung to his neck, his shoulders, as if for dear life, and he slid his hands down the backs of her thighs and easily lifted her up, pulling her to him, sliding his erect shaft inside her, when she hadn't even been aware he had undressed. The breath rushed from her

lungs and her eyes slammed closed at the sensation of
him filling her. He was thick, stretching her to receive
him, pressing deeper and still deeper. Her sensitive
inner thighs were rubbed by the fine hairs and hard
muscle of his as he began to move, sliding out and in
again. His pace was slow as she clung to him, then
picked up as his body played hers like a maestro at
his chosen instrument. Higher and higher he made her
soar, as he drove into her harder and faster. She sank
her nails into his broad shoulders and felt unable to
get close enough to him. To be possessed fully enough
by him.

His mouth found her neck, and kissed and nibbled
upward to her chin, insisting she lower it so he could
feed from her lips again. When she did, his tongue
mimicked what their bodies were doing.

She cried out, but his kisses swallowed the sound,
and then everything in her seemed to explode in unbearable pleasure. Sensation reached critical mass,
then detonated, and the ripples that followed made her
body turn to liquid fire. Nothing but feeling existed
in her. She was entirely enveloped in the ecstasy of
physical pleasure, of release.

She was pure sensation. Just as he'd instructed.

She clung to him, limp and more satisfied than
she had ever been in her life, and he held her in his
arms, kissing her hair and her face, his arms so tight
around her that she felt like a tiny thing, all wrapped
up in strength. She wondered if a dusty university

basement, or even her own little house in Binghamton, could ever feel this secure, this safe.

This perfect.

And then their bliss was shattered by the sound of something clattering. They both turned to see the statue lying on the floor beside the table, and it must have hit a nearby chair on the way down, because it was broken in two at the neck.

"Hell!" James lowered her to her feet and turned, unashamedly naked, to pick it up. "It's okay." He looked inside one half, then the other. "It's all right, nothing spilled out. It's all in the lower half."

Self-conscious, cold and alone now, Lucy hurriedly gathered up her borrowed clothes. She pulled on the jeans, the tank top. Nothing underneath. She felt wild, untamed. Primal. Her hair blew as the ocean breeze picked up strength. She quickly turned to close the porthole, shutting out the wind.

"Thank you. We can't risk a sudden gust blowing away my people's savior."

"That's not going to happen," she said softly. And inwardly she thought it *couldn't* happen. Because *he* was his people's savior. Him, James William Poe. He was the one. And she was so proud of him that she felt her chest swelling with it before she reminded herself that she had no right to feel so proprietary. He didn't belong to her, nor she to him. They were two different people—different species, even—on totally opposite paths. This…this beautiful interlude was only that. A brief, magical oasis in the midst of chaos and war and death. And when it was over and peace had been restored, they would go their own ways and cherish the memory.

She would not have a single regret.

He met her eyes, part of the statue in each hand, and said, "It's time, Lucy."

She didn't ask him again if he was sure. She wouldn't insult him that way. She'd made her arguments. He'd made his choice. She wasn't even entirely sure he was wrong.

He turned to face the table. Lucy walked up to take her place beside him, determined to be of whatever help she could, for as long as this interlude might last.

James tipped one half of the broken statue up and poured its contents onto a crisp white bedsheet that he had spread over the table. Right in the center. Then he looked up at Lucy, standing directly across from him, and she held his eyes, biting her lip.

It had been good between them. He'd known it would be, had sensed that it would be fiery. Amazing. Special. More than just sex. But the reality of it had been even better than he had imagined. And he had been imagining it. A lot. Making love with Lucy had felt natural and easy, as instinctive as breathing— and yet at the same time exciting and thrilling almost beyond endurance. He liked sex with her. He liked holding her and kissing her. He liked her, period, and he thought it was mutual. But he was already sensing that she was…pulling back. Withdrawing from him. And he didn't know why.

She didn't have a clue what a gorgeous, sexy woman she was, he thought. She saw herself as the nerdy, buttoned-up professor.

Clueless to her own charms, really.

And right now she wanted to ask him not to do what he was about to do. But she was trying not to. He wondered if she knew how much he appreciated that.

It was quiet on the *Nightshade*. Dark. They'd turned off all the lights, except for a soft yellow night light, and shut down the engine, so they wouldn't draw any attention that might evolve into an interruption at the crucial moment of this miracle he was about to try to perform. Well, partly that. It was also partly a precaution to ensure that Utanapishtim wouldn't be startled if and when he woke up.

He knew that the ancient one would. His only fear was that he would raise some kind of mindless monster, like the corpses back in Byram.

He picked up the statue's head and shook it, to ensure any bits it might contain joined the rest. As he did, the wind picked out outside, howling past them and heaving the boat without warning. Lucy grabbed the table, and James grabbed Lucy, as they both lost their balance.

Then the boat stilled again, and she met his eyes, her own wide as she whispered, "What the hell was that?" She looked around as if expecting to see a ghost.

"Just a gust, Lucy. Just a gust. We're fine."

"Are you sure?" She looked at the ashes. "I mean, I didn't think I believed in gods and curses before now, but hell, I've been living with vampires for the past week. I've seen the dead raised and your sister blowing things up with her freaking eyes. Are you sure someone's not trying to tell you not to proceed?"

He drew a deep breath and opened his mouth to say of course he was sure, but then he didn't. Couldn't. "No," he said at length. "No, I'm not sure at all. But you know I have to do this, right?"

She drew a steadying breath and nodded once, firmly. "Yes. I know."

"Ready?"

She had painstakingly drawn lines of cuneiform on a piece of paper, spelling the words *Friends* and *Safe*, to show the Ancient One when he awoke, but James knew she couldn't hope to write out entire conversations without several hours—if not days—and a half dozen reference books by her side. This was going to have to do until they managed to get the Old One to Gilgamesh, which they could do in less than an hour's time.

"I'm as ready as I'll ever be," she said.

Nodding, James opened his hands and extended his arms, holding them palms down over the small pile of ash and bone fragments. He stared at the dust on the table, and he willed the power to rise up from within him, to surge up from the earth far below, up through the ocean water, up through the hull of the boat, into the bottoms of his feet and up through his body. He willed the power to rain down from the white light somewhere in the universe, through the atmosphere and the sky, through the boat's cabin and upper deck, and to enter through the top of his head to beam down into his body. He visualized the energies meeting in his solar plexus, swirling together and blazing ever more brightly, shooting as one up to the very center of his chest and then splitting into twin beams that shot into his shoulders, down his arms and into his hands. He visualized portals opening in his palms to let that light out, and he felt his palms heat and tingle in response.

And then the glow began to emanate from his hands.

He watched, unable to look away as the ashes seemed to absorb the light. To glow with it themselves, and then to demand more. It felt as if the ashes were sucking the light from his hands, rather than simply receiving it. It was a startling feeling. Entirely different from the way he usually felt during a healing.

He thought about stopping, right then, breaking the contact, stopping the flow. But he was mesmerized by then, and dying to see what would happen next. Then the ashes began to crawl like microscopic bugs. He thought he was imagining it at first, the movement was so slight, as if each granule had somehow come to life and begun to wriggle, to squirm. Were his eyes playing tricks on him? Or was it real?

"Something's happening," Lucy whispered.

Okay, it was real. She saw it, too. And then he knew it was true with even more certainty, because those granules were skittering across the sheet, moving apart, spreading out, forming a sort of oblong shape… and then spreading out more, as he recognized the picture they were drawing.

Ash—flat, one-dimensional ash—painted itself outward from the shape he now realized was a human torso. And it continued moving, growing, expanding, shaping itself into arms and legs and a head.

"It's like some kind of demon-possessed Etch A Sketch," Lucy muttered.

James nodded, unable to take his eyes off the spectacle unfolding before him, beneath his hands, which were pulsing now with white heat. He willed the power to keep flowing, even though it was starting to take an incredible effort. He pushed the light outward, and the shape, the drawing, began to rise up from the sheet, growing thicker, taking on three dimensions, filling out. Fingers took form, the features of a human face growing clear. The ash was multiplying itself, there was no question. There was far more now than there had been before.

And now a body lay on the table, an ash-gray body that seemed as if it would disintegrate if he so much as touched it. So he didn't. He kept his hands hovering just above it, lifting them higher as the body thickened, and still he kept channeling that light. It felt as if the body on the table was sucking him dry, and yet he pushed on.

The ash grew denser, its texture changing now, color seeming to bleed into it from the very room around them. He saw translucent skin, fingernails and deep black strands of hair writhing from the head. And deep inside that conglomeration of ash, James saw the bleached white of bone appearing, then vanishing again beneath the pink of muscle, the blue of veins twisting and swirling into shape like a thousand tiny snakes scurrying to take their places. Organs appeared, purple and healthy. The heart formed, and then suddenly, with a powerful sucking of energy from his hands, that heart began beating.

Beating!

Tha-thump. Tha-thump. Tha-thump.

"Oh, my God," Lucy whispered.

James knew without looking that her head came up then. He felt her tearing her gaze from the miracle taking place on the table between them to look at him. He felt her attention, but he couldn't return it. He was locked on to what he was doing, and he couldn't stop. What was most alarming was that he tried to. And couldn't. It was as if he'd grabbed hold of a live wire, and now it was feeding from him, controlling him so he could not let go.

The figure's skin turned opaque, then pink and then copper, and then eyebrows sprouted, thick and black. Lashes curled from the eyelids. A shadow of beard appeared.

"James, are you all right?"

He couldn't answer her. He couldn't speak. He finally managed, with great effort, to rip his eyes from the powerful naked body on the table between them and look into hers. Without the ability to speak, he tried to tell her that he was dying. That this was going to kill him. That this creature was draining the very life force from his body. And that he was sorry for that—sorry for leaving her behind.

Lucy's eyes widened, and she reached down, grabbed James by the wrists and pulled upward with all her might, grunting with the effort.

The grip of the creature was broken all at once. James flew backward, as if released from a powerful grasp without warning. He hit the wall and sank to the floor, and then he just lay there, gasping for breath, trembling with muscle fatigue and weakness.

Lucy raced around the table, and leaned over him, her eyes searching his face, one hand pressing to his cheek. "James, my God, you're white as a sheet! Are you all right? Please, say something."

He stared at her, trying to gather his wits, to catch his breath, to form words. He was shaking right to the very core. And then his attention was caught by what was happening behind her.

As he stared, riveted, the body on the table slowly sat up. Its eyes opened, black as the night itself, staring straight ahead and then scanning the room, taking in everything all at once. It got to its feet and looked down at itself, naked, copper-skinned. Massive. It opened and closed its hands, staring at them as if in wonder, and then it turned its vivid onyx eyes on James, met his stare, held it.

And James couldn't look away.

Until the creature, the five-thousand-year-old thing that James Poe had somehow raised from ash, tipped back its head, its long ebony hair trailing down its back. And then, its face contorting in some kind of unspeakable anguish, it released a roar that was deafening in both decibel level and in the utter agony it contained.

17

Lucy had never in her entire life been as terrified as she was when she heard that blood-curdling roar and realized that James had done the impossible.

Frozen in fear, she almost couldn't move. But she had to move. *It* was right behind her. She forced herself to turn, to face it.…

Her eyes fell upon a hairless, powerful, naked chest, then rose as she tipped her head back, her gaze rising over thick neck, shoulders bulging with muscle and a face that was undeniably human. And Middle Eastern. And furious as it stared back at her.

No. Not it. Him. He was a man, and his expression looked like one of pain. Emotional pain, perhaps. Maybe physical, too. Who knew? She dug in her pocket for the paper she'd scribbled on earlier, the lines that spelled out the words for *friends* and *safe* in cuneiform. She sent up a silent prayer that she had accurately matched the form of the text to the period during which this man had lived, or at least to one close enough to it that it would be recognizable to him.

Then again, according to legend, his life had spanned so many years that he could be familiar with the styles of several different periods. He had been the first immortal, after all. She used to think the Sumerian myths she'd studied and taught—about the flood survivor, the Epic of Gilgamesh—were just that: myths. But now she knew they were real. All of them, real. Even she couldn't deny that any longer. Not with Utanapishtim, the Flood Survivor, standing right in front of her.

She unfolded the paper even as he stared at her, and then at James, behind her. James scrambled to his feet then, gripping her shoulders and trying to get between her and the creature, but she shook her head. "No, no. He's not going to hurt me." She held up the paper, held it toward the ancient one's face, and she made her voice as gentle as she could. "We're friends, Utanapishtim. Friends." She pointed at the symbols as she said the word.

Scowling, he snatched the sheet from her hands, staring at it, blinking, but more interested in the paper, its thinness, its texture, than the words she'd written.

"You…" He jabbed a finger toward James, ignoring her. "You…" he said, then slapped his own chest. "This?"

"Good God, he speaks English!" Lucy was stunned. "How is that possible?"

Utanapishtim's eyes narrowed on her. "I…" He tapped his ears with his palms.

"Hear?" she asked.

"Mmm. I hear. Long time." He cleared his throat, his voice hoarse, no doubt because he hadn't spoken for thousands of years.

"He wasn't dead," James said softly. "My God, he wasn't dead at all. The tablet says that the punishment from the gods for breaking their edict that he never share his immortality with anyone was that he would die, yet remain immortal."

Utanapishtim nodded slowly. "Im…prisoned."

Imprisoned, Lucy thought. All those years he'd been conscious, aware within the prison of that stone statue.

Utanapishtim's eyes dampened, but they were also wild, frightening. "How…long?"

"Five thousand years, maybe more," James said softly.

The man only stared blankly at him, then shifted his gaze to Lucy, as if awaiting her explanation, and she realized he had no way of knowing what a year was, much less what their numbering system meant. "A year is…a sun cycle. From planting to growing, then to harvest, to resting and to planting again. That's one year." She held up a single finger to show him one.

"Mmm. What is…five tousun?"

She blinked and lowered her eyes. Then she found her pencil and started writing on the sheet of paper.

Utanapishtim watched with great interest as she drew
the Sumerian symbols for 5000 on paper, no doubt
curious that she wasn't engraving them on wet clay
with a stylus reed.

If he was this impressed by a simple pencil and
paper, Lucy thought, he was going to be overwhelmed
when he saw actual modern technology.

Unsure whether it was wise, but convinced he
had a right to know, she showed him what she had
written.

His eyes shot to hers, then back to the number again
and he shook his head in disbelief.

"I know it's shocking."

"Aiee, so long!" He shook his head in denial. And
then he closed his eyes and backed up to the wall,
hugging himself, and rocking, and chanting in his
own tongue.

Lucy started toward him, but James stopped her
with a hand on her shoulder when she was still a few
feet beyond the reach of Utanapishtim's powerful
arms. "We will help you, Utanapishtim." She spoke
carefully, enunciating each word. "We will. I know
it will be hard, but—"

He was completely unresponsive.

"Why don't we give him some space, some time?
Maybe something to eat?" James suggested.

The huge man moaned deep in his chest and continued muttering. It sounded to Lucy like a series of
prayers. Repetitive, but beautiful.

James took her arm, leading her out of the room and pulled the door closed behind them.

"No," she said, covering his hand on the doorknob before he'd finished. "Leave it open. If it's true what he said—"

"You're right. He's been imprisoned long enough."

"Too long," she whispered.

Leaving the door open, they went up the stairs to the deck above, leaving the ancient man, the first Noah and the first immortal, to his misery. Lucy realized there was no way for her to measure what Utanapishtim must be feeling. No way she could even try. He wasn't from her culture; his ways of thinking were entirely alien to her. Even if she could guess how she might feel waking up after five thousand years trapped inside a stone statue, essentially buried alive, conscious but immobile and blind—even if she could somehow wrap her mind around that, it still would not bring her even remotely close to what Utanapishtim was feeling.

And then her attention shifted completely when James took a step and collapsed to his knees.

"James!"

She crouched down next to him, her hands on his shoulders, her eyes searching his face, but it wasn't easy, with his head hanging so low. She pressed a hand to his cheek. "What is it? Was it the resurrection?"

He nodded but didn't speak.

"It drained you, didn't it?" she asked, but it wasn't really a question. "I knew it. I could see it. It was as if you were bleeding your own energy into him, as if he were taking your life to restore his own." Then she blinked, stunned by what she had said. "He truly was the first vampire. Only it was life itself, not blood, he needed to survive."

"To *re*vive, at least. There was no mention in the writings of him having to drain anything from anyone to stay alive. He was normal, a day walker, an omnivore, just an immortal one, as far as we know, until the gods cursed him for sharing his gift."

"For creating the vampire race," she muttered, sitting down on the deck beside him, leaning back, closing her eyes.

"Do you really believe that? That my race, my people, are so evil that the gods would punish the man who created the first of them?"

"Of course I don't." She straightened and looked him in the eye, insisting he see that she hadn't meant it that way. "I've seen your people, James. I've met them. I know they're not evil."

"Thank you for that," he said, watching her face.

"It's nothing but the truth. However, we have to remember that we're dealing with a superstitious man from a time and place where everything from a scorpion sting to a toothache was considered sent by the gods or by demons. Everything was a reward or a punishment to the ancient Sumerians. And I'm telling you, James, that is what he's going to believe, or perhaps what he already does."

James stared at the open hatch, the stairs beyond

it. "I wonder if he knew, when he gave the gift to Gilgamesh, that it would cost him his soul," he whispered. "Or that the great king and every immortal who came after him would need to feed on human blood in order to stay alive? Or that they would only be able to live by night?"

"I wonder if he knew there would be others at all," Lucy said. "He may have assumed Gilgamesh would keep the gift to himself, not share it and create an entire undead, immortal race."

"He vowed to...share not the gift."

They both looked up fast, Lucy shooting to her feet and away from the hatch door as if it had burned her. Utanapishtim was standing there, halfway up the steps, staring at them. He was completely naked and apparently unconcerned about it as he came up the last three steps, onto the deck itself. His hairy thighs were like tree trunks, and he towered over her, standing six-five at the very least.

James got to his feet and stepped between the two of them.

Utanapishtim seemed to search the night sky, probably for the correct words to speak. "I meant not to make...immortal race."

"I know that," Lucy said softly. "But it happened all the same."

"I gave...only to my king."

"Yes."

"He swore...only Enkidu, he said."

"Enkidu was already dead," Lucy explained. "The

king could not bring him back. But when someone else he loved was about to die, he…"

"He…" At a loss for the right word, Utanapishtim mimed snapping something in two.

"Broke," Lucy said.

"Mmm. Broke. He broke his promise," Utanapishtim moaned. "For that…I have…" He grimaced as if in pain.

"Suffered," Lucy said. "You have suffered terribly. But it wasn't a punishment sent by the gods. There is another reason for your suffering."

"No other…reason. I saw…Great Flood. Felt its… waters. I know the Anunaki." He looked at her face, and then at the sea and sky around them. "Do not taunt them, woman. The gods hear all."

Lowering her head, she wondered how she would ever convince a man from ages past to understand science and logic, when all he'd ever known were superstition and magic. To him, the flood itself was proof the gods existed. To her, it was just a flood, brought about by a period of global warming and the partial melting of the glaciers.

And yet, how could she explain Utanapishtim's immortality? The fact that he spoke and understood English alone was testimony that what he said was true: that he'd been conscious on some level, even while his body had been reduced to ash. For centuries the sculpture in which he'd been entrapped had been in the possession of an American collector. English had been spoken all around him for generations, until the last heir left the naked priest king to his favorite museum.

If Utanapishtim wasn't immortal, how had that happened?

"My...offspring. You call...vahmpeer."

"Vampire," she said.

"Drinkers of...blood. Like demon Lilith."

Lucy shook her head quickly. This was just the sort of interpretation she'd been afraid he would begin to put on things. "No. No, Utanapishtim. The vampires do not harm anyone. They are good people. Good people, Utanapishtim."

He didn't seem convinced of that. "Yet you are not...vahmpeer?"

"No. I'm as you were. Before the gift of the gods, before the flood."

He nodded, then shifted his black eyes to James. "You?"

"My father is a vampire. My mother only half."

"I know not...half," Utanapishtim said.

Lucy was amazed at the hunger for knowledge she glimpsed in those opaque black-fringed eyes. She held her hands out, palms up. "Vampire," she said, raising one open palm. "Human," she said, and raised the other. Then she cupped her hands together.

Utanapishtim grunted, nodding, and sat down on the deck. Then he put a hand on his stomach. "My... hunger burn like fire. My—" He tapped his head.

"Brain? Head? Mind?"

"Mmm, mind. My mind hungers also. You have... tablets?"

"Books?"

"I do not know books." Utanapishtim sighed, frustrated, and lowered his head into his hands.

"I'll show him," James said. "Though hearing our spoken language all those years won't help you much with learning to read our writing, Utanapishtim."

Utanapishtim, however, was still holding his head, and nodding it up and down, hands completely covering his face. He was once again muttering in Sumerian.

"I'll find food," Lucy said, sending a quick look farther along the deck, to where a second set of stairs led down to the galley. "James, why don't you find him some clothes, and...some books."

In the midst of his muttering, Utanapishtim lifted his head from his hands long enough to command, "Be fast, woman."

Lucy was surprised by the order, but she reminded herself that he had been a king once. He was bound to expect his orders to be followed, his authority to be respected. "Yes. I'll be as fast as I can." She took three steps, then paused to send a worried look back at James.

He stood tall and strong, as he had done ever since Utanapishtim surprised them. She knew he was determined not to reveal his weakened state to the other... man. And he'd been doing such a good job of it that he had momentarily even managed to make her forget.

But he'd been on his knees only moments ago, weakened, his energy drained by the first immortal.

And yet he stood there, looking as strong as he always was. And she knew why. He didn't want Utanapishtim getting the idea that he could get away with anything. For Lucy's sake, he needed to meet the man as an equal.

With her eyes, Lucy asked James if he was going to be all right, darting a meaningful glance Utanapishtim's way.

James caught her look, read her meaning and winked. "Be fast, woman."

She smiled, admiring him more than she ever had before. Of the two men, James was the one with the aura of leadership about him. Quiet authority, confidence in his own power. She felt better, suddenly, about leaving him with the hulking, confused, living, breathing artifact and hurried on her way.

James watched the Ancient One for a long moment before nodding and taking him below again, where he went through drawers until he found a pair of jeans big enough for the man. He held them out, and Utanapishtim looked at them, then tipped his head in an inquisitive way. "What is?"

"To wear. To, um, cover yourself." James gestured at the khakis he wore.

Utanapishtim looked at James's pants, then at the jeans he was holding out and his expression turned to one of horror. "No! It will…bind my—" He didn't know the word, so he grabbed his genitals and shook them with a low growl.

James felt his brows arch and tried not to show his amusement. "Maybe some sort of a…toga?"

"I know not…toe-gah."

Sighing, James pulled the bedsheet from the table and held it up. "Better?" He watched the other man's face, saw it relax in relief.

"Better," Utanapishtim said, pronouncing the *t*'s harder than James had as he took the sheet. He inspected the fabric, then nodded with approval.

Good, James thought. He didn't yet know the extent of this being's powers. It wouldn't do to piss him off. Besides, he needed Utanapishtim's help. And yet he kept finding feelings of hostility toward the old one bubbling up from some unseen well in his gut. Why?

Who was he kidding? He knew why. He'd seen the way Utanapishtim had looked at Lucy. Pure male appreciation, and probably no small amount of curiosity about her, her bearing, her clothing, her ponytail. Probably best to deal with it now, before Utanapishtim got any ideas about her.

"Utanapishtim," James said.

The ancient one, who was expertly wrapping the sheet around himself, creating a one-shouldered toga without even a knot or a pin, stopped and looked at James.

"I raised you from ash." As James said the words, he picked up half of the broken statue, running his fingertips inside to show the old one the ashen residue there.

"Mmm. Woman—seer woman—find me. Burn me. To...protect me, she sayed. But I...feel it. I feel the fire." He closed his eyes as a full body shudder racked him.

Not only buried alive, but burned alive first. "I am sorry," James said.

Utanapishtim grunted, nodding and continuing to clothe himself.

"Nonetheless," James went on, "know this, Utanapishtim. I was the one who found you. I used my power to restore you to life, to give you back your body."

"You...power?" Utanapishtim asked, his attention now caught.

"Yes. My power." James looked at his hands. "I can...heal the sick, raise the dead, with my hands."

Utanapishtim's eyes narrowed. "You...give me you power."

"No. I cannot."

"I take you power!" The huge man surged forward, reaching for James.

James dodged him and held up his hand like a weapon. "I freed you from that statue that was your prison. I can put you right back in there."

Utanapishtim stopped in his tracks and looked at James, his eyes widening. Then, slowly, he nodded his surrender. "What...want you...from me? Why you find me? Raise me?"

"Many things, Utanapishtim. Many things. But one thing first. That woman…" James pointed in the direction Lucy had taken. "She is my woman."

Utanapishtim held his gaze, his own slowly easing from one of dark fury to something that might have been…teasing? "The right of the king—"

"You're not a king anymore, Utanapishtim. You're a man who needs me. You need me to help you find your way in this world. It is nothing like the world you knew. And I will help you—if *you* will help *me*." James lifted a hand, forefinger pointing in a way that every male of every age would understand, then picked up half the broken artifact in his other hand. "But if you touch my woman, I'll put you right back inside this statue forever," he said.

Utanapishtim narrowed his eyes and leaned slightly down, bringing him nose to nose with James. "You… brave. You challenge me—as Enkidu did Gilgamesh. But you…weak. Cannot fight me…now."

James looked up, frowning. How did Utanapishtim know? Could he sense the weakness he himself was trying so hard not to reveal? He added extra-sensory perception to his mental list of the old one's powers.

"You raise me," Utanapishtim said with a slow nod. "If I…desire…you woman, I will…allow you…fight me for…own her." He bowed as if he had bestowed a great gift.

"Utanapishtim, we don't own women anymore. They are equal to men in this time. They are free to come and go as they please, to choose the man they wish to be with."

The ancient one's face split into a smile. "You... James of the Vahmpeers. You make me to laugh."

"It's not a joke."

Utanapishtim chuckled aloud, slamming James on the back with one hand. "Woman. Free to choose. Ahahaha! Why she choose any man, then?" He laughed some more, then caught his breath, swiping a tear from the corner of one eye. "Keep you woman, James of the Vahmpeers. You are freed me prison and made me to laugh. You are worthy to you Loo-see."

It was going to be a long, slow, uphill battle, teaching this guy, James thought miserably. Oh, not the language. He was speeding along on that. But the twenty-first century? No way. This once-great priest king was in for one hell of a culture shock.

"Now, show me...this." Utanapishtim turned toward the television set, eyeing it.

"I don't think you're ready just yet, my friend. But let me try to explain."

Utanapishtim held up a hand for silence, moving toward the flat screen and placing his palms on it. As he did, he closed his eyes for a long moment, and when he opened them again, he whispered, "Ahhhh. Is magic." He walked directly to the remote control on the wall, picked it up and eyed it for a moment, and then he aimed it at the TV set and turned it on.

James stood there gaping. "How...how did you—?"

"Like you...I am...power. I...take inside by..." He pressed his palms together.

"By touching?"

"Mmm. Touching. Yes. I touching and I...I...what word? What word?" He spotted a book on a stand and went to it. He held the book, which was about yachting, between his palms and closed his eyes, and when he opened them again, mere seconds later, he nodded once. "Now all this," he said, opening the book and fanning the pages, staring at them in wonder as he did. "All this." He snapped the book closed again. "In here," he said, tapping his head with the other hand.

"Just like that?"

"I...take."

"You absorb knowledge by touching. Like a sponge absorbs water."

"Ahh. Yes. I touch. I take. Absorb. Good word. Knowledge, yes. Words. Power."

"Power?" That was amazing, James thought, what he'd just demonstrated. But what did he mean by that last part? He could absorb power by touching? What kind of power did he mean, or was he even using the word correctly? And what other abilities might he possess? "Do you have any other...powers, Utanapishtim?" James asked.

Utanapishtim looked away. "I hunger. And I... want up there." He pointed toward the ceiling. "Out. Open."

Nodding, James decided he'd best tackle one topic at a time. Utanapishtim wasn't going to tell him any more than he wanted to anyway. It was clear the man wasn't going to have any trouble learning—not if he could absorb knowledge by touch. God, that was amazing.

At least they'd settled the issue of a hands-off policy where Lucy was concerned.

He understood the man's desire to be outside, beneath the stars, after five thousand years in captivity, so he led his newly resurrected guest back to the upper deck, where they sat in chairs, but only after Utanapishtim spent a few minutes studying his. They stared out at the waves rippling beneath the starry sky, smelling the aroma of sizzling beef wafting up from the galley, and James said, "I wish to tell you why I raised you, Utanapishtim."

Utanapishtim gave a regal nod.

"There is a prophecy—a story written from very long ago—that says my people will be destroyed. That they will be…no more."

"Did vahmpeer anger the Anunaki?" Utanapishtim asked.

"No. It is an enemy who will destroy them. Not the gods. The prophecy says that only you, Utanapishtim, can save us. That is why I brought you back."

Utanapishtim considered his words for a long moment, and then he spoke at last. "It is for the gods to decide."

"But they are your people, too," James said.

"I know not…vahmpeer. I know not…they worthy. The Anunaki know."

"It is written that—only you can save us, Utana-pishtim."

The ancient one shook his head. "I...defy gods. I...suffer. No. I no anger Anunaki again." And in that moment he looked more like a frightened, battered, abused child than a mighty immortal king and father of the undead.

Lucy arrived with a large tray bearing three plates of food. Steaks, potatoes, green peas. There were napkins, silverware, ice-filled glasses and a pitcher of water. She set the tray on the nearest table, and before she could move to hand Utanapishtim a plate, he had snatched the steak right off one, then shifted it lightly and quickly from one hand to the other, in deference to its heat.

Lucy handed a plate to James, then took her own. Sinking into a nearby chair, she began to eat, using her fork and steak knife, all the while watching the king use his fingers.

Utanapishtim tore off a bite of the steak, chewing, swallowing, nodding. "Good," he growled, and devoured more. He finished every bite, gulped down his water, belched loudly, then sat back in his seat. "Good woman," he said at length, speaking not to her but to James, and adding. "You chosen well." Then, looking at Lucy, he said, "I given you for James of the Vahmpeers," he told her. "Serve him well, woman."

Lucy choked on her steak, and James jumped up and slammed her on the back, twice, until a piece of meat came flying out of her mouth.

She stared at Utanapishtim, wide-eyed. Then she looked at James, who shrugged and said, "I tried to explain things to him. He thought I was joking."

She lowered her head, smiling to herself.

That was not the reaction he had expected, James thought as he watched the reactions cross her face, and then he forgot to think anything. God, she was beautiful. Okay, okay, he was getting off track. He dragged his attention back to the conversation. "You're not indignant?" he asked her.

"Why would I be? He's only a reflection of the society in which he lived. No, I was just thinking how interesting it's going to be when he meets Rhiannon."

James winced at the thought, which instigated another. "Not to mention my sister. I hope to God she doesn't blow him up."

"I know not 'blow him up,'" Utanapishtim said. "But I know 'sister,' James of the Vahmpeers. She is like you, yes?"

"Brigit is…nothing like me."

18

By the time he finished his third plate of food, Lucy was relieved to see Utanapishtim finally beginning to slow down. Maybe his stomach was nearing maximum capacity. She had cooked almost everything in the galley and was honestly running out of options. They were only about an hour from the island, and the sun was rising far away on the eastern horizon, a fiery red-orange ball just beginning to emerge as if from the watery depths.

Utanapishtim set his food aside as he caught sight of the sun. His eyes took on a distant, reverent look, and he rose from his chair and moved to the rail. Facing the rising sun, he opened his arms wide and began to speak in an ancient Sumerian dialect. His tone was different from when he spoke to either of them. It was softer, submissive, maybe even fearful. Brushstrokes of blazing yellow and orange painted his face in light. Tears dampened his velvet black lashes as he stared into the sunrise.

"Utu agrunta è-ani, igisha ganeshè…"

"What's he saying?" James asked, leaning closer to Lucy and speaking very softly.

"This is amazing," she whispered. "Hearing it spoken—God, I never imagined… This is beyond belief."

"Yes, I know, but what is he saying?"

Lucy strained to understand the words, seeing them phonetically in her mind, trying to recall translations. "It's hard, I'm used to translating from looking at the text, not hearing it aloud."

"Igi sha gane shè hé-em shi bar re…"

"It's a prayer—to the sun god, Utu," she whispered. "May the sun god, rising from the watery deep… um…open his beautiful eye upon me. When the king raises his head…to heaven, may all praise him duly when he lifts his eyes…and his glance flashes…like lightning."

Utanapishtim lowered his hands, folded his arms across his chest, forming an X over his heart, a fist on each shoulder, and he bowed his head. Then he stood in silence for a moment.

"We have to be careful with him, James," Lucy whispered. "He still sees himself as a king, the chosen one of the gods. And we have no idea what powers he has."

"I know a few."

She shot James a look, her eyes wide. "You do?"

"Lucy, it's amazing. He can absorb knowledge,

everything contained in a book—or even a device—just by laying his hands on it."

"What do you mean, even a device?" she asked.

"He put his hands on the TV for five seconds, and then he was using the remote and channel surfing. And I've been watching him touch things. He's been through every book in the library. He's touched the engines of this boat."

"My God, that's amazing."

"Yeah, and it's not all. He keeps trying to touch me, Lucy, but I've been dodging him."

"Why?"

"He said he could absorb words, information, knowledge...and...power."

She frowned, seeing the worry in James's eyes. "You realize his English is—"

"Amazing, and getting better by the minute," James said. "Not perfect, though, so I'm guessing it's the ideas, information, rather than grammar and syntax, he absorbs from the books. But before that, when I told him I'd used my healing power to raise him, he asked me to give my power to him, and when I said I couldn't, he said he would take it and he came at me."

She frowned hard, shooting another look at Utanapishtim. "How did you avoid him?"

"Threatened to put him right back in that damned statue. I was bluffing, but apparently I've got a good poker face."

"Hell." She thinned her lips. "He could be dangerous."

"I have no doubt he is," James said. "We've just got to get him on our side—and find out what other powers he has."

"And what his vulnerabilities are, as well," Lucy added. "The sun clearly isn't one of them." She found it very odd that she could so easily take her eyes from a man who was a walking, talking archaeological find and yet get so easily trapped in James's deep blue eyes. She was lost there then, though he was unaware of it.

"If anything, he seems to be drawing strength from it," he said, watching Utanapishtim and in the process giving her time to adjust her focus before he caught her staring at him in what probably looked like abject adoration.

She shook it off. "We need to get him to the island. He'll have time to get his bearings today, before everyone rises. And by nightfall maybe we'll have softened him up about whether to help us or not. And then, once he meets them, they'll win him over. Just like they did me."

"I agree."

She was staring at him again. Dammit.

He must have sensed her gaze, because he met it faster than she could look away, and his lips pulled into a tender smile. "We really did it, didn't we?"

"We? *You* did it, James. I was barely any help at all."

He shook his head slowly, pressing a palm to her cheek. "I couldn't have done it without you. If I manage to save my people, Lucy, it will be because you helped me. I wouldn't even have known where to find Utanapishtim's remains without your help. I can't begin to figure out a way to thank you."

She felt her blood rushing to her face and had to lower her eyes. But her smile would not be contained. "We're not finished yet, James. But I promise, when all this is over, I will come up with a way for you to repay me."

"It won't be enough."

She raised her head again and met his eyes as he went on.

"Whatever you ask for, it won't be enough," he said, and his eyes were darkening, sliding over her face and lingering on her lips. He bent closer, his lips brushing hers, and she swayed against his body.

Utanapishtim shouted as if in pain.

They pulled apart, startled. The old one was holding his head between his hands, his eyes closed tightly. "By the teeth of Enki, what is that?"

They rushed to his side. "Tell me what's happening to you, Utanapishtim," James said, his tone respectful but strong.

"Pain. Cries. Shouts. Voices, many voices. Entire worlds shout my ears all together. It…aiee, it loud!"

"We're nearer the mainland than we've been so far," Lucy said. They were moving alongside a peninsula jutting out from the mainland, and the island was just beyond.

"They die! They burning! I feel they pain!" Utanapishtim shouted.

"It's the vampires!" James shouted. "The ones being burned in their homes. They're his offspring, and he's connected mentally."

Utanapishtim had fallen to his knees by then, and James fell beside him, put his hands on the man's shoulders—in spite of the risk, Lucy thought in awe— and closed his eyes. "Focus on me, Utanapishtim. Maybe I can help you."

As Utanapishtim opened his eyes and met James's steady gaze, Lucy saw James's expression change from worry and concern to extreme pain. Whatever Utanapishtim was feeling, James was feeling it, too.

James grimaced in pain, but, grating his teeth, he managed to whisper, "Hundreds of them are dying by fire. Some…burning alive. Others running from the buildings into the killing rays of the rising sun. And Brigit—"

"Brigit?" Lucy slid a hand over the nape of James's neck. "Where is Brigit? What's happening to her?"

But James only grunted in pain, and then his hands began to glow. He looked down at them, where they were pressed to Utanapishtim's shoulders, and he seemed surprised. He moved to pull them away, but Utanapishtim closed his own hands over them, holding them there.

The glow brightened, and then it died as James

broke free, stumbling away from the big man and falling to the deck.

"What just happened, James?" Lucy asked.

Breathless, he said, "I don't know."

The sun rose higher, Utanapishtim's face easing as his tense muscles uncoiled. He sank to the deck beside James, his back against the railing. Lucy crouched in front of him.

"It's over," James said. "It's over. The voices have stopped."

He addressed Utanapishtim. "Those were the voices of your offspring, Utanapishtim. Your people. My people. But now it's day. They must sleep by day, and their voices go silent until nightfall. By then, I will have taught you how to block out the voices you do not wish to hear."

Utanapishtim nodded, still holding his head as if it ached. "But they...burning."

"Yes."

"Explain," Utanapishtim commanded.

Nodding, James said, "Humans, ordinary men, have learned of the existence of the vampires—your children, Utanapishtim—for the first time. Some want to wipe your people from existence, and so they wait for sunrise, when your children are helpless, and then they set fire to their homes. Even by day, a vampire will wake when being burned alive. He will feel the pain until he has burned to dust and nothing remains. It is...it is quick. But it is a horrible death, all the same."

Utanapishtim lowered his head and held up a fore-finger. "One voice calls for help, still."

"Yes, I hear it, too. It's my sister's voice. It's Brigit."

Lucy went rigid. "Where is she, James?"

"That way," he said, lifting an arm and pointing away from the sunrise, toward the hazy coastline visible in the distance. "The mainland."

Lucy raced up the steps onto the bridge, right up to the helm, and hoped she'd picked up enough from watching James and Willem to pilot the yacht herself.

She pushed the throttle forward.

As the wind blew her hair behind her, she wondered who this woman was, coming to life inside her? Because she was angry, whoever she was. Angry and ready to fight to protect Brigit, a woman she barely knew, and to avenge the innocent dead.

Something new and exciting was happening inside her. Something far removed from the cowering, frightened woman she had been before. The one who hid from trouble, avoided confrontation and protected herself above all else.

As she looked below and met James's eyes as he stared up at her from the deck, she thought he had a lot to do with the changes going on inside her. He was a hero in his own time. The kind of man who would become a legend, the kind they would write stories and songs about in the future. He was the salvation of his kind, even though his kind were a kind she'd never known existed.

He was amazing. And he made her want to be amazing, too. More than that, he was looking at her as if he thought she already was. But she knew she wasn't. She wanted to be, though. She wanted to be worthy of the look in his eyes. She didn't think she ever had been, never in her life. And she wondered if she was kidding herself to think she could ever be worthy of standing beside a man like him.

And that was sad beyond measure. Because even though he was different, not quite human, she was pretty sure she was in love with him.

Lucy piloted the boat with James watching over her, correcting her errors, giving instructions. But mostly he and Utanapishtim focused on their sense of Brigit. They sat side by side, only acknowledging her when she needed to correct course, and then often only by lifting an arm, pointing a finger. Lucy was almost jealous of the connection James and Brigit seemed to share. She'd been feeling her own burgeoning bond with James, but this was different. This was a bond of blood and more. It went to the cellular level. They were family, those two. And their bond was far stronger than the link she shared with James because of the Belladonna Antigen.

She couldn't read his thoughts. He could read hers, though, she reminded herself. Sure, he'd promised he wouldn't pry, and she believed him. Still, she carefully avoided thinking too much about her feelings for him or, God forbid, the L word. Even though he was far too busy right now to notice either of those things floating around inside her mind.

As they neared shore, she looked for a suitable place to leave the yacht, and spotted a rocky outcropping that seemed isolated and a bit wild. A lighthouse stood there, but there was no town close at hand.

"I'm going to take us in there," she said, pointing.

James finally blinked out of his stupor long enough to meet her eyes, and then to look where she was pointing.

"No, don't. There's a lighthouse, so there'll be rocks too. We're better off anchoring farther off shore. We can take the dinghy in."

She nodded and reduced speed, finally cutting the engine altogether when he signaled that she'd gone far enough.

Then, James turned to Utanapishtim. "This is a different world than you have ever known, Utanapishtim. More importantly, it's a world at war—anyone who appears different is under suspicion and liable to be attacked. And you're dressed…in a way that makes you stand out. It would be better for you to stay here, to wait for us to return with Brigit."

Utanapishtim met his eyes, looking stunned. "What king will…hide…safe, while his soldiers fight?"

"Actually, all of them, nowadays," Lucy muttered. "But it wasn't the case in your time, was it?"

"In my time, you, woman, would to be stayed behind. Safe."

"I've spent most of my life staying safe," she said. And then she shot a look James's way. "No more."

James stared at her, searching her face as if sensing a change.

And he ought to. She felt as if her entire worldview were in the midst of a great upheaval, the results of which were only beginning to settle in, changing who she was, what she was, right to the marrow.

"Make no mistake, Lucy, I will keep you safe." He almost reached for her, but his hand paused in midair, and he glanced at Utanapishtim. "Would you at least consider changing your clothes? Dressing as I do?" The look on Utanapishtim's face answered for him, and James gave up. "Let's stick together, then. All three of us."

Utanapishtim grunted his assent.

They beached the dinghy near the lighthouse, dragging it up onto the rocky shore, leaving it behind several large boulders that, James thought, would shield it from view from almost all directions. And then they trekked inland, keeping to the wooded areas. He felt his sister's fiery energy as he hiked farther, and soon he sensed that she wasn't far away, having made her way to the coast as best she could. She was hurting, and she was furious, and she was not alone. Those were the things he managed to pick up from her as he moved closer.

But he was worried.

With a hand on his shoulder, Lucy asked, "What's wrong?"

"Brigit. She's beaming her location to me openly, with every bit of mental power she possesses, in spite of the moratorium our people have placed on open telepathy."

Utanapishtim was looking at him, questions in his eyes.

"Others...find her?" he asked.

"Yes, others might. There *are* humans who possess the power of telepathy. Only a few, but they do exist." He stared off into the distance. "I just hope to God none of them are picking up on Brigit's vibe and coming after her. Or if they are, I hope we get there first."

"Why...hu-muns...hate so the vahmpeers?"

"Because they fear us," James said.

"Make...no...reason." Utanapishtim seemed doubtful.

James didn't blame him for his skepticism. It took two sides to fight a war, and Utanapishtim must assume that he was getting only half the story. The undead weren't entirely blameless. There had been plenty of incidents when the vampires had not been as innocent as James had chosen to depict them. But he had reasons for not bringing up every infraction. He needed Utanapishtim on their side.

And he sensed he might be losing the man.

Then he was distracted by another matter entirely.

His twin sister was near. He felt her, and then he looked up ahead and he knew. He pointed to an abandoned church, which was only a mile or two from where Will and Sarafina's home had stood. "She's in there."

"There?" Utanapishtim said, pointing, too. "Is… temple?"

"Yes. A place of worship."

"Is…?" Utanapishtim held up his thumb and forefinger. "Small. What god…live there?"

"None of the gods you knew," James said. "The people today worship different gods."

Utanapishtim stared at the church, at its steeple. "Then…why Anu has not…?" He pounded his fist into his open palm. "Struck down it?"

Lucy put a calming hand on his arm. "This land is far from the land of Anu and the Anunaki, Utanapishtim. This is a temple to one of the gods of this land."

He nodded, clearly mulling that over, as the three of them approached the front door of the abandoned church.

And then it flew open and Brigit flung herself into James's arms, weeping. Shaking, too, so hard that it frightened him. He closed his arms around her, lifting her off her feet, feeling her pain and bleeding with it.

"It's okay, it's okay. I'm here now."

Sniffling, she pulled away just far enough to meet his eyes. Her face was smeared in black, her clothes scorched, torn and sooty. The skin had peeled off her forearm in one place, and there were angry pink patches on her hands and neck, as well.

"God, I'm so glad to see you."

"Me, too." He looked nervously behind them. It was daylight, and there were clearly people after her. "Get back inside. Come on, so I can tend to your wounds." He set her down, then saw her finally notice his companions, even while stepping aside to let them pass.

"Professor Lucy. I'm surprised you're still around." And then she glanced at Utanapishtim, and her eyes seemed to get stuck on him. James watched her take him in from head to toe, saw her noting his odd attire before she seemed unable to look away from his face.

"You…you're…" She managed to dart a quick glance at James. "Is he…?"

"Ziasudra, otherwise known as Utanapishtim," James said.

"No shit." Brigit closed the church door after the three of them went inside, and then she moved closer to the huge man. She lifted a hand to touch his face, though her words were for James. "I can't believe… you actually did it."

Utanapishtim let her touch, did not back away, but he held her eyes. "I did not give you permission to touch me, woman."

She grinned at him. "Feisty, isn't he?"

"Maybe you shouldn't talk about him as if he isn't here, Brigit," Lucy suggested. "He's a king, and also sort of your forebearer."

"True enough." Brigit lowered her head in the barest mockery of a bow. "Your highness," she said.

"I do not know…highness." And then Utanapishtim winced and backed away from her. "You are… pain. I—I tire of…suffering."

"Come on, Bridge," James said, leading her to the nearest pew and telling her to lie down. He held his hands over her, vaguely aware of Lucy and Utanapishtim walking farther into the church, looking around curiously. "Tell me what happened while I work," he told her.

"I drafted a lot of vamps to help me out."

"The resistance, I know." His palms weren't tingling, weren't glowing. He rubbed them together rapidly, until they grew warm, and tried again.

"The idea was," Brigit said, "to start giving these mortal vigilantes a taste of their own medicine, but the cowards only attack by day. So what good is a resistance made up of creatures who can only fight by night? Dammit, I need humans, not vampires, and I don't have any."

"Where are they now? Your soldiers?"

His hands still weren't glowing. She sat up, gripping his wrists and turning his hands upward. "Having trouble, bro?"

"I don't know what's wrong."

She shrugged. "We heal rapidly anyway, you and I. Look, it's already getting better. Give me an hour, I'll be good as new."

But James was troubled. And he kept thinking of when Utanapishtim had fallen on the deck of the *Nightshade* and had held James's hands to him. He looked up at the man, who was standing nearby, watching them curiously, met his eyes, tried to see any sign of guilt there, not that Utanapishtim would be likely to feel any. But James has no doubt, the bastard had stolen his power.

And then Brigit caught his attention with a single word.

"Gone," she whispered.

His eyes shot back to hers. "Your entire team?"

"Nearly." She lowered her head then, and he knew she was trying to hide her tears. But she couldn't hide anything from him. "We were holed up in an abandoned house, and the assholes burned it. I don't even know how they knew we were there. We lost a dozen good people. I managed to carry four of them out before the flames got too bad, but they were badly burned, too, between the damn inferno and the sun."

"And the vigilantes?" he asked, noting that Utanapishtim was coming closer now. The resurrected king was watching Brigit's every move, listening intently to her every word, fascination in his black eyes.

"I sploded 'em," Brigit said, using their childhood term for her destructive gift. "That's one—"

Utanapishtim held up a hand, interrupting her. "I know not…sploded. What means it?"

"As I started to say," Brigit went on, irritated, "that's one gang down, about twenty to go, and that's just in the Northeast. They're popping up all over the place. I'll get them all as soon as I get enough intel to know where to look."

"Intel…?" Utanapishtim asked.

Brigit ignored him and kept talking. "I kept the leader alive. He's in the basement, tied up and trembling, surrounded by sleeping vampires who'd just as soon drain him dry as look at him."

"You take prisoner. Leader. This wise, for female. Now, say me what means sploded," Utanapishtim ordered.

James looked at his hands and wondered how the hell he was going to regain what Utanapishtim had taken from him. "Don't tell him, Bridge."

Ignoring the warning, Brigit said, "Okay, watch this, King Tut." She pointed at a lectern standing in the corner of the church, and then she turned her hand, palm up, touched her fingers lightly to her thumb and then, as she flicked them open, a beam shot from her eyes, following the direction of her fingertips and the lectern exploded into a thousand bits.

From the far side of the church, Lucy shrieked and jumped. "Shit, Brigit, give a little warning, would you?"

"Sorry, Prof." Brigit looked at Utanapishtim. "That

was just a little one. I can cause a lot more damage if I want to."

He nodded. "This I know… You not only one have power of splode."

Brigit grinned. "You've known others?" she asked.

"One other." He shifted his eyes to James. "This place…not safe, James. I feel—"

"I feel it, too," Brigit said, turning her head, looking around.

"It's daylight," James said. "We can't move your four sleeping soldiers until dark. Not safely."

"Maybe we can." Lucy, who had been wandering around the church, exploring, held a length of green canvas in her hands. "There are several of these tarps back here. Apparently they used them to cover the organ. If we wrap the vamps up, we can each carry one of them to the dinghy. Just like we did when we took Sarafina and the others out of that cave after the fire. You say there are four vampires here, Brigit?"

"Yes, fighters, too. Two male, two female." Brigit eyed Lucy. "And while I'm sure that James and I and Utanapishtim can each manage to carry one, I doubt you can. You don't have preternatural strength like we do."

"You have hu-mun prisoner," Utanapishtim said. "Make him carry."

Brigit lifted her brows at him. "Good thinking, Kong."

He made a fist and thudded it against his own chest. "Utanapishtim."

Brigit shrugged. "Whatev. C'mon, they're this way."

She led them through a door beyond the nave, which led to a very rickety and dusty flight of steps leading down into utter darkness. James followed directly behind her, then turned to call up to Lucy, "Be careful, it's very dark."

"I'll just wait at the top, then," she said softly.

He thought there was something odd in her voice, then realized what it was. She was getting tired of being the only one of them without any sort of supernatural ability. He supposed he could understand that, even though he'd been determined to exist in complete denial of the powers he possessed, with the exception of his power to heal.

A power he'd lost. The reality of that ached in his chest, but he had no time, just now, for grieving.

He continued down the stairs and saw a man, a mortal, tied to a chair. He was a man James had seen before. Just a glimpse, though, as they'd sped away from the scene of the shooting at Studio Three. He had a scar running from the outer corner of his left eye, down across his cheek, to the center of his chin, and pale gray eyes. He was not a redneck, and he was not uninformed about vampires, nor acting out of fear or ignorance.

He was DPI.

19

An hour later they were nearing the spot where they'd left the dinghy. Lucy had said nothing about the scar-faced man up to that point, although she'd been stunned when she'd seen him. She'd been waiting for a moment when she could get James alone. And it finally came.

She was walking beside him, Brigit leading the way, a canvas-wrapped vampire over her shoulder. It was surreal to watch her carrying a vampire that was taller, broader and no doubt far heavier than Brigit herself. She was a small woman, petite, and those blond curls were a total contrast to her personality, much less her power. It was like watching a toddler pick up an adult. It just made no sense.

Brigit was several yards ahead of them now, moving fast, maybe running on adrenaline.

Behind then, Utanapishtim walked more slowly, apparently in deference to the struggling, scar-faced mortal just ahead of him, who was suffering under his own vampiric burden.

Finally there was enough distance between Lucy and James, and the others, that she felt she could speak freely. "I know that man," she whispered.

He shot her a curious look.

"He was in the room where I woke up—after the shooting. After you healed me. The room where I was held. He was there with a woman, and while she did most of the questioning, I got the feeling he was the one in charge."

James nodded. "I saw him, too, outside the studio in all that chaos. He was one of the men in black. He's government. DPI."

She felt a rush of relief that her own suspicion had just been confirmed. "Then that means DPI is behind this vigilante nonsense, doesn't it, James?"

"I wouldn't be surprised. Probably pretending to be a regular guy, egging them on. Hell, look at his clothes."

She glanced behind them. The scar-faced man was wearing jeans and a T-shirt with a flannel shirt over it, buttoned all the way up. As if he knew what red-necks wore, but not how they wore it. His mouth was moving, but she couldn't hear his words.

"He's running his mouth, James. What's he saying?"

"Nothing good." James turned, looking back at them. "Shit. I didn't realize Utanapishtim had dropped back. He was behind me a minute ago."

"We're almost there," she said.

"Let's drop back a little, all the same. I don't like this."

"Not me," she said. "I've kept my head down since you guys brought him up from the basement. I don't think he's recognized me yet. And I'd just as soon he didn't."

"Don't kid yourself, Lucy," James told her. "He knows exactly who you are. These guys aren't that easily fooled."

The two of them slowed down. Utanapishtim and Scarface slowed down, too. Lucy didn't think that boded very well. Clearly, whatever Scarface had to say, he didn't want to say it in front of James and Lucy, and just as clearly, Utanapishtim wanted to hear the man out.

James stopped in place, waiting, facing the other two, making it impossible for them to lag behind without being obvious about it.

"Where are you taking me?" Scarface demanded when they caught up. "I've been asking this guy, but he refuses to say a word."

"I can't tell you that," James said softly. "But you'll be safe, I promise."

"Safe? Are you crazy? I'm being held prisoner by vampires, for God's sake."

"Obviously we're *not* vampires," James said, with a nod at the sky above. "Sunshine, remember?"

"You're not human. I know that much. That blonde… the things she can do. Are you two…related?"

James tipped his head to one side. "You know we are. And why don't you stop playing games? Just as you know I'm not human, I know you're not some yahoo with an ax to grind."

"I resent that."

"You would if you were one of them. But you're not. You're government. DPI."

"I don't know what you're talking about."

"You do, and you'll talk, pal. Believe me. You're going to tell us everything we want to know."

The man seemed to go a shade paler, and he sent a look toward Utanapishtim. "I told you so."

"James!" Brigit called from up ahead.

Looking forward, James saw that she had stopped, and lowered her undead passenger to the ground. She ducked behind a boulder, then peered out around it.

"I need to go see what's up. Watch him," he told Lucy.

She nodded, and James jogged up ahead, still carrying his unconscious vampire refugee over his shoulder, until he reached Brigit, where he set his burden down beside the other canvas-wrapped vampire.

Lucy kept on walking, but being more or less alone with the scar-faced man made her nervous.

"You're not one of them," he said to her. He was moving slowly, clearly struggling to bear the weight of the bundle over his shoulder.

She looked at him, then at Utanapishtim, who was still listening to every word, following behind, soaking it all up and not making a single comment. He carried his own burden as if it were a twig.

"They're my friends," Lucy said to Scarface. "You, on the other hand, are not."

"You're so wrong about that." He lowered his voice to a whisper. "We were trying to save you from them when we took you in. Still are. All this stuff we've leaked to the press about you being wanted—it's bull. We're just trying to get you to come in…so we can protect you. They're going to kill you, Lucy. You know too much."

"And you know far too little," she said.

"Listen, listen, I'll…I'll make you a trade. You help me get away, and I'll make you a trade, okay?"

He was back to a normal tone of voice again. The others were too far away to hear—or maybe not. Utanapishtim was closer and, she thought, trying to listen in.

"You have nothing I could possibly want," she said.

Scarface looked quickly ahead at the others, then spoke. "I have the book," he whispered, and he patted his breast pocket. "The one that tells all their secrets, the one no one is supposed to have."

"You get the tiny version?" she asked, with a derisive look at his shirt pocket.

He tugged on something, revealing just the edge. "Electronic version, right here on my phone." As he moved, the canvas bundle shifted on his shoulder and a pale, slender hand fell free.

Lucy lunged, tucking the hand back in even as smoke began to spiral from it. "Be careful!" she snapped.

"For God's sake, will you focus here?" Scarface demanded. "You've chosen the wrong side in this, and you'll know that if you just read the book. I'll give it to you. Just let me go and it's yours."

"I'm not letting you go." And besides, she thought snidely, she already had the very same material on her own phone. In fact, she had Lester Folsom's own "eyes only" version.

She caught herself, realizing that she'd processed that thought very loudly. She wondered if anyone else had picked up on it and glanced ahead, knowing she probably ought to tell James she was in possession of the book.

Would he be angry that she'd kept it from him? Would he insist she destroy it, or hand it over to Rhiannon or one of the other vampire elders? She didn't want to give it up. She wanted to read it first—find out everything that James might not have told her already. And even knowing parts of it would no doubt be biased and untrue, books were sacred to her. Knowledge was everything.

She would finish reading it, and then she would tell him and let him do whatever he wanted with the thing.

"Come on, Lucy. You're a scientist. Don't you want to know the truth about them?"

Utanapishtim stepped up behind the man, gripped

his shoulder. "Silence, prisoner. Wish you to die now?"

"I'm going to die anyway, if you don't let me go. You don't know what they're capable of. They'll drink my fucking blood, for God's sake."

"Loo-see, go there." Utanapishtim pointed ahead, to where James was speaking to Brigit. "You belong... beside...you man. Go."

"But James asked me to watch him."

"I king! You go!"

He growled the words, jabbing his forefinger in James's direction, and Lucy jumped into motion, but first she snatched the phone from Scarface's pocket.

He glared at her.

"Sorry, pal. You've got nothing left to bargain with now."

She took the phone with her to where James and Brigit were crouched behind a boulder. Utanapishtim had spoken with so much authority that it had seemed far beyond her ability to argue with him. By the time she was catching up with James, it was a done deal, and just as well. She'd been shaken by the scar-faced man. But she had at least taken the precaution of confiscating his bargaining chip. God forbid he give it to Utanapishtim, with his ability to absorb every bit of information it contained just by holding the device in his hands.

What would he believe of his offspring if he were fed all the lies about them contained in that book? True, she hadn't finished it, but what she had read so far had depicted the vampire race as animals. As soulless, murderous savages without feelings.

She made it to the boulder and came to a stop. "What is it?" she asked the twins. To her surprise, the sea was just a stone's throw away below them.

"Just a passing group of humans," James said. "We think they were just hikers, but given the circumstances..." He looked at Lucy. "What have you got there?"

She handed it to him. "The electronic version of Folsom's book. Scarface offered to trade it to me in exchange for letting him go. I took it from him so he wouldn't try to tempt Utanapishtim with the same offer."

James took it, looked at it and then flung it as hard as he could. The device sailed through the sky, arcing overhead, then plummeting downward again and falling into the sea with a "plip." "That takes care of that problem," he said.

Lucy licked her lips, realizing he would do the same to her personal edition of the book if she told him she had it.

"That information might have been useful, James," she pointed out.

"Information? It's propaganda. Our secrets are ours, Lucy. To keep or to share, our call. Not some retired DPI goon's."

"But there might have been things on there about them, things we don't know."

"Once DPI, always DPI. Believe me, he didn't give away a thing that could help us. They never do."

"Knowledge is power, James."

"I have all the power I need, thanks. Or at least, I did."

What was that supposed to mean, she wondered, lowering her head. "Books are sacred to me."

"That wasn't a book. It was a phone." He hooked a finger under her chin and smiled, as if trying to tempt her out of her displeasure.

"It was a book, and you know it."

His face turned serious then. "It was a weapon meant to be wielded against my people. And I destroyed it. It was the right call, Lucy."

"Destroying knowledge in any form is never the right call."

"Will you two go get a freaking room or something?" Brigit turned, irritated, and then her eyes widened as she looked beyond them. "Utanapishtim! Heads up! Scarface is getting away!"

James and Lucy whirled to see the mortal darting around a sand dune and heading into the woods. The vampire he'd been carrying lay bundled on the ground.

Brigit ran like a flash to where Utanapishtim was and lifted her hand, palm up, fingers touching her thumb, toward the fleeing prisoner, but Utanapishtim reached out, closed his hand around hers and pushed it down.

"No need...to keep him."

"Who the fuck are you to make that decision?" Brigit shouted.

Utanapishtim backed up a step, as if stunned by her words, not to mention her tone. "I am king. You… are…of me, woman. Remember it."

Brigit stared at him, her eyes blazing mad, and he stared right back at her.

"Let it go, Brigit," James said softly. "There wouldn't have been room in the dinghy for him anyway.

"I needed him." She jerked her hand free of Utanapishtim's and used her finger to poke him in the chest. "You'd best watch your step, King Shit. Because you don't know fuck about what's going on here."

Lucy stared at the pair of them, her eyes rounding with fear, until Brigit turned and marched back toward the boulder, where she reclaimed her undead passenger and began striding onward, picking her way down the steep slope toward the beach below.

It was only a few hours later, late in the afternoon, when the dense bank of misty fog that surrounded the island came into view. James stared at it so intently that Lucy knew he was trying to feel for his relatives' energies, because navigating by sight was absolutely impossible.

Standing beside him at the helm, Lucy asked, "Isn't there some sort of sonar system you could use to pick your way to shore?"

"The yacht isn't equipped with sonar." He met her

eyes, and his were warm with approval. "But that was a good idea."

"And it gave me another," she said. "Can the vampires' power block military sonar from detecting the island?"

"I don't know. I doubt it. But then, I don't know every vampire or what each one is capable of, so it's impossible to say." He stared through the heavy fog, eyes straining. "There's just no way to dock until the vampires awaken and Rhiannon is able to part the mists long enough to let me find my way in by sight." He shrugged. "It's only a slight delay."

"It is. And this is a good day, for you." She smiled at the light in his eyes. "You're returning to your people with your mission accomplished. Like a conquering hero. Like Gilgamesh himself, so long ago. You're saving them, James. And I owe you a huge apology."

His smile faded as he blinked at her. "For what? Helping me pull off the impossible?"

"For doubting you. For questioning your judgment in balancing what means were justified to get to this end."

He lowered his head briefly. "You were right about some of it. Raising the dead didn't work out so well."

"The mortal dead, yes. But your sister obligingly returned them to the grave where they belonged, except for that mother you reunited with her husband and children. It all worked out fine in the end. You were right all along. And I'm sorry for doubting you."

"Just don't let it happen again, woman." He delivered the dictate with a hint of Utanapishtim's exotically unidentifiable accent, and she laughed with him, even while giving a quick glance behind them.

But there was no one in sight. Utanapishtim was asleep, exhausted, in one of the cabins below. Brigit was in another, also napping, equally exhausted after a night of battling mortal vigilantes and rescuing vampires from the flames. The four surviving members of her resistance team were divided up between the two remaining cabins, unconscious until sundown.

Leaving just the two of them alone at the helm, Lucy thought.

James dropped anchor where they were and shut off the yacht's engines. He led Lucy down to the deck-level wet bar, just behind the bridge, and poured them each a glass of wine. Then he held up his glass. "To victory."

"To victory." She clinked her glass against his, then took a deep drink.

He did the same, then said, "I'm sorry about destroying that phone."

"But you still think it was for the best."

"Yes. I know you disagree, but that's okay with me."

She nodded, feeling a little guilty that she still had her own version of the book. And yet also feeling entirely justified in keeping that information from him.

For now. Her phone was tucked away in her bag, in one of the cabins down below. She told herself that she would finish her reading and then delete the thing, though she didn't think in the end she would have the willpower to do it.

"What's on your mind? You look pensive," James said.

She shook free of her thoughts and tried to refocus on what they'd been discussing last. "I...I was wondering why Utanapishtim didn't return from the grave the way those others did, mindless and out of control."

"I think it's because they'd really died. Not only physically but spiritually—the part of them that was them, the soul, for want of a better name, had moved on. I guess with the first woman, it was so soon after her death that I was able to pull her soul back into her body. But with those others, the soul didn't return. I restored the body, but it was just animated meat and bone. No soul."

"And with Utanapishtim?"

He nodded, sipping, thinking. "He never really died. I mean, his physical form was gone, but his spirit remained...trapped with his ashes, where it would have stayed forever."

Lucy frowned. "I wonder...if there's any way to set him free. I mean, eventually he's going to die. He can't live forever."

"Why not?" James asked. "Seems to me it's either that or return to his living death. God, can you imagine how awful it must have been? All those centuries, conscious yet imprisoned? Buried alive, basically."

"It's a miracle he's not completely insane." She shivered. "He's not quite right though, even now. Sometimes, there's something in his eyes that just… it scares me, James."

Something scraped the side of the anchored vessel, and James swore under his breath, rushing to the side to look over it. Lucy could see the island now—just glimpses amid the mist every now and again. "Should I wake the others, let them know we're here?"

"Let them sleep awhile, Lucy," James said. "We have three hours until sundown, after all. And this island will be bustling by then. I think maybe you and I ought to sleep, too."

She dipped her head a little, wondering if that was all he wanted them to do and hoping not. "I wish we could debark and find a cozy spot on the island for our…nap," she said softly. "I'm craving solid ground beneath my body."

"I'm craving you beneath mine," he said. He pulled her into his arms then, holding her close to him and smiling down into her eyes. "I haven't stopped thinking about it since we—"

"Neither have I, James," she whispered.

He bent his head and kissed her mouth. He took his time, his tongue moving deep, tasting her thoroughly.

"All the cabins…" she said between kisses, "are… occupied."

"You taste like wine. Better." His hands moved over her body, sliding down to cup her backside, squeezing her closer. "We don't need a cabin."

"You're right, we don't," she whispered. "The sitting room. We can shut the door."

"What's wrong with right here?" he asked, but he didn't make her answer. He scooped her up in his arms and carried her, kissing her all the way, down the stairs, past all four closed cabin doors and into the sitting room. Then he kicked that door closed behind him and lowered her onto the pristine white carpet.

20

"**J.W.**! Get your ass up. King Louie's gone."

"What?" James came awake slowly, having been carried into sleep on a wave of utter bliss. He was lying on the soft, luxuriously plush carpet, Lucy's head resting on his chest, his arms wrapped tightly around her naked shoulders. The throw they'd borrowed from the sofa was the only covering either of them wore. Somewhere along the way night had fallen.

He flashed alert as he focused on his sister's voice, coming from beyond the closed door. "Brigit?"

"Will you get up? We have a problem."

Lucy was coming awake, too, by then, and as she sat up and began pulling on her clothes, James got to his feet. He yanked on his jeans, sent a quick glance Lucy's way and then, as soon as she was decent, he opened the door.

"What's wrong?"

"Utanapishtim's gone," Brigit said. "See for yourself."

She waved a hand toward the open door of the cabin where the old one had retired. James surged past Brigit, noting the mussed bedcovers, and then a bag, dumped out in the center of the mattress. Lucy's bag.

"Oh, no," Lucy whispered. "It wasn't even in this cabin. I'd tucked it into a closet in another room. No, no, no, he couldn't have…"

"What the hell?" James sorted through the pile of her possessions, picking up the object she seemed intent on as she drew near. Her phone, still turned on. Frowning, he picked it up and looked at the screen. It was filled with text, and as he scrolled upward, he found headers and realized what he was looking at. An electronic version of that damned book.

Lifting his gaze, he met Lucy's stricken eyes.

"You had this? This whole time?"

"I was going to tell you but—"

"When? Dammit, Lucy, I told you how I felt about this. How could you keep this from me? Much less keep it around, running the risk Utanapishtim might get his hands on it and take it as gospel before we've had the chance to—"

The roar of an explosion split the air, cutting him off midsentence. All three of them went silent, staring upward.

James pushed the two women aside and raced up the steps to the deck above, only to discover that the boat had been docked. "Who the hell piloted us to shore?"

"I don't know," Brigit said. "The vamps we brought with us were gone, too, when I woke up. Probably rose at sunset and were eager to get to the island. They could have done it."

"Either them or Utanapishtim. If he touched the damned boat, he'd instantly know how to operate it." He was at the gangplank now, which linked the yacht to an outcropping of rock on an unfamiliar part of the shore.

He raced down it, searching the horizon for the source of the explosion, and was just in time to see the flash of another, followed by screams and sensations of the pain and anguish of his people. His family.

"What the hell is he doing?" James raged.

"It's my power!" Brigit shouted, racing to join him.

Lucy was right behind, struggling to catch up as another explosion rocked the ground they stood on, and then another and another.

Brigit's eyes were wet, her face twisted in fear. "He has the same power as I do. I can feel it. God…" Her eyes fell closed, body arching forward, hugging in on itself as if involuntarily. "Stop it!"

They were running then, all of them, even Brigit, still clutching her middle as if in pain. Across the rocks that guarded the island, racing along paths through the woods and on toward the ruins, where the refugees had been encamped. But when they got there they saw only wreckage and ruin. Burned-out campsites and vaguely familiar shapes burned into the grass—people-shapes. Utanapishtim had turned a mighty power against his own people. Smoldering ash was all that remained.

"Some of them got away," Brigit whispered, moving up beside James, clutching at his arm.

Lucy was on his other side, trembling, tears flowing like rivers down her face. He was constantly aware of her there, of everything she felt. And yet he was furious with her for this.

Brigit nodded, pointing toward the far side of the island, the thickly wooded end. "They went that way."

"He didn't, though." James tried to pick up a sign of the man, to sense him. "God, why did he do this?"

"We have to go after the survivors," Lucy said. "James, they may need help."

"I have to go after Utanapishtim," he told her, his tone low, his heart as much an ashen ruin as the vampires Utanapishtim had destroyed. "I did this." His throat closed up on the words. "*I* did this."

"You couldn't have known," Lucy told him. "If he…absorbed all the information in that book, then he might assume that what it says about vampires is the truth. Hell, that's even the title. *The Truth*. How can he be expected to distinguish the difference? He'd believe everything he read, believe he'd spawned an evil, bloodthirsty race of undead demons. That's what he'd believe, because that's what the book said about them—about you."

James tilted his head sideways, searching Lucy's eyes. "And yet you kept it. In spite of my warnings, you kept it—and you didn't even tell me."

"I knew you'd destroy it," she whispered. "I wanted to finish reading it first. I thought there might be information that could…"

He stared at her in disbelief, wondering how he had let himself believe there might be something between them. How could he not have been aware that she considered him a different species? Something inhuman. She didn't even trust him enough to tell him the truth. And that had gotten people killed.

"How could you betray me—and my people—this way, Lucy? I thought you were on our side."

"I am." The hurt flashed in her eyes; he saw it and felt a spasm of remorse ripple through him. "I didn't mean for this to happen," she said, eyes lowering, tears glimmering on her lashes.

They'd been moving rapidly as they talked, but they paused now, as Brigit said, "There!" She was pointing dead ahead, and they all looked that way just as Utanapishtim stepped from the shadows and sent a blast of white-hot energy beaming from his eyes into a clump of brush.

The brush exploded, but James felt no pain in its wake. Thank God.

"'May all praise him duly when he lifts his eyes,

and his glance flashes like lightning,'" Lucy quoted. "It was part of his prayer that first day on the ship."

"He's just like me," Brigit whispered. "That's what he meant when he said he knew of one other person who shared my particular power. He was talking about himself. God, he's just like me."

And as she said it, Utanapishtim turned, spotted them and ran back toward the shore. He sprinted up the gangplank and boarded the yacht. Within seconds he was at the helm and powering up the ship as if he were an expert, backing the yacht straight out from the harbor.

"We can't let him get away!" James shouted. "He's completely out of his mind!"

"We have to know what else he read," Lucy said. "We have to know what set him off."

As she spoke, she was tapping the screen of her phone.

"What we have to do is find the survivors. God, my parents were on this island," Brigit shouted.

"It's all here," Lucy said slowly. "I didn't know, because I never finished reading the damn book. But it's in here." She lifted her eyes to James. "The missing segments of my tablet, and someone translated them. James, Utanapishtim isn't only the one who can save your people. He's the only one who can destroy them."

She shook her head slowly, staring at the phone. "It's all right here. According to Folsom, the government removed those segments of the tablet back in the fifties, when it was first recovered. They must have had teams of translators. They read the whole thing, then removed key phrases, just breaking them away, then planted the rest at my school and waited, knowing that someday someone would translate it. Finally I did. And they also knew how you would interpret what remained. They knew you would find and resurrect Utanapishtim, and they knew what would happen when you did. They tricked you, James. They used you to bring about the destruction of your own people. And they used me, too."

"I…resurrected the only being who could destroy my entire race?" he whispered. He fell to his knees. To go from being his people's savior to their destroyer in a single hour was more than he could bear. "God, no."

"There's more," Lucy said softly. And then she read aloud.

"'There is no redemption for the Ancient One, unless he undoes all he has done, beginning with the eldest one.'" She shook her head. "Obviously the translator has taken liberties here. It probably wasn't meant to rhyme, but I imagine it's close."

"He breaks his curse by undoing what he has done," James said. "He believes he must destroy the race he inadvertently created. Undoing his sin against the gods by destroying his own kind. 'Beginning with the eldest one,'" he said softly.

"He's going after Gilgamesh," Brigit said. "But I thought he was here, on the island."

"He must have left. Either way, I have to go after him—them," James said. "Brigit, take Lucy and go after the survivors, see if you can find out where Damien is. Do what you can for them, and then catch up with me. I'll stay on Utanapishtim's trail."

"I'm the one who should go after him," Brigit said softly.

"I did this." James took his sister by her shoulders, and stared into her eyes. "Please, give me a chance to make it right." And then he faced Lucy and, his heart in his eyes, he said, "You were right. Even though you broke my trust, betrayed me in a way I don't know if I can ever forgive, you were right, Lucy. My ego did this. My blind determination to fulfill what I thought was my destiny, to be my people's hero, so my fucking life would finally make some kind of sense."

"There's more." She held up her phone.

"I don't give a shit what that damned book has to say." James turned and began running back toward the shore, no doubt in search of a boat. Brigit was already running off to find the survivors of the brutal attack.

Lucy raced after James. "Wait!" she cried. "I'm going with you. And if you argue, you're just wasting time. You can't stop me." There were tears in her eyes.

James nodded, feeling too broken, too defeated, to argue. He hadn't saved his people. Instead, he had brought about the end of his race. God, he'd been such a fool. "All right." Then he dragged his eyes from her determined expression and stared after his sister.

As if sensing his eyes on her, Brigit stopped, turned and called out to him, "Be careful. And you, Professor, make sure you don't do something else stupid and get my brother killed, okay?"

"I'll do my best."

With that Brigit turned and ran off, following her senses to the vampires who'd escaped Utanapishtim's deadly gaze.

James raced along the shore, Lucy following him, until he came to a small motorboat, checked that it was full of gas and, as soon as they were both aboard, fired up the outboard motor and aimed the bow toward the mainland, following the still detectable wake of the departing yacht. Still detectable to his eyes, at least.

"It's not your fault, you know," Lucy said. She sat near the bow, facing him as he sat near the stern to steer. The boat was no more than a supersized rowboat with an outboard attached.

He looked heavenward for an answer. "In what universe is this not my fault? Tell me, will you, because I'd really love to know."

"Don't be sarcastic, James. I'm not the enemy here."

"You could have fooled me."

She lowered her head. "I know. I know I screwed up. God, if your family aren't okay, I don't—"

"They're all my family. And they're not okay."

"You had no way of knowing. The translation was…incomplete. So it was my fault," she said. "If I'd refused to publish what I had until the missing segments had been accounted for…"

"No, this…this war still would have started. Folsom's book is what kicked all this off. And you had nothing to do with that."

"Neither did you." She held his eyes. "Say it. Say this wasn't your fault."

He took a breath, nodded twice. "This wasn't my fault." His lips thinned. He swallowed what felt like bile. "I can say it, but that will never make me believe it."

"We have to get to the university, James. We'll find what we need there, I know we will. The solution must be in the remaining pieces of the tablet. There are so many parts that have never been translated. One of them must explain how we can stop Utanapishtim."

"I have to stop him from getting to Damien first."

"But you don't know how to stop him. What other powers might he have? What can kill him?"

"We know something can. He was killed once."

"But he wasn't!" she argued. "Not really. His body was destroyed, but his soul remained trapped, imprisoned—"

"Unable to do any harm. If that's the best we can do, then—"

"We can't return him to that. God, James, that would be inhuman."

Her words rang in the air between them. He didn't answer, but he knew they were at odds again. To him, the end—removing Utanapishtim from existence to protect his people—justified the means. Even if those means condemned a man to an eternity in a living hell. Buried alive.

To her, he knew, nothing justified that. Nothing. She lowered her head, closed her eyes, but tears wet her lashes all the same. "When we get to the mainland, I'm going home," she said softly.

"You're wanted, Lucy. They'll arrest you."

She shook her head. "I'm not going to stay. I just…I need to go back there. One last time." Then she met his eyes. "Besides, I've been taking care of myself for a lot of years now, so, you know…"

He had no business worrying about her. That was what she was saying. He got that. So he just nodded and said nothing more.

21

Lucy took a bus to Binghamton by way of Timbuktu, or so it seemed. It took most of a day to get there. But at least she'd been able to buy a ticket with what remained of her cash, using a false name and convincing the sales agent that she had lost her ID and was in a real jam. He'd taken pity on her.

She never would have thought herself capable of embarking on such a wild journey as the one she'd just been on. A journey that had left her life in ruins, her heart in pieces and was now coming to an end with absolutely nothing gained. And yet, she wasn't finished. Not completely. She intended to see this through, to try to make right, in the only way she could, what she had done so very, very wrong.

She was going to the university, to the dusty, familiar basement, to find her beloved clay tablets, and she was going to sit there and translate until she either found an answer or ran out of shards.

Or ran out of time.

She didn't know for sure if her house was being watched. She presumed it had been, at first, but maybe they'd given up after so many days of her not showing up. She hitched a ride from the bus station with a biker and had him drop her off several blocks from her house, and then she walked along a road that ran parallel to hers, cut through the woodlot in between and emerged on the edge of her own small backyard.

And then she stood there in the shelter of the trees, looking at what had been her haven. The tiny cracker-box house with its pristine white paint and neat black shutters. Its organized, color coordinated window boxes were sprouting weeds, and the once perfectly manicured lawn was shaggy. Newspapers had piled up on her front stoop, and the mailbox was overflowing. The place was a mess.

For just a moment she stood there, thinking it was an exact match for what had happened to her neat, organized, tightly controlled life. It, too, had got away from her. It had spiraled into chaos. She'd spent the past week scared to death, frantic, excited and… alive, she realized slowly. More alive than she had ever been. Awash in emotions and sensations she had never before allowed herself to experience. Emotions that included a blinding, dizzying passion for a man who was like no other she had ever known.

Or ever would.

He undoubtedly resented her now, maybe even hated her, for ruining his chance to save his people. Much more, for the lives that had been lost because of her foolish mistakes. First in publishing her translation too soon, never knowing the deadly impact it would have on a race of people living today. And secondly, and even less excusable, leaving that ebook on her phone within Utanapishtim's reach. She couldn't undo those mistakes. But maybe she could keep things from getting any worse.

From the woodlot beyond the backyard, she watched the house for several long minutes. She moved along the edge of the woods so she could look past her house and see the road out front. There was, as she had feared, a dark sedan parked directly across the street.

Well, it was still her home. And she needed it desperately right then. So she moved back through the woods until the house itself blocked her from the street and dashed right up the middle of the tiny backyard, ducking low until she reached the back door.

Her key was already in her hand. She inserted it in the lock, opened the door and slipped silently into her house, feeling as nervous as a cat burglar. Closing the door behind her, she leaned back against it and sighed. The relief of home washed over her. God, if only she could curl up into a ball and stay right there.

But she couldn't.

She kept very low as she moved through the house, never turning on a single light nor moving in any way that could be seen from outside. As much as she wanted to bask in her haven, she just didn't have time. She had to be fast, and she had to be efficient. She crept up the stairs to her bedroom to get clean clothes and packed everything essential into a backpack she found in her closet. A couple of changes of clothes, all her important papers from their fireproof lockbox under the bed, including her birth certificate, social security card, passport, diplomas and degrees. She added a hairbrush, extra socks and running shoes.

Then she took that bag with her and headed into her bathroom for a quick shower, keeping the water cool enough so it wouldn't steam up any windows and give her presence away.

She slicked her wet hair back and fastened it behind her head with a black band, then stuffed a few more essentials into her backpack. Toothbrush, toothpaste, deodorant. Just the basics. She quickly changed into cargo pants and a black tank top, with thick cushy socks and tall black lace-up hiking boots. She added a khaki Binghamton Mets baseball cap and a pair of dark sunglasses.

As an afterthought, she stuffed an empty duffel into her backpack, in case she needed to take some things from her office. Finally, stopping in the kitchen, she shoved a box of granola bars and several bottles of green tea into the bulging bag, snagged a jacket from the hook near the back door and crept outside again.

"Goodbye, house," she whispered. "You've been good to me." But there was something inside telling her that she had outgrown this little nest of hers. This hiding place—which was what it had been. A cocoon where she had secreted herself away from life. From living.

The woman who emerged from that back door, she felt, was not the same one who'd left this house by the front door so short a time ago. Not even close.

She knew things, had seen things, she had never known or seen before. She'd come to understand things she had never even considered. And she'd shifted her vision about what was right and what was wrong in the world, seeing things now as varying shades of gray, not pure black and white like before.

Sometimes the ends really did justify the means. James had shown her that. And shown her, too, that there were still real heroes in this world. He was one of them, she had no doubt of that, no matter how badly his efforts had turned out. He'd failed. And he believed that proved that her doubts about him had been right all along.

But she believed she'd been wrong. James was more heroic than any man she had ever known. She hoped she would get a chance to tell him that one day. She wished she had done so before leaving him this last time. But the pain of walking away had left her too raw to say anything at all.

She was in love with him. She knew that now.

For whatever that was worth.

Her bicycle was leaning against the side of the house, and she wanted it in the worst way. It would make traveling a whole lot faster and easier. She dislodged her backpack and lay on her belly in the grass, sliding along the side of the house and gripping the bike by its front wheel. And then she inched it toward her slowly, very slowly, bit by bit, avoiding any sudden motion that would give her away.

Eventually she managed to get the bike all the way to the backyard, easing it around the corner and then, finally, she stood upright. She slid her backpack on once more and walked the bike into the woods out back, through them and out to the road. There she mounted and rode, heading for the university and hoping to God she could blend in with summer session students long enough to get to the basement of her building undetected.

"Damien, thank God I've found you." James stared at the man in blatant relief when he answered his own door. "But why are you back here? In your own house? Don't you know the danger you're in?"

Damien, the first true vampire, the onetime great King Gilgamesh, met his eyes, his own grim, and nodded at the suitcases piled on the floor behind him while pulling James inside and closing the door. "I'm aware and taking precautions. Shannon stayed behind, in case one of those vigilante groups targets me while I'm here."

"Stayed behind…?" James closed his eyes. "Where?"

"What?"

"Where did she stay behind, Damien?"

"On the island, of course. She wanted to return

with me, but I wouldn't allow it. She was safe there, and I thought it best to leave it that way."

"And you haven't heard from her since?"

"We've all agreed not to use mental communication, as you well know, James." And then his eyes narrowed. "Why? What the hell is happening?"

James lowered his head. "Utanapishtim…is alive. I…I raised him."

"For the love of the gods…"

"I took him to the island. But he wasn't…he wasn't right. He wasn't sane, and he got hold of a copy of the book—that damned Folsom book, and—"

"And what?" Damien gripped James's shoulders, staring into his eyes. "He couldn't have read it—he wouldn't even know the language."

"He knows the language. He absorbs knowledge by touch. And he apparently believed what the book said."

"Which was what, exactly?"

"That he'd been cursed by the gods for creating the vampire race, and that his only means of redemption was to destroy it utterly."

Damien waited, his eyes already seeming to reflect what James was about to tell him.

"He attacked his own people—the refugees on the island. He…has the same ability as Brigit. He can blast things to bits by directing a beam of energy from his eyes, and he—"

"Where's Shannon?" Immediately Damien closed his eyes and called out to her.

"She won't respond if she's alive, Damien. She won't risk giving away the location of the island to the mortals."

Damien nodded, acknowledging the truth of that. "Then you need to tell me. Were there any survivors?"

"Yes." James swallowed hard. "But many were killed. I don't even know about my own family yet. We only know a group got away and headed for the other side of the island. And that Utanapishtim took a yacht and headed for the mainland, rather than going after them. I assumed he would come here."

"Why would he come after me?"

James shrugged. "Because the same passage from that book that told him he'd been cursed for creating our race, and that he must eliminate us all to undo the curse, also told him that he needed to start with the eldest one first. And that would be you."

"Then he *will* come here."

"If he can find you. And he seems to have a sense of all of us. He can hear vampires, home in on them. And I believe he can also take their powers." He met Damien's eyes. "I believe he has already."

Damien blinked in shock.

"There's more," James began.

"I'm sure there is. And I know you're working hard to save your people—our people—but right now my only concern is Shannon."

"The missing parts of the tablet, Damien—the missing parts were taken deliberately. The DPI has them, and they left the rest knowing that someday it would be translated, and that we would believe raising Utanapishtim was the only way to save our kind. But the opposite was true. Raising him was the way to begin the destruction. And I did it, Damien. I did it. I played right into their hands."

Sighing, Damien squeezed James's shoulders. "You couldn't have known. I was fooled, too, James. And I'm far older and more experienced than you."

"I let my ego—"

"Pssh, ego. You're the best of all of us. Always have been. You didn't do this for ego, James. You did this to save your people because you thought it was your destiny. And I'll tell you something, my friend. You're not finished yet." He blinked and said, "And speaking of destiny, where is your professor?"

James averted his eyes. "She's gone. She's done all she can for us, and—and she's gone back to try to rebuild her life. What's left of it, anyway. Yet another bit of destruction left in my wake, I'm afraid."

"No, she's not gone. You're not finished with that yet, either." Damien clapped his shoulder hard. "I have to return to the island. I have to find Shannon. I don't have time to wait here for Utanapishtim to show."

"If he's determined to get to you, he'll go where you go. He'll follow you right back to that island and finish what he started there. He's not sane, Damien."

"Why the hell not? He was when I knew him. And he died shortly thereafter, so he should be just the same as—"

"He never died. He was conscious, aware, but entombed. Even when his body was burned, he remained."

Damien's face contorted. "For five thousand years?"

James nodded.

"You resurrected a monster. You realize that?"

"I made a mistake, I know that now."

"And you just expect me to wait here for him to come to me? Not even knowing if my wife is dead or alive? And as the authorities are moving against us?"

James blinked. "What authorities?"

"Hell, you've been out of touch. I keep forgetting." Damien shook his head slowly. "Just today, while we slept, the White House Press Secretary said that the government now admits to the existence of vampires. He conveyed a plea from the president himself to the vigilantes to stop with their attacks."

"It's bullshit."

"No question," Damien said. "They've put out arrest warrants for any and every vampire—for our own protection, they say. They claim they've set up a safe house for us, and that they want to begin having discussions with our leaders. They're asking us to trust them, promising to arrest the vigilantes and prosecute them for violating our civil rights."

"Do you believe them?"

"No, and I've just emailed an electronic recording to a local TV station saying so. They wanted to know why it wasn't a video." He smiled bitterly, shaking his head at the ignorance of the mortal world.

"I thought everyone knew vampires don't show up on film."

"Apparently not. But meanwhile, they're quietly rounding up members of the Chosen."

"What?" James was stunned.

"I hate to think why, and we don't know where, but they've been disappearing, ordinary people with ordinary lives. The only common denominator among them is that they have the antigen. Most probably don't even know what it means. And I caught wind they're going to raid your professor's university, confiscating any remaining pieces of that tablet that might be there. They're calling the information a matter of national security and using the Patriot Act to justify taking it."

"When?" James asked, his heart suddenly seeming to seize up in his chest.

"Tonight. Why?"

James lowered his head swiftly. "God, no."

"What?"

"Lucy...I think it's a fairly safe bet that she'll be there. At the university."

"Well, she's not safe there, James. You need to get her out. And I need to get to that island and find Shannon." Damien turned, reached for a single bag and strode toward his own front door, leaving everything else behind.

But James stopped him, a hand on his shoulder.

"We have to find Utanapishtim, Damien. We have to kill him."

Damien lowered his head. "And how do you suggest we do that? Kill him, I mean."

"Lucy thought the answer to that would be on those tablets—the pieces she hadn't translated yet. But you must know how it was done the first time."

Damien nodded. "He was beheaded."

"Then get me an ax."

Damien stared at James as if he had never met him before; then he walked out the door and around the corner of the house to a woodpile. He tugged an ax easily from where it was embedded in a log and held it out. "I thought you were a healer, James. The good twin."

"I was. But I told you, he took that from me."

"Are you sure?"

James lowered his head. "I hoped I was wrong, but…yes, I think so. I know when he could have done it. And then later…"

"It doesn't matter. You're still good, you can't turn your back on your own moral code. Believe me, I know."

"My goodness has cost countless vampires their lives. Maybe even my own family. I'm through being good." James took the ax from Damien's hand.

"I want you to let this go, James. I want you to go to the university and find your Lucy," Damien said. "You've delivered your warning. You've done all you can. But you have to know that there are more important things than the greater good."

"What could possibly be more important than saving our people, Damien?" James asked softly.

"Love, James. Love is more important. I've lived longer than anyone on this planet—other than Utanapishtim himself—and I'm telling you, that is the one thing I know for sure. Love is…it's everything, James. It's everything."

James felt those words sink into his heart like hot arrows, and they stayed there while he bled from the wounds. "Brigit went after the refugees on the island. She intended to find them, help them and then catch up with me. This will be her first stop. When she arrives, she'll have news of Shannon for you. Give her another couple of hours, all right?"

"All right."

James looked at the ax. "You sure you don't need this?"

"I have others. If he comes for me, I'll be ready. Go. Find the solution for this if you can, but remember what I said. Solve *this* first," he said, with a hand to his heart.

22

Lucy left her bike beyond the nearly empty parking lot nearest the Archaeology/Anthropology building and walked past the handful of cars, hoping no one would recognize her. Passing a parked VW Bug, she caught a glimpse of her own reflection in a window and stumbled to a clumsy stop as she stood there, staring. No, no one would recognize her, she realized. She barely recognized herself.

But it *was* her own reflection staring back at her. Not the old one, though. Not the bookish, shy, introverted and usually nervous professor. This woman was an adventurer, an avenger, a woman who ran with vampires and their kin.

And now she was trying to save their whole race, just the way James had been trying to do. Who the hell had she become? Had she bitten off a chunk of his delusions of grandeur? Had his cause been infectious somehow?

Or was it just her tendency to root for the underdog

and sympathize with anyone persecuted for being different? After all, she'd always been different, too.

Right now she only knew she had to try to make up for the wrong she'd done to James, and the wrench she'd thrown into his plans. Hell, into his destiny.

She walked on, leaving her reflections—both literal and figurative—behind.

The building was closed for the summer, but she had a key. All the professors in the department did, so they could come and go if they needed to, though use of the offices during the summer months was discouraged. It was when the maintenance crews had the run of the place, giving it a summer scrubbing, painting where it was needed and adding new coats of shellac to the hardwood floors.

She went around to the back, rather than entering through the front doors, then skirted the loading dock with its big overhead door and overall-wearing handymen wandering in and out. The side entrance would be fine. It was a simple door in a solid brick wall, and you could walk past it without even noticing it was there. She slid her key card into the slot, the lock clicked, and just like that she was inside, with no one the wiser.

She avoided the workers easily as she made her way to the stairwell, and tried to be quiet as she opened that door and headed down to the sublevel. The basement. Her real domain.

She had to use her key card again to enter the work and storage room that held all the untranslated fragments of ancient stone. When she stepped inside, she was holding her breath, though she didn't realize that until she finally let it out with a whoosh. She'd half expected that same alien feeling to overtake her here as it had at home. The feeling that she'd outgrown the place, that she no longer belonged here.

But no. This place still fit. It fit like her father's old worn-out fedora had fit his head. She'd never felt worthy to wear it, but it hung in her home, over the mantel, above a photo of her and her parents, the three of them arm in arm in the desert.

Sighing, she shook off the memories, unsure why thoughts of her family had chosen to plague her just then, when she had so much else going on. Lives at stake, lives only she could save.

Maybe.

She slid her backpack off and set it on an empty chair, flipped on the high-intensity overhead lights and moved to the wall full of drawerlike bins in the back. They flanked a second door, which led out into parts of the vast university basement the students never saw and, eventually, to the loading dock just outside.

It wasn't the door but the bins on which she focused. Each drawer was tagged with the alphanumeric code that told her where its contents had been recovered, and when. She knew the section with the bins from the 1954 dig in Northern Iraq. She knew it well. She spent most of her time working on the hundreds of bits of clay tablet from that section.

In fact, she'd spent countless hours scanning

broken clay pieces in search of those that might possibly belong with the tablet she'd translated. The one that had given her fifteen minutes of fame and then proceeded to tear her life to bits. There were a hundred still to be checked, give or take. She pulled out that bin, took it with her to the table and unloaded each piece with care. Then she grabbed her supersized magnifying glass and her stiff-bristled brush, put on her headlamp and sank into a chair that bore the imprint of her backside, thanks to all the hours she'd spent there. And then she began searching for answers. Automatically, she reached up for her glasses before reminding herself that she no longer needed then. Thanks to James. For a moment the memory of his healing touch washed over her, warm and soothing. Recalling the look in his eyes brought tears to her own, but she brushed them away.

She was still there, bending over a chunk of stone where she'd glimpsed Utanapishtim's original name, Ziasudra, when she heard voices outside in the hall.

"Open it."

The tone was commanding, male—and she'd heard it before. It was Scarface! She was on her feet, grabbing handfuls of clay fragments from the table and stuffing them into her pockets, the only thing she had time to do.

"The artifacts in this room are priceless," said another familiar voice. Frank Murray, one of the BU deans. "And, I assure you, utterly useless to you.

There are only a handful of people in the entire world capable of translating—"

"I said, open the door."

"Yes, yes, I'm trying."

Grabbing her backpack, Lucy darted to the rear of the room, slid through that second door and closed it quietly, then belatedly realized her headband lamp was still in place. She yanked it off, moving quickly through the basement toward the loading dock in the rear, where all the workers were, unfortunately, milling about.

She could hear Scarface and the dean behind her. Scarface was shouting and getting excited. Clearly he could that see someone else had been in the room. They would be coming after her momentarily.

She picked up the pace as she climbed the ramp to the loading dock, emerging into the outdoors and quickly hid alongside a large truck. It was dark, but the workers were still there. They often put in long hours during the summer months, in order to be done by the time the place came back to full screaming life in the fall. No one saw her. And Scarface was coming, with a half-dozen underlings in tow. She had to get out of sight.

Making a quick decision, she jumped up onto the truck's step, opened the passenger door and got in, then ducked low, scooting over until she was sitting on the floor between the seats.

There she quickly transferred all the clay fragments from her pockets into her backpack. She tucked the headlamp in there, as well, then unzipped another compartment to retrieve her baseball cap and sunglasses.

As she did, she saw something from the corner of her eye. Folded and stacked neatly in a box beneath the seat were a pair of overalls, a pair of safety glasses and a hard hat.

Smiling as she began pulling them on over her own clothes, she thought maybe being heroic wasn't so hard after all. Five minutes later she was climbing down from the truck and moving toward, rather than away from, the clusters of workers, all of whom were dressed just like she was.

"I want this entire area searched," Scarface was ordering three men who trailed him. "Professor Lucy Lanfair is a fugitive, and I believe we have her cornered here. Get on it."

Lucy blended in with the workers until she saw that the agents were questioning each of them. Every single one of them. Work had stopped, and everyone in overalls was being herded into smaller groups around the truck. She found herself herded right along with them.

"All right, no one is leaving until you've all been questioned and cleared," said a suit-wearing agent who looked like he would tip over in a stiff wind. "Do not try to blow this off. We've got men stationed at each of the campus exits. This won't take long, so just consider it your way of helping your country. Once you've been cleared, you'll be allowed to leave the premises immediately."

He was interrupted by another man, who came out of the building with a small group behind him.

"The building's clean, sir. No one in there."

"Move to the next one," the suit said, pointing. Then he looked at the workers again and pointed to one man. "You, you're first. Come here."

As the man moved away from the group, muttering under his breath, the others drew together, broke out packs of cigarettes and complained about government bullshit.

Lucy was caught. She knew it, and she didn't know what to do about it. She couldn't walk away without being questioned first, or they would notice and the hunt would be over. Hell, what was she going to do?

Then it came to her. They'd finished searching the building. They wouldn't be likely to go back in there. So if she could just manage to get back inside, she might be safe. It would be the last place they would expect to find her. All she needed, really, was a distraction. A way to focus their attention elsewhere long enough for her to dart back inside.

And then her prayers were answered in the worst possible way.

"What in the living hell...?" someone said, and then, one by one, every head turned toward the commons, where a large copper-skinned man was striding toward them, wearing nothing but a bedsheet.

Utanapishtim. What was he doing here?

"You!" said one of the suits, pointing at Utana-pishtim. "Hey, hold up there. Where the hell do you think you're going?"

Utanapishtim's eyes narrowed. "Where the hell I wish, hu-mun."

"Oh, is that how it is?" The agent's hand slid to the weapon at his side. "I'm gonna need to see some ID, pal."

The beam came out of nowhere. The federal agent froze in place as his body seemed to vibrate, but only for an instant. Then he exploded, and bits of him flew everywhere.

"Shit," Lucy muttered, as everyone flew into motion, diving for cover. She dove, too, racing back into the basement before anyone even looked her way. She slipped inside and pressed her back to the door behind her. Breathless, scared to death, she yanked off the safety glasses and hard hat, tossing them aside.

And then she heard gunfire and closed her eyes. God, she hated guns.

It was over soon, though, as explosion after explosion rocked the building like a series of earthquakes. She headed into her beloved basement room and nearly cried at what she saw there.

Every bin had been emptied. The containers lay scattered about the floor, tipped and toppled, their contents gone. And the men hadn't been careful, either. There hadn't been time. They must have simply dumped the piles of delicate hardened clay into whatever boxes or bags they were using to transport them.

Crucial information would be lost forever, chipped away, and even a single line or character could change the entire meaning of a translation.

The damage would be irreparable. Not to mention the countless hours of labor that had gone into sorting and cataloging each fragment. Years of work, wasted. Gone.

Except for those few dozen pieces she'd managed to secrete in her backpack.

It was devastating.

Shaking off her grief, she moved toward the door to the hall, planning to go upstairs and try to find an exit she could use, or a place to hide.

But before she could leave, the back door was blown right off its hinges, and she spun around, pressing her back to the door.

Utanapishtim himself stood there.

Drawing a breath, trying to stop her trembling, Lucy looked him squarely in the eyes and lifted her chin. "How did you find me?"

"I…" He made a cupping motion, palm to palm. "Ab-sorb…all knowledge from small box…in your bag."

She nodded. "My address, campus address, probably my entire playlist." She closed her eyes, shaking her head slowly. "It never occurred to me." And then she swallowed, cleared her throat. "If you've come to kill me, I have a dying wish, Great King. I wish that you would listen to my words before I die. For you have been grievously misinformed."

"I seek not you death, Loo-see. But...I wish to hear these words."

She nodded. "The book you found, the one you read on that small box you took from my bag...it was a book filled with as many lies as truths."

"It say 'The Truth.'"

"That was just what it was called. Anyone can call a book 'The Truth.' It's a name. I could name my dog Inanna, but that wouldn't make my dog a goddess, would it?" He was frowning at her, as if perplexed, and she knew she was speaking far too fast, so she tried to slow down. "The man who wrote those words hated your people. He spent his life trying to wipe the vampires from existence. But they are not the monsters he says they are."

Utanapishtim lowered his head but kept his eyes on her. "I...create them. I...defy the Anunaki, and I have suffer...they wrath for five tousund years."

"I know. I know, Utanapishtim, but—"

"Why the gods would punish me so...if vahmpeers was good? Was right?"

No point in telling him there were no such things as the Anunaki. Hell, she wasn't even sure she believed that anymore herself. "I cannot know the minds of the gods, Utanapishtim. But I do know your people. I used to believe as you do, but now I know better. They're good. And they're yours. Your blood. Your offspring. Your children, Utanapishtim."

"I...cannot disobey the gods. Not...again." He shuddered as he spoke. "I will not be sended into the

death that is alive no more. I want only…release."
Then he lifted his eyes to hers. "I then join my children in afterlife. In Land of Dead. Is where they belong.… Is where I belong."

His pain was palpable in his words. And it was terrifying to him, she knew, the thought of being returned to that state of living death. No wonder he was willing to wipe out his own rather than risk that happening.

She wished she could make him understand. "You don't have to destroy them. I believe we can find a way to free you from this curse, if you will just let me—"

"Enough!"

He barked the word, and she flinched, raising an arm to cover her face as if that would stop his deadly gaze.

He paused, and his eyes looked truly sad. "I come not for you, Loo-see. You…still hu-mun. I come for James."

"He's not here."

"Will here be soon."

"What makes you think—"

"Where else James go? Know you not, woman? You are…his heart."

She blinked against a sudden rush of hot moisture and averted her eyes. "You're wrong."

"No, he's not." James had silently entered from behind Utanapishtim and stood now by the back door, an ax in his hand. "He's wrong about a lot of things, Lucy, but he's dead on target about that."

"James…"

She whispered his name on a choking sob, wanting to run to him but afraid to move. Did he mean it? And did it matter, at a time like this?

"You killed innocents out there, Utanapishtim," James said softly. "The carnage outside is… It's brutal."

"It…ness-ary." The king bowed his head slightly, one hand rising as if he was about to press it to his forehead, but he stopped himself in midmotion. "They try stop me."

"You could have backed off, regrouped, waited for me in ambush somewhere," James said. "Those actions would have been preferable to the annihilation of the innocent."

"I…there was no time."

"There's all the time in the world. We're immortal. You know that. But don't you see, Utanapishtim? You're not thinking clearly."

Utanapishtim's head snapped up, eyes narrowing. "You…question decision of you king?"

"You're not my king, Utanapishtim. Never were."

"Don't antagonize him," Lucy whispered. She was working her way around the room, trying to get to where James stood. She was edging along the wall, wanting nothing more than to be in his arms.

"Think you I not have pondered this, James of the

Vahmpeers? I have thought on this. My decision has made."

"You've thought on this with a sick mind, Utanapishtim! All those centuries, captive in that stone statue, it twisted your brain.—"

"Nothing twist mind of king. I am like Anunaki."

"I know. I thought I was like a god, too, for a while. I let my ego get away from me. But I'm not a god, I'm a man. Just like you. You are a man, Utanapishtim, and now you are also a murderer of innocents. What you plan to do is genocide, and you must stop it now."

"The gods demand—"

"I don't give a damn what the gods demand!"

"Then die!" Utanapishtim's eyes narrowed on James and began to glow. And in that instant Lucy launched herself as if from a rocket, diving into the path of that beam, only one thought, only one emotion, driving her: that she could not stand by and watch the man she loved blasted to bits.

The last thing she heard before the hum that tried to blow her head open was James screaming her name.

23

James had mentally braced himself for the blow when Utanapishtim's eyes had begun to shine. And then, like a slow-motion nightmare, he'd seen Lucy lunging into the path of that killer beam.

She shouted, "Utanapishtim, no!" as she leaped in front of the man.

And even as James screamed her name and lunged for her, she took the blow meant for him. The beam of light hit her, and her body went stiff and began to vibrate. James raced toward her, noting that Utanapishtim's expression had turned to one of horror and the beam from his eyes had flickered.

And then another beam shot from behind James, blasting past him and hitting Utanapishtim square in the chest, sending the great man flying backward to slam into a wall and crumple to the floor. James shot a stunned look behind him, only to see Brigit striding into the room like some kind of warrior woman—one who was royally pissed.

Utanapishtim lay on the floor, beaten, stunned, looking shell-shocked and as if he might have finally suffered a complete break with reality. He was muttering, "I intend not her. Not Loo-see. Not Loo-see." And then he lapsed into Sumerian—or something James presumed was Sumerian.

He didn't care. He refocused on Lucy, kneeling beside her where she'd fallen. Gathering her into his arms, he lifted her upper body from the floor, pushed up her scorched tank top. Her belly was badly burned, a large black spot smoldering, smoking, raw flesh visible beneath the charred skin.

She opened her eyes, looking up at him, and he could see the pain in her eyes. "You can heal it. I know you can."

Meeting her eyes, he felt tears brimming in his own, because he was so afraid he couldn't. He pressed his palms to her belly, waiting for the white light to come. And when it didn't, he blinked rapidly.

Brigit put her hand on his shoulder. "Do it, J.W. What are you waiting for?"

"I'm trying."

"Well fucking try harder, bud. She's circling the drain."

He tried, he focused, he searched inside himself for the pool of energy he'd always been able to tap into, to reroute, to press outward into those who needed it. And for the second time in his memory, he felt only emptiness inside him. There was nothing there.

"It's...gone. He took it from me, back on the

yacht. I was afraid of that when I tried to heal you in that church and couldn't.… I just didn't want to believe…"

Brigit met his eyes, her own wide with disbelief as she processed that. She pressed her lips together, gave a firm nod. "You're gonna have to do it the other way, big bro."

"What other way?" Then realization entered his eyes. "Oh, no. Hell, no. I don't even know if I can. Or if she'd want it." Then he shot a look Utanapishtim's way and realized the other man was gone. "He took my power. He can use it. Utanapishtim! Where are you?"

"Shit, he's gone. I'm going after him," Brigit said. "Meanwhile, you'd better ask her while she's still able to answer you. It's time to fang up or shut up, J.W."

"Wait, Brigit! I've never—"

But she was gone. And James was left holding the woman he loved—yes, loved. He knew that now. And she was dying. Right in his arms, she was dying.

"I'm sorry, James," Lucy whispered. "I just couldn't bring myself to give up that stupid book of Folsom's. Books have always been everything to me. But I know now there's something far more important."

"Love," he said. "Love is more important."

She smiled softly, closing her eyes. "I'm so sorry. I ruined everything."

"No, you didn't."

"I did. And now I'm dying, and you've lost your power, and…it could have been so good. If I'd lived…

if you wanted me…we could have had…" She closed her eyes, but tears squeezed through her thick lashes all the same. "I love you, James."

"I love you, too."

"I wish I could stay with you." She closed her eyes briefly, then flashed them open again. "I get it now. I do. I get it. I've felt so guilty all this time that my parents died and I lived. But now…now I understand they couldn't have borne it any other way. Now…I know what it is to love someone more than you love your own life. To be willing to sacrifice everything for another human being. I couldn't have lived if I had let you die, James. I am so happy, so proud, that I was able to prevent it. To be the hero for once in my life." She smiled through her tears. "I know how they felt, dying for me. They were happy. They were happy they managed to save me. And it feels so good to finally understand that. To understand what they did. Thank you for that, James. Thank you. I'm not a coward after all."

He felt hot tears running down his face. "You never were." And then she was fading, and he shook his head. "You can't leave me," he whispered. "I don't want to go on without you, Lucy. I don't know if I can. You're like…the part of me that's been missing. You understand me like no one else ever has.… I can make you one of us. One of them. You're one of the Chosen. That means—"

"I know what it means."

He nodded. "I've never…but I can try."

She opened her eyes and stared into his. "I trust you. I trust you with my life, my eternal, immortal life, James. And I would be honored to join your people."

James closed his eyes and summoned forth the vampiric part of his soul. He felt his jawline shift, felt his razor-sharp incisors extend, felt a powerful hunger piercing his awareness. And as he looked downward and she met his eyes, he saw the glowing red reflection of his gaze in hers. For the first time he thanked his stars for the part of him that was preternatural, undead. Vampire. For the first time he truly and completely loved and accepted the part of himself he had formerly rejected and tried to ignore. The part he'd hated all his life. The part he'd thought he was too good for.

The bloodlust raged, and for the first time he welcomed it, rather than meeting it with disgust and forcing it into submission. He surrendered to it, embraced it. He let it take him over, make him hard, aroused, hot, hungry. He was, in that moment, entirely vampire. And he relished it fully, as he had never ever done before. It and it alone was going to save Lucy's life. The vampire in him was the only reason he could have her now. And for that, he loved it.

He bent to her throat, a low growl of desire and hunger rising from deep within him. Opening his lips, he sucked her neck, taking the skin into his mouth, between his teeth. Pressing just slightly, he felt the thrum of that river of blood rushing through her veins.

He felt it pulsing faster as she anticipated what was to come. Her heart raced like a frightened rabbit's, and he relished that, too. And then he sank his fangs into her flesh and he fed from her, drinking.

And it was good. It was so, so good. Her blood filled him, warming his body, thundering through him, becoming power, becoming energy, becoming strength. He lifted his head from her neck, tipped it back and roared like a lion celebrating a kill. And then he lowered his gaze to her again.

She was white as a ghost, and her heartbeat had slowed to almost nothing. He'd drained her, imbibed her, and every time her heart thudded against her chest he felt it, heard it. It stuttered. It paused. It stopped.

He picked up the ax he'd dropped beside her and drew his wrist over the sharp edge, slicing a vein. Forcefully, he pressed his flesh to her mouth.

"My blood, your blood. My life, your life. Drink, Lucy. Drink me into you and come back to me, my love."

Epilogue

Everything was different when Lucy opened her eyes to find herself in James's arms. He was different. Stronger, deeper, sadder—and also wiser—and it showed in his eyes. He'd acknowledged and incorporated the beast within him. Embraced it to save her life. Appreciated it and was, even now, getting to know the vampiric part of himself just as she was.

Because she was different, too. Very different.

"I...I feel so strange."

He held her, rocked her. "I know. You've changed. You're a vampire now."

She lifted her head and blinked, looking around her. "We're not at the university anymore."

"No. You had to sleep the sleep of the undead while the change took hold. And now we're on the island, but not for very long."

Sitting up, Lucy saw a campfire snapping and crackling nearby, sending sparks into the air. She felt and smelled and tasted it. Rhiannon was poking a long stick into the coals and staring into the flames.

And as she widened her scope, Lucy looked around at the others. James and Brigit's parents were there, Edge and Amber Lily. Willem and Sarafina. Brigit and others, a couple of dozen at the most.

"They survived," she whispered. "Your family, your friends. They're okay." She was smiling at the people around her, though they all looked sad.

"They're…the only ones."

Blinking in shock, Lucy shot her attention back to James. "What?"

He nodded sadly, but before he could say more, Rhiannon had spotted them and was coming toward them. "Is she ready?"

"I think so, yes."

Rhiannon met her eyes, and then, to Lucy's stunned surprise, she smiled very slightly and extended a hand. "Welcome to your new family, Lucy Lanfair."

Lucy took her hand, and Rhiannon pulled her to her feet, led her to the fire, James at her side every step of the way. "Everyone, this is Lucy, our newborn fledgling and J.W.'s mate."

And then she proceeded to introduce everyone. When she had finished, Rhiannon turned to Lucy and said, "You now know the names of every vampire still in existence, little one. We've been calling out mentally, to no avail. Every vampire we know of back on the mainland has been wiped out by vigilantes, or by Utanapishtim, in his rage. The Chosen are being rounded up now, as well, by the government, and the gods only know what they intend to do with them. There's no sign of preternatural life anywhere but here. The refugees on this island are the only vampires remaining, as far as anyone knows."

Lucy could not contain her tears. She couldn't bear the thought of so much death, and her emotional pain was as magnified as everything else seemed to be. Though now, she knew, was no time to be noticing that she could hear the flap of an insect's wings a mile away, or the swish of a fish's tail in the ocean depths. That she could smell the scent of every plant and animal on this island, and distinguish between them, as well. And then she realized why her emotions were so overblown. She was feeling the grief of every vampire around her.

James closed his hand around hers. "We have to decide how to proceed," he said. "But we cannot do so from here. I fear it's too close to the mainland, and of course Utanapishtim may be able to find his way back here. We have to move."

Damien stepped forward then, and he held a clay tablet in his hands. Someone must have retrieved it from the ashes of the mansion in Byram, where she had last seen it, Lucy thought. That reminded Lucy of the pieces still resting in her backpack, and she quickly spotted it, resting near a tree. Thank God.

"As far as the world of man knows," Damien said softly, "they have wiped us out entirely. They know of Utanapishtim, though of course most of them have no idea who or what he truly is. All they know is that some kind of supernatural being is blasting a path of destruction through anything in his path."

"We shall strive to keep it that way," Rhiannon said softly. "We must remain in the shadows, hiding our presence more carefully than we ever have before. If they realize any of us are left, there will be no peace for us or the world until every vampire is gone. We're sailing North. Cuyler Jade has a home above the Arctic Circle. We'll be safe there, for now."

"But what about Utanapishtim?" Lucy asked. "He can track you, he can sense you—I mean *us*." And that thought made her shiver.

Rhiannon turned to Damien, who held the tablet and read, "'The two who are opposite and yet the same. One light, one dark, the first the destroyer, the second the salvation.' It makes sense now." He turned to stare directly at Brigit.

She lifted her brows in question.

"Yes, my child," Rhiannon said softly. "You're the one destined to save us all. You—with your power of destruction—are the only one who can destroy Utanapishtim once and for all. It's your destiny, not your brother's, to be the salvation of your race."

Brigit's brows pressed together, her head tipped to one side, and she said, "Well, then we're all fucked. I'm the evil twin, remember?"

The vampires huddled together around the fire, comforting and being comforted. Someone began talking about one of the dead, telling stories of their deeds, then another jumped in, and still more. All night long they spoke of those who'd died, and James held Lucy close as they listened.

Lucy felt for all the world as if she'd been born at a funeral. And she wondered what the future held for her, for James. For his kind. *Their* kind.

She knew only one thing for sure. Whatever time remained to her, she would spend it with this man— this man who was, to her, an angel. Good through and through. This man she loved. The only man she had ever, or would ever, love. And whether that time was short or long, she intended to relish every single second of her new life.

Because she finally was alive. She was alive as she had never been before. And she would rather die with these supernatural beings, in the arms of this superhuman hero, than return to the sleepwalk she had called her life before.

She would love, and she would live, with every fiber of her being for every moment she had left, spending her life right by his side from now…until forever.

Everyone ought to live that way, she thought as she turned her face up to James's in search of his lips. Even ordinary humans. Otherwise, what was the point of living at all?

* * * * *

Read the exciting conclusion to
Children of Twilight,

Twilight Fulfilled,

coming in October 2011
only from
New York Times *bestselling author*
Maggie Shayne
and
MIRA Books.

USA TODAY bestselling author

JENNIFER ARMINTROUT

Buried in the Heartland is a town that no one enters or leaves. Graf McDonald somehow becomes its first visitor in more than five years… and he was only looking for a good party. Unfortunately, Penance, Ohio, is not that place.

Jessa's the only one to even remotely trust him, and she's desperate for the kind of protection that Graf can provide. Supplies are low, the locals are ornery for a sacrifice and there's a monster more powerful than Graf lurking in the woods. New men are hard to come by in this lonesome town, and this handsome stranger might be Jessa's only hope for salvation.

AMERICAN VAMPIRE

Available wherever books are sold.

www.MIRABooks.com

MJA2878

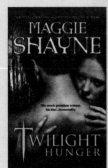  

REQUEST YOUR
FREE BOOKS!

2 FREE NOVELS
FROM THE SUSPENSE COLLECTION
PLUS 2 FREE GIFTS!

YES! Please send me 2 FREE novels from the Suspense Collection and my 2 FREE gifts (gifts are worth about $10). After receiving them, if I don't wish to receive any more books, I can return the shipping statement marked "cancel." If I don't cancel, I will receive 4 brand-new novels every month and be billed just $5.74 per book in the U.S. or $6.24 per book in Canada. That's a saving of at least 28% off the cover price. It's quite a bargain! Shipping and handling is just 50¢ per book in the U.S. and 75¢ per book in Canada.* I understand that accepting the 2 free books and gifts places me under no obligation to buy anything. I can always return a shipment and cancel at any time. Even if I never buy another book, the two free books and gifts are mine to keep forever.

191/391 MDN FDDH

Name	(PLEASE PRINT)	

Address		Apt. #

City	State/Prov.	Zip/Postal Code

Signature (if under 18, a parent or guardian must sign)

Mail to the **Reader Service**:
IN U.S.A.: P.O. Box 1867, Buffalo, NY 14240-1867
IN CANADA: P.O. Box 609, Fort Erie, Ontario L2A 5X3

Not valid for current subscribers to the Suspense Collection
or the Romance/Suspense Collection.

Want to try two free books from another line?
Call 1-800-873-8635 or visit www.ReaderService.com.

* Terms and prices subject to change without notice. Prices do not include applicable taxes. Sales tax applicable in N.Y. Canadian residents will be charged applicable taxes. Offer not valid in Quebec. This offer is limited to one order per household. All orders subject to credit approval. Credit or debit balances in a customer's account(s) may be offset by any other outstanding balance owed by or to the customer. Please allow 4 to 6 weeks for delivery. Offer available while quantities last.

Your Privacy—The Reader Service is committed to protecting your privacy. Our Privacy Policy is available online at www.ReaderService.com or upon request from the Reader Service.

We make a portion of our mailing list available to reputable third parties that offer products we believe may interest you. If you prefer that we not exchange your name with third parties, or if you wish to clarify or modify your communication preferences, please visit us at www.ReaderService.com/consumerschoice or write to us at Reader Service Preference Service, P.O. Box 9062, Buffalo, NY 14269. Include your complete name and address.

MAGGIE SHAYNE

32980	TWILIGHT PROPHECY	___ $7.99 U.S.	___ $9.99 CAN.
32875	BLUE TWILIGHT	___ $7.99 U.S.	___ $9.99 CAN.
32872	EDGE OF TWILIGHT	___ $7.99 U.S.	___ $9.99 CAN.
32871	TWILIGHT HUNGER	___ $7.99 U.S.	___ $9.99 CAN.
32808	KISS ME, KILL ME	___ $7.99 U.S.	___ $9.99 CAN.
32804	KILL ME AGAIN	___ $7.99 U.S.	___ $9.99 CAN.
32793	KILLING ME SOFTLY	___ $7.99 U.S.	___ $9.99 CAN.
32618	BLOODLINE	___ $7.99 U.S.	___ $8.99 CAN.
32498	ANGEL'S PAIN	___ $7.99 U.S.	___ $7.99 CAN.
32497	DEMON'S KISS	___ $7.99 U.S.	___ $9.50 CAN.
32266	TWO BY TWILIGHT	___ $5.99 U.S.	___ $6.99 CAN.
32244	COLDER THAN ICE	___ $5.99 U.S.	___ $6.99 CAN.
32243	THICKER THAN WATER	___ $5.99 U.S.	___ $6.99 CAN.

(limited quantities available)

TOTAL AMOUNT	$ _____
POSTAGE & HANDLING	$ _____
($1.00 for 1 book, 50¢ for each additional)	
APPLICABLE TAXES*	$ _____
TOTAL PAYABLE	$ _____

(check or money order—please do not send cash)

To order, complete this form and send it, along with a check or money order for the total above, payable to MIRA Books, to: **In the U.S.:** 3010 Walden Avenue, P.O. Box 9077, Buffalo, NY 14269-9077; **In Canada:** P.O. Box 636, Fort Erie, Ontario, L2A 5X3.

Name: _____

Address: _____ City: _____

State/Prov.: _____ Zip/Postal Code: _____

Account Number (if applicable): _____

075 CSAS

*New York residents remit applicable sales taxes.
*Canadian residents remit applicable GST and provincial taxes.

MIRA

HARLEQUIN®
www.Harlequin.com

MMS0511BL